"No question about it, Peter Ca[...] writer. But there's a sadness jus[...] sadness of all wasted human pote[...] another, he will soon be recognized as one of our very best young fiction writers."

—Howard Frank Mosher, *Cleveland Plain Dealer*

"Cameron's prose is neat without being fastidious; it is full of observations that ring like porch chimes and flicker like fireflies, evanescent yet indelible." —*The New Yorker*

"These stories are expertly paced, they display a subtle understanding of psychological relationships, and they show Cameron's remarkable ability to convey, with great pathos and without sentimentality, some of the central quandaries of contemporary life."

—Greg Johnson, *Atlanta Journal and Constitution*

"Cameron is one of the best writers about middle-class youth since Salinger." —*Booklist*

"Cameron has a wonderful ability to take the tiny, fleeting moments of our lives and show us how rich and meaningful they are. His writing is concise, witty, and compassionate. Peter Cameron's words are worth thousands of pictures. We need all the Peter Cameron we can get."

—Jane Erikson, *Arizona Daily Star*

PETER CAMERON has written three novels, *Leap Year*, *Andorra*, and *The Weekend* (available in Plume edition), and two collections of stories, *One Way or Another* and *Far-flung*. His fiction has appeared in *The New Yorker*, *Rolling Stone*, *The Paris Review*, *Grand Street*, and *Prize Stories: The O. Henry Awards*. He lives in New York City, where he works for Lambda Legal Defense and Education Fund.

Also by Peter Cameron

Andorra
The Weekend
Far-flung
Leap Year
One Way or Another

The Half You Don't Know

SELECTED
STORIES

Peter Cameron

A PLUME BOOK

PLUME
Published by the Penguin Group
Penguin Books USA Inc., 375 Hudson Street,
New York, New York 10014, U.S.A.
Penguin Books Ltd, 27 Wrights Lane,
London W8 5TZ, England
Penguin Books Australia Ltd, Ringwood,
Victoria, Australia
Penguin Books Canada Ltd, 10 Alcorn Avenue,
Toronto, Ontario, Canada M4V 3B2
Penguin Books (N.Z.) Ltd, 182–190 Wairau Road,
Auckland 10, New Zealand

Penguin Books Ltd, Registered Offices:
Harmondsworth, Middlesex, England

First published by Plume, an imprint of Dutton Signet,
a division of Penguin Books USA Inc.

First Printing, January, 1997
10 9 8 7 6 5 4 3 2 1

Ⓟ REGISTERED TRADEMARK—MARCA REGISTRADA

LIBRARY OF CONGRESS CATALOGING-IN-PUBLICATION DATA
Cameron, Peter.
The half you don't know : selected stories / Peter Cameron.
p. cm.
ISBN 0-452-27732-9
I. Title.
PS3553.A4344H35   1997
813'.54—dc20   96-26346
CIP

Printed in the United States of America
Set in Ehrhardt
Designed by Julian Hamer

PUBLISHER'S NOTE

BOOKS ARE AVAILABLE AT QUANTITY DISCOUNTS WHEN USED TO PROMOTE
PRODUCTS OR SERVICES. FOR INFORMATION PLEASE WRITE TO PREMIUM
MARKETING DIVISION, PENGUIN BOOKS USA INC., 375 HUDSON STREET,
NEW YORK, NEW YORK 10014.

for Andy

Contents

I now hasten to the more moving part of my story. I shall relate events, that impressed me with feelings which, from what I had been, have made me what I am.

—Mary Shelley,
Frankenstein

Homework

My dog, Keds, was sitting outside of the A & P last Thursday when he got smashed by some kid pushing a shopping cart. At first we thought he just had a broken leg, but later we found out he was bleeding inside. Every time he opened his mouth, blood would seep out like dull red words in a bad silent dream.

Every night before my sister goes to her job she washes her hair in the kitchen sink with beer and mayonnaise and eggs. Sometimes I sit at the table and watch the mixture dribble down her white back. She boils a pot of water on the stove at the same time; when she is finished with her hair, she steams her face. She wants so badly to be beautiful.

I am trying to solve complicated algebraic problems I have set for myself. Since I started cutting school last Friday, the one thing I miss is homework. Find the value for n. Will it be a whole number? It is never a whole number. It is always a fraction.

"Will you get me a towel?" my sister asks. She turns her face toward me and clutches her hair to the top of her head. The sprayer hose slithers into its hole next to the faucet.

I hand her a dish towel. "No," she says. "A bath towel. Don't be stupid."

In the bathroom, my mother is watering her plants. She has arranged them in the tub and turned the shower on. She sits on the toilet lid and watches. It smells like outdoors in the bathroom.

I hand my sister the towel and watch her wrap it around her head. She takes the cover off the pot of boiling water and drops lemon slices in. Then she lowers her face into the steam.

This is the problem I have set for myself:

$$\frac{245(n + 17)}{34} = 396(n - 45)$$

$$n =$$

Wednesday, I stand outside the high-school gym doors. Inside students are lined up doing calisthenics. It's snowing, and prematurely dark, and I can watch without being seen.

"Well," my father says when I get home. He is standing in the garage testing the automatic door. Every time a plane flies overhead, the door opens or closes, so my father is trying to fix it. "Have you changed your mind about school?" he asks me.

I lock my bicycle to a pole. This infuriates my father, who doesn't believe in locking things up in his own house. He pretends not to notice. I wipe the thin stripes of snow off the fenders with my middle finger. It is hard to ride a bike in the snow. This afternoon on my way home from the high school I fell off, and lay in the snowy road with my bike on top of me. It felt warm.

"We're going to get another dog," my father says.

"It's not that," I say. I wish everyone would stop talking about dogs. I can't tell how sad I really am about Keds versus how sad I am in general. If I don't keep these things separate, I feel as if I'm betraying Keds.

"Then what is it?" my father says.

"It's nothing," I say.

My father nods. He is very good about bringing things up and then letting them drop. A lot gets dropped. He presses the button on the automatic control. The door slides down its oiled tracks and falls shut. It's dark in the garage. My father presses the button again and the door opens, and we both look outside at the snow falling in the driveway, as if in those few seconds the world might have changed.

My mother has forgotten to call me for dinner, and when I confront her with this she tells me that she did but that I was sleeping. She is loading the dishwasher. My sister is standing at the counter, listening, and separating eggs for her shampoo.

"What can I get you?" my mother asks. "Would you like a meat-loaf sandwich?"

"No," I say. I open the refrigerator and survey its illuminated contents. "Could I have some eggs?"

"O.K.," my mother says. She comes and stands beside me and puts her hand on top of mine on the door handle. There are no eggs in the refrigerator. "Oh," my mother says; then, "Julie?"

"What?" my sister asks.

"Did you take the last eggs?"

"I guess so," my sister says. "I don't know."

"Forget it," I say. "I won't have eggs."

"No," my mother says. "Julie doesn't need them in her shampoo. That's not what I bought them for."

"I do," my sister says. "It's a formula. It doesn't work without the eggs. I need the protein."

"I don't want eggs," I say. "I don't want anything." I go into my bedroom.

My mother comes in and stands looking out the window. The snow has turned to rain. "You're not the only one who is unhappy about this," she says.

"About what?" I say. I am sitting on my unmade bed. If

I pick up my room, my mother will make my bed: that's the deal. I didn't pick up my room this morning.

"About Keds," she says. "I'm unhappy, too. But it doesn't stop me from going to school."

"You don't go to school," I say.

"You know what I mean," my mother says. She turns around and looks at my room, and begins to pick things off the floor.

"Don't do that," I say. "Stop."

My mother drops the dirty clothes in an exaggerated gesture of defeat. She almost—almost—throws them on the floor. The way she holds her hands accentuates their emptiness. "If you're not going to go to school," she says, "the least you can do is clean your room."

In algebra word problems, a boat sails down a river while a jeep drives along the bank. Which will reach the capital first? If a plane flies at a certain speed from Boulder to Oklahoma City and then at a different speed from Oklahoma City to Detroit, how many cups of coffee can the stewardess serve, assuming she is unable to serve during the first and last ten minutes of each flight? How many times can a man ride the elevator to the top of the Empire State Building while his wife climbs the stairs, given that the woman travels one stair slower each flight? And if the man jumps up while the elevator is going down, which is moving—the man, the woman, the elevator, or the snow falling outside?

The next Monday I get up and make preparations for going to school. I can tell at the breakfast table that my mother is afraid to acknowledge them for fear it won't be true. I haven't gotten up before ten o'clock in a week. My mother makes me French toast. I sit at the table and write the note excusing me for my absence. I am eighteen, an adult, and thus able to excuse myself from school. This is what my note says:

Dear Mr. Kelly [my homeroom teacher]:
    Please excuse my absence February 17–24. I was unhappy and did not feel able to attend school.
                    Sincerely,
                    Michael Pechetti

This is the exact format my mother used when she wrote my notes, only she always said, "Michael was home with a sore throat," or "Michael was home with a bad cold." The colds that prevented me from going to school were always bad colds.

My mother watches me write the note but doesn't ask to see it. I leave it on the kitchen table when I go to the bathroom, and when I come back to get it I know she has read it. She is washing the bowl she dipped the French toast into. Before, she would let Keds lick it clean. He liked eggs.

In Spanish class we are seeing a film on flamenco dancers. The screen wouldn't pull down, so it is being projected on the blackboard, which is green and cloudy with erased chalk. It looks a little like the women are sick, and dancing in Heaven. Suddenly the little phone on the wall buzzes.

Mrs. Smitts, the teacher, gets up to answer it, and then walks over to me. She puts her hand on my shoulder and leans her face close to mine. It is dark in the room. "Miguel," Mrs. Smitts whispers, "*tienes que ir a la oficina de* guidance."

"What?" I say.

She leans closer, and her hair blocks the dancers. Despite the clicking castanets and the roomful of students, there is something intimate about this moment. "*Tienes que ir a la oficina de* guidance," she repeats slowly. Then, "You must go to the guidance office. Now. *Vaya.*"

My guidance counselor, Mrs. Dietrich, used to be a history teacher, but she couldn't take it anymore, so she was moved into guidance. On her immaculate desk is a calendar blotter with "LUNCH" written across the middle of every box, including Saturday and Sunday. The only other things on her desk are an empty photo cube and my letter to Mr. Kelly. I sit down, and she shows me the letter as if I haven't yet read it. I reread it.

"Did you write this?" she asks.

I nod affirmatively. I can tell Mrs. Dietrich is especially nervous about this interview. Our meetings are always charged with tension. At the last one, when I was selecting my second-semester courses, she started to laugh hysterically when I said I wanted to take Boys' Home Ec. Now every time I see her in the halls she stops me and asks how I'm doing in Boys' Home Ec. It's the only course of mine she remembers.

I hand the note back to her and say, "I wrote it this morning," as if this clarifies things.

"This morning?"

"At breakfast," I say.

"Do you think this is an acceptable excuse?" Mrs. Dietrich asks. "For missing more than a week of school?"

"I'm sure it isn't," I say.

"Then why did you write it?"

Because it is the truth, I start to say. It is. But somehow I know that saying this will make me more unhappy. It might make me cry. "I've been doing homework," I say.

"That's fine," Mrs. Dietrich says, "but it's not the point. The point is, to graduate you have to attend school for a hundred and eighty days, or have legitimate excuses for the days you've missed. That's the point. Do you want to graduate?"

"Yes," I say.

"Of course you do," Mrs. Dietrich says.

She crumples my note and tries to throw it into the wastepaper basket but misses. We both look for a second at the note lying on the floor, and then I get up and throw it away. The only other thing in her wastepaper basket is a banana peel. I can picture her eating a banana in her tiny office. This, too, makes me sad.

"Sit down," Mrs. Dietrich says.

I sit down.

"I understand your dog died. Do you want to talk about that?"

"No," I say.

"Is that what you're so unhappy about?" she says. "Or is it something else?"

I almost mention the banana peel in her wastebasket, but I don't. "No," I say. "It's just my dog."

Mrs. Dietrich thinks for a moment. I can tell she is embarrassed to be talking about a dead dog. She would be more comfortable if it were a parent or a sibling.

"I don't want to talk about it," I repeat.

She opens her desk drawer and takes out a pad of hall passes. She begins to write one out for me. She has beautiful handwriting. I think of her learning to write beautifully as a child and then growing up to be a guidance counselor, and this makes me unhappy.

"Mr. Neuman is willing to overlook this matter," she says. Mr. Neuman is the principal. "Of course, you will have to make up all the work you've missed. Can you do that?"

"Yes," I say.

Mrs. Dietrich tears the pass from the pad and hands it to me. Our hands touch. "You'll get over this," she says. "Believe me, you will."

My sister works until midnight at the Photo-Matica. It's a tiny booth in the middle of the A & P parking lot. People drive up and leave their film and come back the next day for the pictures. My sister wears a uniform that makes her look like a counterperson in a fast-food restaurant. Sometimes at night when I'm sick of being at home I walk downtown and sit in the booth with her.

There's a machine in the booth that looks like a printing press, only snapshots ride down a conveyor belt and fall into a bin and then disappear. The machine gives the illusion that your photographs are being developed on the spot. It's a fake. The same fifty photographs roll through over and over, and my sister says nobody notices, because everyone in town is taking the same pictures. She opens up the envelopes and looks at them.

Before I go into the booth, I buy cigarettes in the A & P. It is open twenty-four hours a day, and I love it late at night. It is big and bright and empty. The checkout girl sits on her counter swinging her legs. The Muzak plays "If Ever I Would Leave You." Before I buy the cigarettes, I walk up and down the aisles. Everything looks good to eat, and the things that aren't edible look good in their own way. The detergent aisle is colorful and clean-smelling.

My sister is listening to the radio and polishing her nails when I get to the booth. It is almost time to close.

"I hear you went to school today," she says.

"Yeah."

"How was it?" she asks. She looks at her fingernails, which are so long it's frightening.

"It was O.K.," I say. "We made chili dogs in Home Ec."

"So are you over it all?"

I look at the pictures riding down the conveyor belt. I know the order practically by heart: graduation, graduation, birthday, mountains, baby, baby, new car, bride, bride and groom, house. . . . "I guess so," I say.

"Good," says my sister. "It was getting to be a little much." She puts her tiny brush back in the bottle, capping it. She shows me her nails. They're an odd brown shade. "Cinnamon," she says. "It's an earth color." She looks out into the parking lot. A boy is collecting the abandoned shopping carts, forming a long silver train, which he noses back toward the store. I can tell he is singing by the way his mouth moves.

"That's where we found Keds," my sister says, pointing to the Salvation Army bin.

When I went out to buy cigarettes, Keds would follow me. I hung out down here at night before he died. I was unhappy then, too. That's what no one understands. I named him Keds because he was all white with big black feet and it looked as if he had high-top sneakers on. My mother wanted to name him Bootie. Bootie is a cat's name. It's a dumb name for a dog.

"It's a good thing you weren't here when we found him," my sister says. "You would have gone crazy."

I'm not really listening. It's all nonsense. I'm working on a new problem: Find the value for n such that n plus everything else in your life makes you feel all right. What would n equal? Solve for n.

Excerpts from
Swan Lake

What is that called again?" my grandmother asks, nodding at my lover's wok.

"A wok," I say.

"A wok," my grandmother repeats. The word sounds strange coming out of her mouth. I can't remember ever hearing her say a foreign word. She is sitting at the kitchen table smoking a Players cigarette. She saw an ad for them in *Time* magazine and wanted to try them, so after work I drove her down to the 7-Eleven and she bought a pack. She also bought a Hostess cherry pie. That was for me.

Neal, my lover, is stir-frying mushrooms in the wok. My grandmother thinks he is my friend. I am slicing tomatoes and apples. We are staying at my grandmother's house while my parents go on a cruise around the world. It is a romance cruise, stopping at the "love capitals" of the world. My mother won it. Neal and I are making mushroom curry. Neal isn't wearing a shirt, and his chest is sweating. He always sweats when he cooks. He cooks with a passion.

"I wish I could help," my grandmother says. "Let me know if I can."

"We will," says Neal.

"I don't think I've seen a wok before," my grandmother says.

"Everyone has them now," says Neal. "They're great."

The doorbell rings, the front door opens, and someone shouts, "Yoo-hoo!"

"Who's that?" I say.

"Who's what?" my grandmother says. She's a little deaf.

I walk into the living room to investigate. A woman in a jogging suit is standing in the front hall. "Who are you?" she says.

"Paul," I say.

"Where's Mrs. Andrews?" she asks.

"In the kitchen," I say. "I'm her grandson."

"Oh," she says. "I thought you were some kind of maniac. What with that knife and all." She nods at my hand. I am still holding the knife.

"Who are you?" I ask.

"Who's there?" my grandmother shouts from the kitchen.

The woman shouts her name to my grandmother. It sounds like Gloria Marsupial. Then she whispers to me, "I'm from Meals on Wheels. I bring Mrs. Andrews dinner on Tuesday nights. Your mother bowls on Tuesday."

"Oh," I say.

Mrs. Marsupial walks past me into the kitchen. I follow her. "There you are," she says to my grandmother. "I thought he had killed you."

"Nonsense," my grandmother says. "What are you doing here? You come on Tuesdays."

"It is Tuesday," says Mrs. Marsupial. She opens the oven. "We've got to warm this up."

"I don't need it tonight," my grandmother says. "They're making me dinner."

Mrs. Marsupial eyes the wok, the mushrooms, and Neal disdainfully.

"What do you have?" Neal asks.

Mrs. Marsupial takes a tinfoil tray out of the paper bag she is holding. It has a cardboard cover on it. "Meat loaf," she says. "And green beans. And a nice pudding."

"What kind of pudding?" my grandmother asks.

"Rice pudding," says Mrs. Marsupial.

"No thanks," says my grandmother.

"What are you making?" Mrs. Marsupial asks Neal.

"Mushroom curry," says Neal. "We're lacto-vegetarians."

"I'm sure you are," Mrs. Marsupial replies. She turns to my grandmother. "Well, do you want this or not?"

"I can have it tomorrow night," my grandmother says. "If I remember."

"Then I'll stick it in the fridge." Mrs. Marsupial opens the refrigerator and frowns at the beer Neal and I have installed. She moves a six-pack of Dos Equis aside to make room for the container. "I'll put it right here," she says into the refrigerator, "and tomorrow night you just pop it into the oven at about three hundred and warm it up, and it will be as good as new." She closes the refrigerator and looks at my grandmother. "Are you sure you're all right now?" she asks.

"What kind of bush is that out there?" my grandmother says. She points out the window.

"That's not a bush, dear," Mrs. Marsupial says. "That's the clothesline."

"I know that's the clothesline," my grandmother says. "I mean behind it. With the white flowers."

"It's a lilac bush," I say.

"A lilac? Are you sure?"

"It's a lilac," confirms Neal. "You can smell it when you hang out the wash." He opens the window and sticks his head out. "You can smell it from here," he says. "It's beautiful."

"Do you want me to take your blood pressure?" Mrs.

Marsupial asks my grandmother. "I left the sphygmomanometer in the van."

"No," my grandmother says. "My blood pressure is fine. It's my memory that's no good."

I dump the sliced tomatoes and apples into the wok and lower the domelike cover. Then I stick my head out the window beside Neal's. It's getting dark. The lilac bush, the clothesline, the collapsing grape arbor are all disappearing.

"I don't want to be late for my next drop-off," Mrs. Marsupial says. "I guess I'll be running along."

No one says anything. Neal has taken my hand; we are holding hands outside the kitchen window where my grandmother and Mrs. Marsupial can't see us. The smell of curry mixes with the scent of lilacs and intoxicates me. I feel as if I'm leaning on the balcony of a Mediterranean villa, not the window of my grandmother's house in Cheshire, Connecticut, five feet above the dripping spigot.

After dinner my grandmother tells Neal and me stories about "growing up on the farm." She didn't really grow up on a farm—she just visited a friend's farm one summer—but these memories are particularly vivid and make for good telling. I have heard them many times, but Neal hasn't. He is lying on the floor at my feet, exhausted from cooking. My grandmother is sitting on the love seat and I am sitting across from her on the couch, stroking Neal's bare back with my bare foot, a gesture that is hidden by the coffee table. At least I think it is.

"There was an outhouse with a long bench and three holes—a little one, a medium one, and a big one."

"Like the three bears," says Neal. His eyes are closed.

"Like who?" says my grandmother. She doesn't like being interrupted.

"The three bears," repeats Neal. "Cinderella and the three bears."

"Goldilocks," I correct.

"Little Red Riding Hood," murmurs Neal.

"You've lost me," my grandmother says. "Anyway, we used to eat outside, on a big plank table under a big tree. Was it an oak tree? No, it was a mulberry tree. I remember because mulberries would fall off it if the wind blew. You'd be eating mashed potatoes and suddenly there would be a mulberry in them. They looked like black raspberries. In between courses we would run down to the barn and back— down the hill to the barn, touch it, and run back up the hill. You'd always be hungry again when you got back up." She pauses. "We should turn on some light," she says. "We shouldn't sit in the dark."

No one says anything. No one turns on a light, because light damages the way that words travel. Suddenly my grandmother says, "How many times was I married?"

"Once," I say. "Just once."

"Are you sure just once?"

"As far as I know."

"Maybe you had affairs," suggests Neal.

"Oh, I'm sure I had affairs," says my grandmother. "Although I couldn't tell you with whom. I can't remember the faces at all. It all gets fuzzy. Sometimes I'm not even sure who you are."

"I'm Paul," I say. "Your beloved grandson."

"I'm Neal," Neal says. "Paul's friend."

"I know," my grandmother says. "I know now. But I'll wake up tonight and I'll have no idea. I won't even know where I am. Or what year it is."

"But none of that matters," I say.

"What?" my grandmother asks.

"Who cares what year it is?" I say. I rest both my feet lightly on Neal's back. It moves as though he is sleeping. I think about explaining how none of that matters: names or ages or whereabouts. But, before I can explain this to my

grandmother, or attempt to, a new thought occurs to me:
Someday, I'll forget Neal, just like my grandmother has forgotten the great love of her life. And then I think: Is Neal
the great love of my life? Or is that one still coming, to be
forgotten, too?

After my grandmother goes to bed at nine o'clock, Neal
and I redo the dishes. She likes to wash them if we make
the dinner, but she doesn't do such a hot job anymore.
There are always little pieces of muck stuck to her pink glass
plates. Neal washes and I dry. I am using a dish towel from
the 1964 World's Fair. On it, a geisha girl embraces an Es-
kimo, who in turn embraces an Indian squaw embracing a
man in a kilt. My grandmother took my sister and me to the
World's Fair, but I don't remember her buying this dish
towel.

"I think I'm going to move back into the apartment,"
Neal says.

"Why?" I ask.

"I feel funny here. I don't feel comfortable."

"But I thought you wanted to get out of the city in the
summer?"

"I did. I do. But this isn't working out." Neal motions
with his wet, sudsy hand, indicating my grandmother's
kitchen: the African violets on the window sill, the humming
refrigerator, the cookie jars filled with Social Teas. I insert
the plate I am drying into the slotted dish rack. It seems to
stand on its own accord, gleaming.

"Are you mad?" asks Neal.

"I don't know," I say. "Sad. But not mad."

"There is another thing, too," Neal says. He chases the
suds down the drain with the sprayer thing.

"What?"

"I feel like when we're sleeping together she might come
in. I don't feel right about it."

"She sleeps all night," I say. "She thinks you sleep on the porch. Plus she's senile."

"I know," says Neal, "but I still don't feel right about it. I just can't relax."

I sit down at the kitchen table and light one of my grandmother's Players cigarettes. Neal washes his hands, dries them, and carefully folds the World's Fair dish towel. He comes over and curls his fingers around my throat, lightly, affectionately throttling me. Neal's clean hands smell like the English Lavender soap my grandmother keeps in a pump dispenser by the sink. Neal's hands smell like my grandmother's hands.

I exhale and look at our reflection in the window. I only smoke about one cigarette a month, and every time I do I experience a wonderful dizzy feeling that quickly gives way to nausea.

"It's no big deal," Neal says. "It's just not cool here."

I think about answering, but I can't. I close my eyes and feel myself floating. The occasional cigarette is a wonderful thing.

My mother sends me a postcard from Piraeus. This is what it says:

Dear Paul,
Piraeus is a lovely city considering I had never even heard of it. I'm not sure why it's a Love Capital except the movie "Never on Sunday" was filmed here. Have you seen it? Hope you're O.K. Are you taking good care of Grandma?

Love,
Mom

About a week after Neal moves out, the ballet comes to town, and my grandmother asks to see it. There are commercials for it on TV, showing an excerpt from *Swan Lake*, while across the bottom of the screen a phone number for charging tickets appears and disappears. The swan's feet blur into the flashing numbers.

My grandmother claims she has never been to the ballet. I don't know if I should believe her or not. Whenever the commercial comes on, she turns it up loud and calls for me to come watch. I do not understand her sudden zeal for the ballet. She gave up on movies long ago, because they were "just nonsense." Besides, she falls asleep at nine o'clock, no matter where she is.

Nevertheless, I buy three tickets to *Swan Lake* for my grandmother's eighty-eighth birthday. Neal comes to her special birthday dinner, bringing a Carvel ice-cream cake with him. At my grandmother's request, we are eating tomatoes stuffed with tuna salad. She must have seen an ad for it somewhere. I tried to scallop the edges of the tomatoes as she described, but I failed: they looked hacked-at, like something that would be served in a punk restaurant. But they taste O.K.

"It's just like old times, having Neal here," my grandmother says.

"I've only been gone a week," Neal says.

"It seems like longer," my grandmother says. "It seems like ages. We were lonely without you. Weren't we, Paul?"

I don't answer. I never admit to being lonely.

After dinner Neal and I do the dishes because my grandmother is the birthday girl and not allowed to help. Neal is telling her the story of *Swan Lake*. "The chief swan turns into a girl and falls in love with the prince, but then she gets turned back into a swan."

"Why?" my grandmother asks.

"I don't know," Neal says. "It's morning or something. They have to part. But the prince goes back to the lake the next night and finds her, and because they truly love one another, she changes back into a girl. I think that's it. Basically."

"It sounds ridiculous," says my grandmother.

"I thought you especially wanted to see *Swan Lake*," I say.

"I do," my grandmother says. "It just sounds silly." She looks out the window. "What kind of bush is that out there?" She points to the lilac bush.

"A lilac," I say.

"That's a lilac?" she says. "I thought lilacs had tiny purple flowers."

"They do," I say. "But that's a white lilac. The flowers grow in bunches."

"That's not a lilac," my grandmother says. "I remember lilacs."

"It is a lilac," says Neal. "Maybe you're thinking of wisteria. Or dogwood."

"I can't see it from here," my grandmother says. "I'm going to go out and look at it." She gets up and walks down the hall. The back door opens and then slams shut.

"If she asks me that one more time," I say, "I think I'll go crazy."

"I think it's sweet," Neal says. "I think your grandmother's great."

"I know," I say. "She is."

Neal puts the remaining, melting Carvel cake back into the freezer, and then stands there, with the freezer door open, pinching the pink sugar roses with his fingers. "I wish your grandmother knew we were lovers," he says.

I laugh. "I don't think she'd want to know that," I say. I sit down at the kitchen table.

"Why do you say that?" Neal says. "I think you should tell her. I wouldn't be surprised if she had figured it out."

"What do you mean?" I say.

"What do you mean, what do I mean?" Neal says.

"She doesn't know," I say. "No one knows."

"I know no one knows." Neal closes the freezer and sits down next to me. "That's the problem."

I look out the window. My grandmother is walking slowly down the backyard. She is an old lady, and I love her, and I love Neal, too, but I don't see the problem in all this. "I don't see the problem in all this," I say.

"You don't?" Neal says. "Really, you don't?"

I shake my head no. Neal shrugs and gets up. He opens the refrigerator and stands silhouetted in the glow from the open door. He is looking for nothing in particular. Outside, my grandmother reaches up and pulls a lilac blossom toward her face, because she has forgotten what they are.

Neal is disgusted with me, and leaves the ballet at intermission. My grandmother falls asleep as Prince Siegfried is reunited with Odette. Her hands are crossed in her lap. She is wearing a pair of white mismatched gloves—one has tiny pearls sewn on the back of the hand, and the other doesn't.

I watch the dancing, unamused. The ballet is such a lie. No one—not my grandmother, not Neal, not I—no one in real life ever moves that beautifully.

The Middle
of Everything

Three days before his show opened, Jack arrived at his hotel in New York to find a telegram from his grandmother. He was not alarmed. His grandmother believed telegrams were the most civilized form of communication. This telegram, like all of hers, was succinct. It read: "Welcome New York. Awaiting your call." It was signed Mrs. Enid Winns Carter.

In his hotel room Jack was overcome with the paralysis he always felt upon arriving in New York. Lately he had made his home in Mexico, and occasionally, Los Angeles. He hadn't lived in New York City for nearly four years. He never knew where to begin in New York. He always felt as if he were coming in at the middle of everything.

He decided to begin by calling his grandmother. The phone barely rang once before she answered it. "Hello Grandma," Jack said.

"Hello," she said. "How are you?"

"I'm fine," he said. "A little jet-lagged."

"Who is this?" she asked. Mrs. Carter liked to act confused on the telephone. It was her least favorite form of communication.

"This is Jack," Jack said. Since he was her only grandchild, there could be little doubt as to his identity.

"Jack?"

"John," he said. "Your grandson."

"Oh, John!" she exclaimed. "It doesn't sound like you. Did you get my telegram?"

"Yes," he said. "How did you know where I'm staying?"

"Because you always stay at the same hotel. That horrible place downtown." He was staying at the Chelsea. A couple of years ago his grandmother had come into town to have lunch with him and had taken a taxi to the hotel. She refused to get out because she claimed Twenty-third Street looked like a circus. She took the taxi back up to the Sherry-Netherland, where she summoned him for a "civilized" lunch. Now Mrs. Carter avoided the city entirely.

"Can I expect you for dinner?" she continued.

"I should really check in at the gallery," he said.

"Couldn't you do that tomorrow?"

"I suppose," Jack said, who was none too eager to confront his paintings. They always looked inexplicably different and invariably worse in New York. "What time are the trains?" he asked. His grandmother lived in Bedford.

"I don't know," she said. "I haven't taken a train in ages. I suggest you call the train people. That's what they are for."

"I see you insist on looking like a field hand," Mrs. Enid Winns Carter said by way of a greeting. She was standing in the front hall, supported by a cane.

"You can't help getting at least a little tan when you live in Mexico," Jack said.

"Yes, but you could help living in Mexico." Mrs. Carter disapproved of North Americans living in foreign parts. She believed everyone should live where he was born. She had lived in the same house in Bedford since the 1920s. It was a large brick house with many rooms and much furniture. She led Jack, rather slowly, into the living room.

"Where is Aunt Helen?" he asked. His Aunt Helen, who was really his grandmother's cousin, had lived with his grandmother for the last three years.

"Mrs. Whitcomb is drying out," his grandmother said. She always referred to Helen as Mrs. Whitcomb.

"Drying out?"

"She's at that clinic where you have to make your own bed. In California." She pronounced California with five syllables.

"I didn't know she had a drinking problem," Jack said.

"Of course she has," his grandmother said. "What do you think she has been devoted to all these years?"

"Nothing, I suppose," he said.

"Wrong," Mrs. Carter said. "She has been devoted to the bottle. And I don't understand this sudden urge to hop on the wagon. It seems a little late in the game."

"Better late than never," Jack said.

His grandmother snorted.

"How long will Helen be away?" Jack asked. He was worried about his grandmother living alone. She was eighty-six.

Mrs. Carter waved her hand. "Enough of Mrs. Whitcomb," she said. "I want to hear about you. Tell me about your show. Are the paintings big and ugly?"

"They're somewhat smaller this year," he said.

"But just as ugly?"

"You would think so," Jack said.

She smiled. "I still hope that before I die, you will paint me a nice picture. Would you begrudge me that?"

"I gave you the pick of the last show."

"No. I'm not interested in ugly paintings. I want a painting *of* something. I know that makes me hopelessly old-fashioned, but so be it. You know what I would most like? A painting of the house at Benders Bay. Surely you could paint that for me? After all your education and training, which I hasten to remind you I financed."

"I'll pay you back."

"Pay me with a painting of Benders Bay." Benders Bay was the house his grandmother once owned on Fishers Island. "I have a photograph of it, if you have forgotten what it looks like."

"I don't paint from photographs," Jack said.

"Then you could go out there and paint it. Although I wonder if it's still there. Perhaps it's been torn down."

"I doubt it," said Jack.

"Yet it's somebody else's now," his grandmother said. "Anyway," she continued, "I would like you to paint me something before I die."

"I'll go up to Fishers next week and paint you the house," he said.

"That makes me very happy," she said. "You have no idea."

Jack's grandfather had built Benders Bay as a wedding present for his wife. They had gone there every summer from 1923 to 1970, the year his grandfather died. Jack spent the summers at Benders with them. His father worked in the city, and his mother, a beautiful and not untalented actress, was usually in a show. She worked very steadily on Broadway during the '40s and the '50s. When Jack was fifteen she killed herself.

The summer weeks at Benders Bay always followed the same pattern: On Sunday, after the matinee, Jack's parents would arrive. His mother would bring an entourage—people from the cast, or other friends—and the house would be filled with exotic glamorous adults, with noise and music and cigarette smoke, with dancing and charades, with men and women running down to the water in the middle of the night, and reappearing, fully clothed, sopping wet, to dance some more. Then on Tuesday afternoon they'd pack everything up and depart in a caravan of honking cars for Manhattan, and an 8:30 curtain, leaving the elder Carters and Jack behind.

When his grandfather died it was revealed that he had several large debts, and his grandmother sold Benders to pay them. She never returned to Fishers Island.

"I am thinking of selling my accessories," Mrs. Carter said, as they ate dinner.

"What accessories?" Jack asked.

"Accessories," she said. "My gloves, and hats and jewels."

"Why are you going to sell them?"

"Why not?" his grandmother said. "Why keep them? Since you have disowned my great-grandchildren, there is no family to inherit them. And I am told there is an appreciative market for vintage accessories. I have spoken with several dealers."

"I haven't disowned the twins," Jack said. "I just don't have custody. There's a difference." Jack was the father of twin girls, Sigourney and Yvette. Shortly after they were born, he and his wife were divorced; Barbara immediately remarried, and his bitterness somehow poisoned his paternal love. Jack knew this was wrong, he knew that his feelings for these children should be separate from his feelings for their mother, but somehow they were all inextricably tangled, threads with many sharp needles, and he cast the whole net off and moved away.

"Call it what you will," Mrs. Carter said. "I never see them."

"Maybe I'm interested in your accessories."

"Why would you be interested in them?"

"I don't know. Perhaps I'll remarry. There's no need to sell them. You don't need the money."

"Are you contemplating remarriage?"

"No," he said.

"There is no one in your life?"

A vision of Langley, his lover, drying her hair with a

white towel beside the aqua swimming pool, presented itself to him. He smiled. Why did he not want to tell his grandmother about Langley? It was probably her age—an unacceptable twenty-three—but he liked the fact that Langley was a secret, that she was unofficial, that she existed only in the palmy air of, as his grandmother would say, Californeea. "No one," he said, but the vision lingered.

"That is too bad. I wish you were in love. You are always a nicer person when you are in love."

"Isn't everyone?" he asked.

"No," said Mrs. Carter. "Love makes some of us villains. Come upstairs. I will show you my treasures. Whatever you want, you can take. The rest I will sell."

He followed his grandmother out of the dining room and into the front hall. Mrs. Carter had had an elevator chair installed along the banister, which was long and curved. She sat down and buckled a seat belt. "It won't go unless this is fastened," she explained. "Stupid thing." She pressed a button and the chair began to rise. Jack climbed the stairs next to her, one step at a time, trying to match her slow ascent. "For heaven's sake, walk normally," she said. "I'll meet you at the top."

On the second-floor landing he looked down and watched his grandmother rise. She was facing away from him, traveling backward, her hands clasped in her lap, her head bowed. That afternoon when he had driven her into town to buy groceries, she had sat the same way. Her loss of mobility was, in her eyes, a loss of dignity. The chair curved around and arrived at the top of the stairs; she unbuckled the belt and the chair tilted forward, depositing her next to him.

"This way," she said, all business in an attempt to transcend her humiliation. Jack followed her down the hall into her bedroom, then into her dressing room. She approached a large armoire that was made of either ash or pecan: some golden wood that was so highly polished they were both reflected in its veneer. It was dusk, and an imported, antique light filled the room. "Damn it," she said. "I forgot the keys. They're downstairs."

"Where are they? I'll get them."

"They're in my bag, in the front hall, on the credenza."

"I'll be right back."

When he returned with the ring of keys his grandmother was sitting in an easy chair by the window. She held out her hand.

"Why do you keep it locked?" Jack asked.

"I keep everything locked," Mrs. Carter said. She flipped through the keys and found the one for the armoire. "Voilà," she said, handing it to Jack.

He opened the armoire. On the inner side of its doors were beveled mirrors mottled with green moss-like fog. One half of the space was a closet of dresses sheathed in dress bags. Sequins glinted, iridescent as crows' wings, in the darkness. The other half contained drawers of varying sizes. Jack opened one and found a stash of scarves, an unmade bed of glossy silk and lace. He felt his grandmother watching his back. The next drawer contained a jumble of gloves, an orgy of hands, gloves of every length and color, gloves with gauntlets, gloves with pearls and flowers and monograms embroidered on them. "Where did you get all this stuff?" he asked.

She snorted. "There was a time when people bought fine things and kept them."

He slid open a thin drawer. On a field of crimson velvet an army of brooches and earrings were pinned, all of them set with stones glittering in unembarrassed colors. "Are these real?" he asked.

Mrs. Carter didn't answer. She sat with a blank look on her face.

Jack closed the drawer. "Are you tired?" he asked.

She shook her head no. "I am thinking about your daughters," she said, looking out the window at the sun's disappearance.

"Oh," Jack said.

"Do they know they have a great-grandmother?"

"I don't think they remember you," he said.

"Of course they don't remember me. They haven't seen me since they were babies. My question was, do they know of me?"

"I think I've mentioned you," he said.

"Mentioned me? How generous of you."

"They are not a part of my life," Jack said.

"So you *have* disowned them." Mrs. Carter looked at him.

"No," he said. "You don't understand."

"Of course I don't understand, because your behavior is incomprehensible."

"They have a new father. I try not to interfere."

"How very gallant of you."

Jack closed the armoire and locked it. He played with the keys. They were old keys, made of iron. He wondered what else they opened. "I'm sorry," he said. "I wish things were different. I wish I were different."

For a moment neither of them said anything. Mrs. Carter looked back out the window. "I had to have the elm tree cut down," she said. "The town insisted on it. They said it was jeopardizing the electrical wires."

"That's a shame," Jack said.

She shrugged her thin shoulders. "They did a very neat job of it. All in a day."

"I didn't notice it was gone," said Jack.

"It's getting dark," said Mrs. Carter. "Turn on the light."

Jack's show was at the Winterburn Gallery, which was owned by a woman named Olivia de Havilland. She claimed this was her real name, and Jack saw no reason to doubt her, since there were a number of other equally odd things about her that were true. He spent an exhausting day hanging the show with her. She had the unfortunate idea that some of the canvases should be hung very high, and some very low, thus creating, in her words, "a dynamic viewing experience."

Although Jack had sent an invitation to the opening to his ex-wife, he was surprised to see her there. They usually avoided each other. But about halfway through the evening, Barbara entered the gallery, trailing a twin by either arm. The twins were dressed in brightly colored jogging suits; Barbara's newly restored body was tightly swathed in leather. She ignored the paintings and made right for Jack. "Greetings," she said, kissing the air beside his cheek. She indicated the twins and said, "les enfants," as though they were some exotic delicacy.

Jack didn't know what to do. He felt under-rehearsed. He was aware that everyone was watching him and that he was making a poor show. One of the twins—he had no idea which—clutched his leg. He reached down and patted her head. She looked up at him.

"Which one?" he said.

"Sigourney," Barbara said. "See Daddy's paintings," she said to the child. "Daddy painted these."

Sigourney studied a canvas that, thanks to Olivia de Havilland, was hung at her eye level. "I can do better than that," she said.

There was much tense laughter, followed by tense silence. Jack turned to Barbara. "How about dinner when this is over?" he asked.

"What's up?" asked Barbara.

"Nothing," said Jack. "I just thought it might be nice."

"With or without?" asked Barbara.

"With or without what?"

"Les enfants," said Barbara.

"Oh," said Jack. "With."

"If I'd known, I'd have brought the dog," Barbara said.

Barbara suggested a restaurant called Café Wisteria in Tribeca. The twins devoured a plate of cornichons and radishes and disappeared beneath the table. For a while Jack and Barbara concentrated on their food, and listened to the murmurings at their feet. Barbara was the most relaxed person Jack had ever met. Nothing seemed to faze her, which drove him crazy. The rumor was that she was addicted to Valium, but Jack knew for a fact that she wasn't. She just inhabited her life disinterestedly.

"How is Roger?" Jack asked. Roger was Barbara's new—well, not new anymore—second husband.

"Roger's fine. He's in Madrid at the moment. We're buying a house there."

"In Spain?"

"Outside of Barcelona."

"Why?"

"Why?" she repeated, as if she had never considered the question before. "I don't know. No reason, really. We plan to spend half the year there."

"Oh," Jack said. "You'll take the twins?"

"They're a little too young to fend for themselves."

"Of course," said Jack. "I just meant . . ."

"What?"

"I don't know. What will they do in Spain?"

"Learn Spanish, I hope. I don't know. What do they do in New York? Play. Grow up. Don't tell me you're developing an interest in them?"

Jack didn't say anything. A small hand was rolling his sock up and down his ankle. "Actually," he said, "I have been thinking about them. I was wondering if I could take them to visit my grandmother."

"How is she doing?"

"Well. She'd like to see the twins."

Barbara raised the tablecloth and addressed the floor. "Honeys," she said, "would you like to go visit your great-grandma? Jack wants to take you to Bedford."

"Where's Bedford?" a twin asked.

"Not far," said Barbara. "In the country. You get there on a train."

"Are there cows?"

"No, it's not a farm."

"Is there a trampoline?"

"No. Just a big house with your great-grandma, who wants to see you very much. And Jack will take you. Wouldn't that be fun?"

"Who's Jack?"

"You know Jack. Your father. Not Daddy, but your father."

Jack leaned his head down and looked under the table. "It's me," he said. "I'm Jack." The twins looked up at him with identical, confused expressions on their small, perfect faces. "I'm Jack," he said again, and reached his hand down toward them, tentatively, as if to wild dogs.

At the hotel there was a message for him to call Langley Smith. Langley had originally been Jack's student, when he taught painting and lectured on modern art for one ill-fated semester at Bryn Mawr immediately following his exodus from New York. He had met her again, several years later, at the opening of a show of his in Los Angeles. By then she had switched from painting to acting. Her biggest claim to fame was as a guest star on "L.A. Law," playing a woman (unjustly) accused of child molestation.

"Hi baby," Langley said. "How did it go?"

"Not bad," Jack said. "Julian Arnotti bought the two big ones."

"Great," she said.

"How are you doing?" Jack asked.

"Not bad. I was called back again for the part in that pilot."

"What pilot?"

"The one for Lorimar. About the American family in Russia. You know, the dum-dum daddy's an ambassador, the ditsy mother's an alky, there are kids and a dog and a lot of funny commies."

"Who are you?"

"The daughter, if you can believe it. I'm a nympho with a thing for Ruskies in uniforms."

"That's great. And you got it?"

"Yes. Unless they decide to make the family black. As you know, black is very popular out here now. They're negotiating with Richard Pryor, and if he says yes, then it will be black. But I doubt he will."

"Maybe you could be an adopted daughter. That would be interesting."

"I'll suggest it. So when are you coming back?"

"I don't know. In about a week. I'm a little worried about my grandmother."

"Why?"

"Well, my aunt who usually stays with her is drying out at Betty Ford. I don't think she should be living alone."

"Can't you get someone to stay with her? A nurse or someone?"

"I guess so. I'll have to look into it."

"If this Ruskie thing falls through maybe I'll fly out. It would be fun to spend some time in New York together."

"I don't know," he said. "I'm kind of preoccupied."

"You must be tired," Langley said. "What time is it there?"

"One o'clock."

"You want to go to bed?"

"Yes," he said.

"O.K., then. We'll talk later?"

"Sure," he said. "Listen, good luck with the thing. The pilot."

"Thanks," she said. "I'll let you know if I get it."

"Well, good night."

"Good night," Langley said. "I love you."

Jack hung up quickly, hoping his failure to respond to her declaration had gone unnoticed. But of course he knew it had not. And he had some idea of how Langley must feel: Langley, in her bedroom, the TV on, the sprinkler spraying the window; Langley in bed in her Tina the Killer Whale T-shirt, having said I love you to the miles between them, to the darkness, to his inevitable silence. She was better and braver than he, he understood that, but what he did not understand was why she tolerated his constipated dumb love, which he could express only when they lay down together and allowed their bodies to speak. He redialed the number of her house in Topanga Canyon. "Hello," he said. "C'est moi."

"Bonjour moi," Langley said. "What's up?"

"Nothing."

"Oh," said Langley.

"I miss you," he said, after a pause.

"I miss you, too," Langley answered.

"I'm a little drunk," he said.

"Go to bed," suggested Langley. "Sleep it off."

"I wish you were here," he said.

"So do I," said Langley.

"I really wish you were here," he said. "Really."

"I love you," said Langley.

He didn't answer. He just sat on his bed, the drapes drawn, the traffic in the street, the phone pressed to his ear.

"Sleep well," Langley said, and hung up.

While his grandmother and the twins had a tea party in the gazebo, Jack mowed the lawn. The gardener was in the hospital. Although he couldn't hear their conversation, which was obscured by the roar of the mower, he could tell they were having fun. Every time he trudged past the gazebo all three waved at him. His grandmother raised her teacup in salute.

The party was still in progress when he finished the lawn, but before he could join it his grandmother told him to shower and change. Jack still had clothes in the house, which he and his father had lived in from the time his mother had died till the time he went to college. His father died five years ago, of a heart attack while swimming in Long Island Sound.

Except to keep them clean, his grandmother had touched nothing in their bedrooms. His was the same as the day he had left for college, and his father's was the same as the day he went for his swim. Jack took a shower in the bathroom they had shared. There was still a bottle of his father's cologne in the medicine chest. He smelled it and then tentatively put some on his skin, but he didn't smell like his father. He stood naked in the cool bathroom and looked out across the lawn at his grandmother and his daughters in the backyard. They were putting on a show for one another. His grandmother stood up and sang "Getting to Know You." Then the twins performed a sort of tap dance, but without tap shoes or music it was rather thumpy and chaotic.

Jack watched from inside the house, like a voyeur.

He called his grandmother the next day. The phone rang and rang, unanswered. Fearing the worst, he took the first train to Bedford. The front door was unlocked. The curtains in the living room were all drawn and the house was dark. His grandmother lay on the sofa. She sat up as he entered the room.

"Who is it?" she asked, feeling on the coffee table for her glasses.

"It's me," he said, "John."

"Haven't you heard of knocking?" she asked.

"I thought something had happened to you," he said. "I tried to call you, and there was no answer. I thought you were dead."

"Not quite dead," she said. "Just napping."

"Jesus," he said. He opened the curtains.

"Close them," she said. "I'm trying to keep the house cool."

He closed the curtains and sat down beside her on the couch. He realized he was panting and tried to catch his breath. He was sweating, too. "Have you heard from Aunt Helen?" he finally asked. "When is she coming back?"

"Not for a while. Apparently she was moister than any one of us thought."

"Well, I'm worried about you being here alone," Jack said. "I'm planning to go back home, and I don't like it that you're here alone."

"Actually," his grandmother said, "I was thinking about getting a chimpanzee."

"What?" he asked.

"A chimpanzee. For a companion. I've read they make wonderful companions. They're very intelligent, you know, and clean."

"Isn't it against the law to own wild animals?"

"Apparently not chimpanzees."

"I can't believe we're talking about monkeys. You aren't serious about this, are you?"

"Of course I am serious."

"I think it's sick. It's macabre. It's like Nora Desmond in *Sunset Boulevard*."

"Nor*ma* Desmond."

"Whatever."

"What about your promise?" Mrs. Carter asked.

"What?"

"I am changing the subject. You promised to paint me a picture of Benders Bay. I don't suppose you have."

Jack had forgotten all about the painting. "Oh," he said.

"You forgot? I thought so."

"I didn't forget. I just haven't had time. I've been very busy."

"Of course," she said.

"I'll go up this week," he said. "Before I go back."

Mrs. Carter leaned forward and kissed him. "It was very sweet of you to rush out here. I'm sorry I unplugged the phone. I should have told you. I keep it unplugged unless I want to make a call or expect one."

"What if someone has to get in touch with you?"

"They can send a telegram. That is what telegrams are for."

"Telegrams are delivered over the phone."

"What happened to the little men on bicycles?"

"I don't know. They all died."

This news momentarily silenced Mrs. Carter.

"Well, that's a shame," she finally said. "A damn shame." She stood up. "Come," she said. "It's lunchtime. Are you hungry? How about a sandwich?"

That night he called Langley. He explained about the painting, telling her he wasn't sure when he'd be back.

"That's very sweet of you, to do a painting for your grandmother," she said.

Jack let her think that. It was the second time that day someone had told him he was sweet, yet he felt less than sweet. "Did you get the part?" he asked.

"No," she said. "They're postponing production while they rethink the concept. They've decided it's politically incorrect to make fun of commies. I can't believe the end of the Cold War is fucking up my career."

"That's a shame," said Jack.

"That's the breaks," Langley said.

"Listen," he said. "Why don't you fly out here? And we'll go out to Fishers together? We can stay a couple of days."

"I don't think so," said Langley.

"Why not?" he asked.

"I don't know," she said. "I'm just, you know, going through a lot of stuff right now, and I want to get it sorted out."

"What stuff?"

"Just stuff. Life stuff, work stuff." She paused. "Love stuff."

"About me?"

"Bingo," Langley said.

"What's the problem?"

"Oh, I don't know," said Langley. "I don't even know that there is a problem. I'm just thinking about it."

"Well, can't you think about it on Fishers Island?"

"Baby, listen, call me when you get back to L.A. We'll talk about it then."

"You don't think we should talk about it now?"

"No. Have fun. Paint well."

"Wait," he said. "Don't hang up."

"What?" said Langley.

"Listen," he said.

"I'm listening," Langley said.

"I don't want to lose you," he said.

Langley didn't say anything.

"I don't want to lose you," he repeated.

"That's funny," Langley said.

"Why?"

Langley made a small noise that could either have been the beginning of a laugh or a sob.

"What's funny?" he asked.

"Nothing, really."

"Have I already lost you?"

"Maybe," Langley said. "A little."

"Listen, I'll come back tomorrow. I can paint the house later this summer."

"No," said Langley. "Paint it now. I told you I have stuff to think about. It's O.K. I'll be here when you come back."

"Well, don't think about anything till I get there."

"I'm a smart girl," Langley said. "I can't promise you that."

The next day Jack took a train to New London and rented a car and rode the ferry over to Fishers Island. He drove out to Benders Bay and parked at the end of the long, sandy driveway, and looked up at the house, which stood on a bluff above the water. It had not been changed. The lilacs were blooming. There was a strong breeze from the sea and it blew some lavender blossoms across the windshield. Jack closed his eyes. He could smell the lilacs and the salt water and the heat. He remembered a time when he and his grandmother had been playing Scrabble on the terrace. He could remember the same fragrant hot wind, and how every now and then they would have to lean forward, shelter the board, and place their hands over the intricately arranged tiles, so that their words would not blow away.

He got out of the car and assembled his easel and supplies at a point in the road where the house was best silhouetted against the sky. As he began drawing, a woman appeared on the terrace and looked down at him curiously. She began to walk down the driveway, and Jack thought of the questions she was bound to ask him—Who are you? What are you doing here? Why are you painting this house? He put down his piece of charcoal, and tried to think of some answers.

Fear of Math

In order to enter the MBA program at Columbia in the fall, I had to take calculus in the summer. I was offered two options: an eight-week, slow-paced course or a three-week intensive. Although the last math course I took was trigonometry my junior year in high school, I chose the three-week course, on the principle that things you are scared of are things you shouldn't dwell on too long. I'd finish calculus in July, spend August at the beach, and start school with a tan.

The first Monday of class, the air-conditioning was broken. I had made the mistake of wearing a denim dress, and as the morning progressed, I felt the back of it getting wetter and wetter. The teacher must have known about the air-conditioning because he was wearing khaki shorts and a white T-shirt. He didn't look at all like a teacher—he looked more like a very old Boy Scout or a very young forest ranger. No one knew he was the teacher until he started teaching, which he did hesitantly, almost apologetically. I could tell right away he had never taught before.

The class met from nine to twelve and then from twelve-thirty to three-thirty. By noon the blackboard was so dusty from erased equations the teacher had to wash it with a sponge and a bucket of water. I went outside and sat on the front steps of the building and ate my tabbouleh-and-pita-bread sandwich. I read over my notes, which already filled about half of the new notebook I'd bought in Lamston's that morning. I couldn't make any sense of them. I'd have to write neater.

The air-conditioner in the hall worked, so I went back up and stood outside the classroom door and drank from a water fountain. I had to lean way down into the curved white basin to reach the weak spurt of water.

When I stood back up the forest ranger was standing beside me holding his bucket of chalky water.

"Will you do me a favor?" he asked.

"What?" I said.

"Will you dump this in the women's room? The men's is locked."

"Sure," I said.

Instead of handing me the bucket, he started walking down the hall. I followed him. Outside the women's room he gave me the bucket and opened the door. He held it open and watched me pour the water down the sink.

He took the bucket back, and we walked down the hall. "You were smart," I said, "to wear shorts."

He looked down at his shorts, as if he had forgotten he was wearing them. He opened the door of the hot classroom and we went in. We were the only ones there. I sat at the desk I had chosen in the morning—in the back row—and he began filling the blackboard with new, harder, equations.

I was subletting an apartment from a friend of mine, Alyssa. Actually, I wasn't subletting it: her parents owned it, and she had gone to Europe for the summer, so I was staying there, paying the bills, watering the ferns, and feeding the two long-haired, exotic, nasty cats.

It was a huge apartment. The more I saw other people's apartments the more I began to realize how extraordinary this one was: it was full of space. The living room was as big as most apartments, with its two leather couches facing one another across from the fireplace. There was a long hall with a thin Persian runner unraveling along the wooden floor, two bedrooms, an eat-in kitchen, and even a pantry full of glass hutches in which hung dozens of globular wineglasses, like a laboratory.

The evening after the first day of class, I was trying to make cucumber soup without a recipe or a blender when the phone rang. It was an old-fashioned black wall phone in the pantry, where it always seemed to ring louder on account of the glass.

"Hello," I said.

"Is Julie there?" a man asked.

"This is Julie," I said. I never say "This is she." Something about speaking that properly unnerves me.

"Julie? This is Stephen?"

"Stephen?" I repeated. I didn't know any Stephens in New York. I didn't know any men here, actually, except for Ethan, my older sister Debbie's creepy ex-husband, and a cute man named Gerry I met a few nights before in the greengrocer's. I'd helped him pick out a cantaloupe.

"From calculus," the man said.

"Oh," I said. "Which one are you?"

"The teacher," he said. "The one who stands in front."

I laughed, and so did he, then I stopped laughing because I suddenly thought he must be calling to tell me I'd have to drop the class. They must have some system where they weed the hopeless students out immediately. I saw my whole career—business school, New York, executive suites, tailored suits—going down the drain. And so quickly.

"What do you want?" I said rudely.

"I don't know," he said. "To see how I did. I've never taught calculus before."

"Really?" I said. "Never?"

"Well, not for six straight hours."

"Oh," I said.

"So how was I?"

"I've never taken calculus," I said. "Not even an hour. I'm the wrong person to ask."

"Did you understand everything?"

"No," I said.

"Oh. Maybe I should go slower." Then he paused, and said, "Do you want to go out for dinner sometime?"

"Dinner?" I said, as if this was a complicated theorem that needed some explaining.

"Well," he said. "Maybe just a drink."

"No," I said. "Dinner's fine. Dinner's good."

Stephen and I ate dinner the next night in the garden of a restaurant, under a dogwood tree. White blossoms fell into my soup and across the lavender tablecloth when the wind blew. We had met outside the restaurant, and for a minute I didn't recognize him. I had only seen Stephen in his Boy Scout shorts, and that was the only way I could picture him. He didn't look as cute in his green fatigue pants and pink oxford shirt. He could have been anyone.

"So," Stephen said, once our small talk had been run through and our soup delivered. "End my suspense. Why are you taking calculus?"

"I have to," I said. "I'm going to business school."

"I knew it," Stephen said. "Everyone's going to business school. My mother's going to business school."

"Did you teach her calculus?"

"No. I got my math genes from her. My father's mathematically illiterate. He's a painter."

"So am I," I said.

"What, a painter?"

"No," I said. "An illiterate."

"Oh," he said. "Well, you can still learn calculus. It just takes longer."

"Can I learn it by September?"

"Sure. If you get a tutor."

"A tutor?"

"Well, yeah. You're going to have to devote all your time to learning calculus. It's a new way of thinking for people like you. We're talking twelve-hour days, seven days a week."

"Why am I doing this?" I said. "It sounds horrible."

"I don't know," Stephen said. "Why are you doing this?"

I spooned my soup, pushing the blossoms aside.

"I don't know," I finally said. "I felt like my life was going nowhere, like it needed a big change. I've been living in Michigan," I said, as if that explained things.

"Where?"

"Ann Arbor. I went to school there."

"What did you study? I assume it wasn't math."

"French. I can hardly speak it anymore."

"What did you do with a French major?"

"Nothing. I was stenciling wicker furniture. I was making pretty good money, for Ann Arbor, at least, but I got sick of it. There was nowhere to go. So I figured I needed an MBA."

I didn't mention that my boyfriend, Tim, made the wicker furniture and that I had lived with him for five years and been engaged for one of them (the fourth). Most of going to business school had to do with breaking with Timmy.

The waiter came and took our soup away.

"I don't know," I said. "Do you think this is all a big mistake?"

"Fools can get MBA's," Stephen said.

"But they have math genes," I said.

"You have math genes," Stephen said. "They just have to be aroused."

I laughed.

"No, really," he said. "They're there. It's like Pygmalion. I could take you on. I'll transform you into a math whiz."

The leaves of the dogwood tree started shaking above us. I looked up and saw the sky glowing as if the sun had set all over, not in just one spot. I could feel the drops of rain above us, falling: heavy, sooty drops. I stood up and put my bag over my shoulder.

"What's the matter?" said Stephen. He thought I was leaving.

"It's going to rain," I said. "Look."

We were the first couple in the empty restaurant, and we got a table right inside the terrace doors. Watching the rain fall in the deserted garden, I felt wise and intuitive and in touch, if not with calculus, at least with the weather.

The next night—the third night of class—my official tutelage began. Stephen arrived at my door with a calculator and a bunch of freesias.

"This is some building," he said. "The elevator is about the size of my apartment."

"It's not mine," I said. "I'm subletting it."

"Oh," Stephen said. "And I thought I had found an heiress." He handed me the flowers.

"Then you should meet Alyssa." I went into the kitchen but Stephen walked into the living room, then down the hall, and into the kitchen through the pantry. "Do you want something to drink? All I really have is beer and cranberry juice."

"I'll just have water," Stephen said. He took an overturned glass from the dish drain and filled it from the tap. I had been nervous about this rendezvous, but there was something reassuring about watching Stephen's Adam's apple bob as he gulped the water: he did it as if he'd been drinking water in my kitchen for years.

Stephen was a better tutor than a teacher. He began by asking me what I didn't understand. I said just about ev-

erything, so we started at the beginning and as he explained
things I asked questions, not letting him continue until I understood. We moved from the dining-room table to the
living-room couch, and when I finally felt like I understood
the first three days of calculus—about one o'clock in the
morning—I put my calculus book on the floor and my feet
on the couch. We were sitting on opposite ends of the leather
couch, facing each other, our legs entangled between us. He
was the kind of person, I noticed, whose second toe is longer
than his big toe. My toes are perfectly proportional, and I set
a standard by them.

"You have very long toes," I said. I touched them.
"They're kind of ugly."

Stephen yawned and peered down his body at his toes.
"It comes with the math genes," he said. "It's part of the
package."

When I was growing up, my father was an engineer for
NASA, and my mother taught home economics. Now they're
both retired and are in business together. They've bought a
series of what my father calls "exploitable" houses—barns
and shacks and even abandoned churches—which they live
in and jointly convert into luxurious summer homes and then
resell for no small profit. My father does the outside and my
mother the inside, or, as they put it, my father builds the
nest and my mother feathers it. They are never in one house
for more than a year. My mother gets attached to some of
them, but my father insists on selling them. He thinks it's
important for people their age to keep moving, as if you'd
petrify if you lived in the same house for a few years.

I went up to see them—and the boathouse they were
restoring in upstate New York—the first weekend of calculus,
although Stephen thought I should stay in New York and
study. I told him I'd study at the lake. I intended to: I packed
my huge calculus book in my knapsack, and even did a few

problems on the plane, but by the time I switched to a six-seater in Syracuse, calculus didn't seem to matter anymore. In the city, with the straight streets and glass walls and constant noise, calculus could be accommodated, but in the tiny plane, gliding over trees and lakes all fading away beneath me into the growing darkness, calculus faded away, too. The numbers and arrows and symbols seemed foolish, so I put my book away and watched the lights come on in the houses below.

Saturday morning I helped my mother upholster a dock that extended around two sides of the house. My parents were converting it into a veranda, covering it with grass-colored indoor-outdoor carpeting. My mother was treading water, outfitted with flippers, mask, snorkel, and staple gun. She looked like Jacques Cousteau. Her job was to swim under the dock and affix the carpeting to the underside; I was supposed to hold it in place and smooth out the wrinkles.

My job was easy. I found the best way to hold the carpet flat and in place was to just lie on the section we were working on. I unhitched my bathing-suit straps and opened my calculus book. I could hear my mother slurping around in the water beneath me, attacking the dock with her staple gun. When she pulled the carpet for a snugger fit, my mechanical pencil rolled off into the weedy water.

In a few minutes my mother swam out from under the dock. She raised the mask so it stuck out from the top of her bathing cap, and crossed her tanned arms on the dock.

"I lost my pencil," I said. "It rolled off."

My mother looked at my calculus book and said, "Can you really do that stuff?"

"Not yet," I said. "It's supposed to click and all make sense at some point."

"The only nice thing about being an old woman is that I was spared new math. I remember when I had to teach metric conversion I was a loony case. Your father had to do

a guest lecture on the metric system. We made vichyssoise.
All the girls fell in love with him. They had never seen a
man cook before. What ever happened to all that?"

"What?"

"The metric system. Don't you remember? We were supposed to convert. They even had commercials on TV about
it: 'America Goes Metric.' What happened?"

"I don't know," I said. "I guess they gave up."

"I like inches," my mother said. "I'd miss inches. It's
too bad we're not closer to New York. Daddy could help you
with your calculus. He used to help Debbie."

"My teacher says it's all genetic," I said. "He thinks my
math genes just have to be aroused."

"Aroused?" My mother pushed away from the dock and
floated on her back. The skirt of her bathing suit fanned out
around her thighs. I looked up into the bright sky and closed
my eyes. The first night Stephen and I slept together, he
whispered numbers into my ear: long, high numbers—dis-
tances between planets, seconds in a life. He spoke as if they
were poetry, and they became poetry. Later, when he fell
asleep, I leaned over him and watched, trying to picture a
mathematician's dreams. I concluded that Stephen must
dream in abstract, cool designs like Mondrian paintings.

"Have you heard from Tim?" my mother asked.

"No," I said. I could feel the green turf pressing into my
cheek and hear my mother making tiny splashing sounds,
listlessly circumventing the lily pads. "We're not calling each
other."

"Don't you wonder how he is?"

I opened my eyes. My mother was treading water, moving her arms and legs very gracefully and slowly, making the
least possible effort to stay afloat.

"Actually," I said, "I'm seeing someone else."

"Already? Who?"

"You don't know him," I said.

"Well, I assume I don't know him. That's why I'm asking."

"The teacher," I said.

"The calculus teacher? The geneticist?"

"Yes," I said.

"Oh, honey," my mother said. She sounded sad. "Just remember you're on the rebound. Be careful. Especially with a calculus teacher."

"I'm not on the rebound."

"What do you call it, then?" My mother picked a piece of duckweed out of the water, fingered it, then tossed it a few feet away. A small fish rose and mouthed the surface of the water, nipping at it. I thought for a moment. I sat up and put my legs in the water. The fish swam away. I was mad at my mother for bringing up Tim, as I had been doing a pretty good job of forgetting about him.

"It's not a rebound," I said. "It's a new life. It has nothing to do with Ann Arbor or Timmy or wicker."

But my mother wasn't listening. She was looking at the bottom of the lake. "Look," she said. "Your pencil." She did a quick surface dive. I watched her white legs kick down into the dark water. In a moment she popped back up, and tossed my pencil onto the dock.

Stephen and I had, in our one short week together, established a ritual. We went out together after class for a beer. The middle of the afternoon, I discovered, was a nice time to frequent bars. I'd never much liked them at night in Ann Arbor when they were noisy and crowded and dark and sticky. But in the afternoon no one played the jukebox, the sun shone in the open door, and the people in the soap operas swam through their complicated lives on the TV above the bar like fish in an aquarium.

Stephen was drawing a diagram on a soggy cocktail napkin, trying, as always, to explain something I didn't understand. I was half watching him and half watching a large white cat thread himself through the legs of the bar-stools, savoring the touch of each leg against his fur.

"See," Stephen said, pushing the napkin across the table. I looked at it but couldn't make any sense of it, so I turned it around.

"No," Stephen said. "This way." He turned it back around.

Something about the blurry diagram on the cocktail napkin depressed me. I couldn't believe it had come to be an important part of my life. It had no message for me. I leaned back against the vinyl booth.

"Can we forget about it for a while?" I said.

"Sure." Stephen crumpled the napkin and punted it to the floor with his fingers. "What's the matter?" he asked.

"I've been thinking," I said. "Maybe this is a bad idea."

"What?"

"This," I said. "Us."

"Oh," said Stephen. "Why?"

"I just feel like I should get through this myself. I mean I think I should pass calculus by myself and then we can decide if we want to see each other."

"But you can't pass calculus by yourself. You need a tutor."

"I'll get another tutor," I said.

"It's too late to get another tutor. We just have one more week. Julie, you know, no one expects you to pass calculus yourself. It's not some big deal. This isn't the Girl Scout merit-badge contest."

"I know," I said. "I can't explain. I just think this is wrong."

Stephen drained his beer glass. "Why won't you let me help you?" he asked.

"I told you," I said. "I think it's wrong."

"But it's not wrong. There's nothing wrong about it. You just want to get rid of me."

I didn't say anything. I watched the cat. We sat there for a moment. I felt like I was making a terrible mistake, only I wasn't sure what it was: if it had to do with love or calculus. I felt I was probably losing on both counts.

I don't think I've worked at anything as hard as I worked at calculus the next week. The exam was scheduled for one o'clock on the last Friday of class; we had a review session in the morning. I asked two questions. Stephen answered them.

I was sitting on the front steps of the math building re-reading my notes when he came out. He stood beside me. "Come on," he said. "I'm taking you out to lunch."

"I can't," I said. "I have to study."

He leaned over and pulled my spiral notebook out of my hands. "If you don't know it now," he said, "you never will."

We went across the street to the bar with the slinking white cat. We had a nice lunch. We didn't mention calculus.

I finished the exam before the allotted time was up, which I thought might be a good sign. I couldn't tell. I had no idea how I did. I handed it in and took the subway home. I showered and began packing, because I was going up to the lake to see my parents for the weekend. I was just going out the door when the phone rang. I debated answering it. Most of the calls were still for Alyssa, and I had turned the answering machine on. But it's hard not to answer a ringing phone.

It was Stephen, telling me I had failed the exam and, consequently, the course. For a second I was actually shocked, and then I realized how absurd the whole thing was, my ever thinking I could pass calculus, get an MBA, live in New York. I stood for a moment looking at Alyssa's ridiculous accumulation of crystal. I couldn't speak.

"Julie?" Stephen said. "Are you listening?"

"Yes," I said.

"Listen," he said. "I explained the situation to Foster." Foster was the chairman of the department and a dean at the business school. His eleven-year-old daughter sat next to me in class. She was taking calculus, she told me, for fun.

"You explained the situation?"

"I just told him you almost passed—you almost did— and that you needed the grade to start the program."

"What program?" I asked.

"The MBA," Stephen said.

"Oh," I said. "I've changed my mind about that. I'm not getting an MBA."

"What?" said Stephen. "Are you crazy?"

I was starting to cry, so I didn't say anything.

"Julie? What are you talking about? Why don't we go out to dinner and talk about this?"

"I can't," I said. "I'm going up to my parents'."

"Listen," said Stephen. "Are you listening?"

"I'm not deaf, Stephen."

"I'm going down to the registrar. I'm going to register you for the August session. I don't even teach it, so it will be O.K. We won't talk about it now. But think about it."

I told him I would think about it; I told him I would call him when I got back on Sunday. I hung up. I stood in Alyssa's pantry. I thought, If I were the kind of person who broke things I would break a glass, or maybe several. I thought, Maybe I should break some even though I'm not that type of person. It would be therapeutic. But I didn't break any. It wasn't worth the effort of cleaning it up, which I would have done, immediately.

Then I started thinking about Stephen. I wished he hadn't called me. He must have started grading my exam the moment I left. Now he was going down to the registrar, at this very moment. He was being so nice. It made me feel guilty and selfish and mean.

I ordered two gin-and-tonics at once from the steward because I wanted two drinks and was afraid he wouldn't make it up the aisle twice by the time we got to Syracuse. They tasted great, and after a while even the fields below us looked trustworthy and harmless, as though if we crashed they'd just reach up and hold us as we fell.

My father was waiting in his Army-surplus jeep at the airport. I threw my knapsack in the back and climbed in the front and we took off. It seemed like he was driving a little too quickly down the tree-lined road; the wind seemed to rush past awfully fast. The sun was finally setting but the light lingered all over the sky.

"I failed my exam," I shouted to my father.

"Oh, honey," he shouted back. "Can you take it again?"

"Maybe. I'll see on Monday."

We drove a little farther in silence and then turned down the dirt road that goes through the woods to the boathouse.

"Your mother's a little upset," my father said, not looking at me.

"Why? What happened?"

"We had a little argument."

Because my parents never argued in front of me, I thought they never argued. "About what?" I asked.

My father sighed and downshifted. "Your mother wants to settle down. She wants to buy a condominium somewhere." He said "condominium" as if it were a carcinogen.

"Oh," I said.

"I like the way we live. I think it's good for us. I think eventually we should think about settling down in one place. But why now? Look at this—" he motioned out at the land that fell away to the lake that lay as still as a mirror between the trees. "A year ago we didn't know this existed," he said. "I just like finding new things. Making new things."

We pulled into the barn where he parked the jeep, but neither of us made a move to get out.

"I hate to tell you this, honey," my father said. "But I just thought you should know. Mom is in bed. She got kind of upset."

"Oh," I said. My poor father. He sat in his jeep, feeling bad.

"Maybe you should go up and talk to her." For the first time he looked at me. There was just enough light left in the barn for me to see the tears, not falling from his eyes, but sitting in them, glistening.

The electricity in the boathouse was limited to the kitchen, so the rest of the house was dark. I climbed the spiral staircase my father had built to the bedroom. My mother was sitting in bed with her hands folded on the quilt she'd made from scraps of dresses she'd sewn for me and my sister when we were little. Whenever I see the quilt, I can picture some of the dresses, although they were all alike: tiny Peter Pan collars, the fronts smocked, skirts puffed out from the waist. I don't know what happened to them. I wish I still had one or two, just to look at. I sat on the other side of the bed.

"Hi," I said. I leaned over and kissed her. She smiled at me, knowing how silly the situation was: her in bed, me coming to her—it was all wrong, all reversed.

"Did Daddy tell you about our disagreement?" she asked. I said yes.

She looked out the porthole window my father had installed in the crook of the roof, but it was too dark to see anything.

"I'm sorry now I made such a fuss," she said. "It's just that I can't keep doing this. It's not that I don't have the energy or the will. It's just that I can't keep making things and leaving them behind. Does that seem wrong?"

"No," I said. "Of course not."

She looked at me. "Your father loved you kids, adored you, but he was so happy when you went away to school and he retired. We could finally take off and do things and not be tied down, and it was great for a while but now I'm sick of it. I'm sorry but I'm plain sick of it."

I thought, Don't tell me this, don't say any of this. I don't want to know you're unhappy. And then for the second time that day I felt mean and selfish. My mother sighed and looked back out the window.

I stood up. "Do you want anything from downstairs?"

"No, thanks." She turned away from the window, trying to smile. "How was your exam? I forgot all about it."

"O.K.," I said. "I passed."

A month later, I did pass calculus. It was almost easy the second time. I didn't see Stephen very much; he wasn't teaching so he wasn't really around. When we did see each other we felt awkward: without calculus we had little to share, and for all the hours we had spent together, we didn't seem to know each other very well.

That same week, my parents told me they were separating, at least until they could decide upon a way of life that was "mutually enjoyable." I was surprised and a little ashamed to find that I felt more relieved than upset. While I was growing up I had always been so proud of them, and my intact home, but at some point—and I didn't know when—all that had lost its terrible importance.

They finished work on the boathouse and sold it to a movie star. Over Labor Day weekend, my father went off to Maine to look for a very dilapidated, very large farm. My mother came to see me in New York. We went out to dinner

and celebrated my passing calculus. My mother waited until
the bottle of champagne was empty and we were drinking
brewed decaffeinated coffee before she talked about the
separation.

"I feel very brave doing this," she said. "I feel foolish,
too, but I do feel brave. And it's nice that it can end like this,
with no hard feelings. We really do understand each other.
Of course it helps that it's a very specific problem—not something about how we feel about each other."

"But doesn't that make it harder?"

"What?"

"Still feeling the same," I said. "I mean, I'd think if you
hated each other it would be easier."

My mother stroked the tablecloth, forming and then
smoothing wrinkles. Her hands were covered with tiny cuts
and scratches, and I noticed she was still wearing her wedding
ring.

"No," she said. "Although I don't know why. I guess I
like to think things have changed more than failed. I don't
know. Does that make any sense?"

"Yes," I said.

"Debbie doesn't understand at all. She's worried about
me. She wants me to move to Allentown."

"What are you going to do?" I asked.

She opened her pocketbook and took out a brochure for
condominiums on a golf course in South Carolina. There
were pictures of buildings nestled in the rough along green
fairways, and floor plans of different models.

"No two are alike," my mother said. "I'm going down
next week to look at them."

"They look nice," I said.

"The best thing about them is that I can pick out everything myself: the carpeting, the drapes, the Congoleum,
the Formica, the appliances—even the shelf paper."

"That's great," I said. There was a moment when I

thought my mother was about to start crying, so I studied the brochure. When I looked up, she seemed O.K.

"And they do all the work," my mother said. "Everything. They even fill the ice trays before you move in."

My mother left for South Carolina on Tuesday, and Wednesday was registration for the fall semester of business school. For a few panic-stricken moments at breakfast, I thought about not going—about getting out of New York while I was ahead. I could go down and help my mother move into her condominium. But that morning I realized that if I went uptown and registered for accounting and statistics and behavioral management and whatever else, I'd be done with all these second thoughts.

It hasn't been quite like that, of course, but it hasn't been bad. Sometimes I see Stephen around in the late afternoon, and we go across the street to our bar. Now it gets dark while we sit there, but it's still nice. Stephen always asks me if I need help. I tell him no. After the ordeal of calculus, business school is manageable.

What Do People
Do All Day?

"Guess what my monogram is," asks Mark. He is sitting at the porch table eating a bowl of Froot Loops: first the pink, then the yellow, and finally the orange circles. The bowl keeps changing color.

Diane, the babysitter, watches him put a yellow spoonful into his mouth. She is not babysitting for him but for his stepbrother, Will, who is sitting in his high chair watching TV.

"Your monogram?" Diane asks. She has the feeling that Mark is smarter than she is and that his questions have some tricky double meaning.

"My monogram. You know, like on a sweater or something. My initials."

"Well," says Diane. "M for Mark and V for Volkenburg. What's your middle name?"

"Theodore," says Mark. "For Daddy. Get it?"

"What?" admits Diane, feeling dense.

"MTV," says Mark. "M—T—V. Like on cable TV."

"Oh," says Diane. She gives the baby a spoonful of the peaches and yogurt his mother, Helen—Mark's stepmother —had blended that morning. Will allows the tiny leaf-shaped spoon to be inserted into his mouth, but makes no attempt to swallow the pale orange mush. It slides out of his mouth. Mark watches and imitates with yellow, partly chewed Froot Loops.

Helen is a lawyer and works in the city part-time. Diane comes at eight and leaves whenever Helen or Ted, her husband, comes home. Ted, a recently untenured communications professor at Drew, is now looking for work in the "real world": television, cable TV, video. He is having no luck.

Outside the screen windows, in the kidney-shaped swimming pool, Annette is swimming her thirtieth, and final, lap. Annette is Mark's mother—Ted's first wife. She lives around the block and every morning, when she sees Helen's car drive past on the way to the bus stop, she pulls her jogging suit on over her bathing suit, trots through the backyards, and dives into her ex-husband's pool. Technically, she is not allowed to do this. She has Mark all of July and every other week during the school year, but thirty—hopefully fifty by the end of the summer—laps never hurt anyone, especially since she does them when Helen and Ted are out. They never use the pool anyway. Diane and Mark are sworn to secrecy.

Annette gets out of the pool, panting, and dries herself with a towel left out overnight, then wraps it around her waist skirtlike and opens the porch door.

"How many?" Mark asks.

"Three O," Annette says. "What's that?" She nods at Mark's cereal. "Lunch?"

"Breakfast," says Mark. "Froot Loops."

"No wonder you like it here," Annette says. "They let you eat junk."

"It's vitamin fortified," Mark says. "See." He holds up the cereal box.

Annette ignores the box but picks some green grapes

from the fruit bowl. She doesn't seem to notice that she is dripping water on the floor. Diane watches, fascinated. She is intrigued with Annette. She hasn't figured her out yet.

"How's Gerber?" Annette asks the baby. She calls him Gerber because she thinks he looks like the Gerber baby. She always makes it sound like an insult, although secretly she is jealous of how beautiful Will is. Mark was kind of an ugly baby.

"Gerber doesn't like this yogurt," Diane says.

"Let me try it," Annette says. She takes the baby spoon from the Peter Rabbit porringer and tastes the puréed peaches. "It's good," she says. "We should all eat this well."

Diane pulls Will out of the high chair, takes off his sodden bib and sits him on the floor. "He needs to be changed," she announces.

"That's your job," says Annette. "At least you get paid for it. I never got paid for it. I did it for love. For my little poppet." She reaches out and tousles Mark's hair, which is already tufted from sleep.

"I'm not your little puppet," says Mark. He eats the last orange Froot Loop.

"You were," says Annette.

"No," says Mark, "I wasn't."

"Oh, but you were, darling. You used to beg me to call you poppet. You would beg me—when you were as little as Gerber."

"He can't talk," says Mark. "So I couldn't have begged you." He drinks the sweet pastel-colored milk from the bowl. Annette watches him.

"You could talk," she says. "You were very smart. Very advanced." She gets up and opens the refrigerator. "When does she come home today?" she asks Diane.

"She's taking the one-thirty bus."

"Does that mean it leaves or arrives at one-thirty?" Annette takes a swig from a bottle of seltzer, then puts it back in the refrigerator. She enjoys the thought of her spittle mixed, unknowingly, with Ted's. He taught her to drink seltzer from the bottle.

"It leaves at one-thirty," says Diane. She picks up Will. "It gets here at two-forty."

"Good," says Annette. She closes the refrigerator. "That gives me the peak hours by the pool."

"What are the peak hours?" asks Mark.

"Prime Time Tanning Hours," says Annette. "Sun Ray City. Eleven a.m. to two p.m."

The "employment counselor" suggested from the start that Ted shave his beard, but he resisted. He likes his beard. He's had it for a long time. Originally, it was all black, but now it's streaked with silver—silver, not white. At least the half of it that is still on his face.

It is noon and Ted is at his friend's apartment in the city, shaving off his beard. He is between "sessions." Everything in job hunting has an unexpected name: "sessions" instead of interviews, "networking" instead of socializing. Barbara Brown, his counselor, is wonderfully maternal: she gets him coffee every morning for their "strategy meetings," gives him quarters so he can call her from the street "first thing" after every session and "report back in." He will miss her, if he ever finds a job. Ted looks at his half-shaved face in the mirror. Maybe he should stop now and get a job in a circus: half man, half woman. He tries to smile with one half of his face and frown with the other. Then he continues shaving, making long sweeps with the razor he just bought, letting the moist curls of hair fall from the razor down his arms and into the sink. His mouth, uncovered, looks all wrong.

Helen never worries that Will will get hurt or get sick or die. She worries that he will forget her; that he will look up at her—from his crib, if he's napping, from his high chair, if he's having a snack, or from Diane's arms—not with the wonderful smile of recognition he has recently acquired but with a dumb, vacant stare. Sometimes, too, riding home on the bus in the afternoon, she has trouble picturing Will. It upsets her that she cannot commit his tiny body to memory. Perhaps it is because he is changing so quickly. He does look slightly different every afternoon.

This afternoon when she gets home everyone is in the pool. Will has his swimmies on and Mark and Diane are pushing him back and forth. Will is laughing, but when he sees Helen he raises his fists in the air, clutching and un-clutching them. Helen pulls him out of the pool, and holds him, even though he is all wet.

Diane climbs out and pours a glass of water over her head. Helen watches her comb out her long blond hair.

"Why did you do that?" she asks.

"It's seltzer," Diane says. "It rinses the chlorine out."

"Oh," says Helen.

"Can I do that?" asks Mark.

"Sure," says Helen.

Mark gets out of the pool and pours his glass over his head. Scarlet juice drips down his face.

"You don't do it with cranberry juice, dummy," Diane says.

Mark licks his lips and his shoulders, then jumps in the pool. The water around him turns pink, but quickly clears.

"Did Ted call?" Helen asks.

"Yes," says Diane.

"What did he say?"

"He probably won't be home for dinner. Don't count on him."

The receptionist tells Ted where the men's room is, but when he finds it he can't get in. It has one of those combination locks on it that require him to push a number. The receptionist didn't tell him the number. He stands in the hall for a long time, feeling lost. He really needs to go to the bathroom, but for some reason he's scared to ask the receptionist for the combination. Finally, a man appears and, as Ted reads the fire-drill instructions, unlocks the door. Ted manages to grab it just before it shuts.

Diane is waiting in a bar for Ted. When they stopped having their affair, about a month ago, Ted agreed that he would still meet her, alone, once a week. They just talk. He thinks these meetings are unnecessary, but he always shows up. Ted lets Diane pick the place because he is afraid if he picks it they will see someone he knows. Since he started his aggressive search for employment, he is trying to straighten out his life. He is secretly looking forward to the fall: Diane will go back to college—all the way to Ohio; he will (hopefully) have a good new job; and his ex-wife will stop swimming in his pool.

Today Diane has picked a bar in the East Village that is known only by its address. It is five past five; Ted is five minutes late. Ted is usually fifteen or twenty minutes late. Once he was an hour late, and Diane waited the whole time, drinking drafts. When he finally arrived she went to the women's room and threw up. Then she drank some more with Ted.

This afternoon she is drinking a gin-and-tonic and watching MTV. There are two TVs over the door, and the duplication of the already bizarre images lends them a certain choreographed beauty. A man comes in and sits down across from her. It takes her a second to realize it is Ted.

"What happened?" she says. "You've shaved."

Ted rubs his naked cheek and shrugs. "How does it look?" he asks.

Ted looks younger; he looks like a boy. He looks like anything she said could hurt him. "Why did you shave?" Diane asks. "I thought you didn't care."

Ted shrugs again, and orders a Dos Equis.

Diane would like to touch his cheek but she restrains herself. She thinks about sitting on her hands but doesn't. They both look at the TV. On it, Michael Jackson dances down a deserted street, illuminating the squares of pavement with his every step. He scowls down at them, singing.

"Isn't he gorgeous?" asks Diane. "I think he's gorgeous."

Ted looks closely at Michael Jackson. He thinks Michael Jackson looks frightening, not gorgeous, but he doesn't tell Diane this. "When do you go back to school?" he says.

"After Labor Day," Diane says. "In two weeks."

"Are you looking forward to it?"

"I don't know," says Diane. "I suppose. Do you wish you were going back to school?"

"You mean to teaching?"

"Yes."

"No," says Ted. "I'm ready for something new."

"So am I," says Diane.

Ted's beer arrives and he pours it. It overflows. "Tell me something," he says.

"What?"

"Why didn't you get a real job this summer? In an office or something? Why did you babysit?"

Diane smiles. "There are no real jobs," she says. "You should know that. Besides, this is easy. He walks. He talks."

Ted nods.

"How did it go today?" Diane asks. "Did you get a real job?"

"They don't tell you," says Ted. "There are second interviews. There are third interviews. They will get back to me."

"You're in a bad mood."

Ted doesn't answer.

"I try to transcend my bad moods," Diane says. "For the sake of others. Have you ever seen me in a bad mood?"

"No," says Ted.

"I've been in a bad mood all summer," says Diane. "I'm in a bad mood now." She smiles. "But can you tell? I still want to sleep with you. I want to touch your cheek more than anything in the world. But I'm transcending it. I'm sitting on my hands." She looks at her hands playing with the ice left in her glass. "Figuratively."

"Oh," says Ted.

"I think it's really sweet the way you humor me," Diane says. "Really, I do. I appreciate it."

Even though she sounds a little hysterical, Ted does not want Diane to stop talking. He doesn't know what to say to her. But Diane stops talking. She looks over at Ted.

"I've got to go," says Ted.

"You just got here," says Diane. "At least finish your beer."

Ted finishes his beer. He puts the glass down on the table and stands up. "I've got to go," he repeats. "I'm sorry."

"You're sorry?" Diane asks.

"Yes," Ted says.

"That's sweet, too," Diane says.

"If you want a snack before dinner, have one of these," Helen says, offering Mark one of the carrot sticks she is cutting.

"I'm not hungry," says Mark. "I don't want a snack."

"Oh," says Helen. "I thought you might be hungry."

"I'm not," says Mark.

"What did you have for lunch?" Helen asks. She likes talking to Mark alone. It is like a rehearsal for talking to Will when he grows up. It is good practice. Will Will be like Mark? Maybe. That wouldn't be bad. Mark is sweet. He gave her a card on Mother's Day that was a real Mother's Day card.

Ted told Mark he could write in STEP before MOTHER, but Mark said no. She keeps the card in her bureau drawer. It has roses on it, and one of the roses has a plastic dewdrop on it.

"I had frozen pizza," Mark says. "But it was about three o'clock."

"What time did you get up?"

"I don't know," Mark says. "Eleven."

Helen is happy because Ted just called from the Port Authority to say he would be home for dinner. Will is sitting on the kitchen floor playing with the latches on her briefcase. In a few minutes he will want to be picked up. Mark is sitting at the kitchen table counting the money he's collected from his paper route. He is using the calculator she and Ted gave him for his birthday. It beeps, not unbeautifully, each time he pushes a button.

Annette left her sunglasses by the pool. At least she thinks she did. She can't find them anywhere in the house, and if Helen finds them by the pool her name will be shit. She'll know they're Annette's because they have her initials stuck to the corner of one of the lenses: AEV. What a dumb thing to have on my sunglasses, Annette thinks. I should have known better. She'll have to get Mark to hide them till tomorrow. Annette dials Ted's number but Helen answers. It figures. Annette hangs up, but then she realizes she has every right to talk to her son and Helen won't even think it's strange she's calling. She dials again. Once more Helen answers.

"Helen? This is Annette. We were just cut off." She shouldn't have said that. Now it is obvious that she hung up.

"Hi," says Helen. "How are you?"

"Fine," says Annette. "Is Mark there?"

"He's right here," says Helen.

"Hello, this is Mark speaking," Mark says, as he has been taught to say.

"Hello, Mark Speaking," says Annette. "This is Mommy Speaking. Listen. Just say yes or no, Mark. Don't repeat what I say."

"O.K.," says Mark.

"Yes or no," says Annette.

"Yes," says Mark.

"I think I left my sunglasses by the pool. I don't want to leave them there overnight. Did you find them?"

"No," says Mark.

"Do you see them? They would be on the picnic table. Or under the chair. The one I lie on."

"I can't see from here," says Mark.

"No," corrects Annette. "That was a no. Nada. Negative."

"What?" says Mark.

"Nothing. Honey, could you go outside and see if they're there? Not right now—wait a few minutes. If you see them just hide them someplace till tomorrow. O.K.?"

"O.K.," says Mark. "Yes."

"I love you, honey," Annette says. "I'll see you tomorrow."

"O.K.," says Mark. "Yes."

Helen and Mark and Ted are playing Spud in the backyard. Actually, since neither Helen nor Ted remembers exactly how to play, it's a variation of Spud: they take turns throwing the ball high up into the air, clapping first once, then twice, and so on, and then trying to catch the ball. Will is crawling around, getting in the way, his fat knees grass-stained. After a while it gets too dark to play Spud so Ted and Mark start playing a violent game which mainly involves running around, screaming, and tackling each other. Helen takes Will inside for his bath. She fills the kitchen sink with warm soapy water, undresses Will, and slips his perfect body into the water. Will loves water. He spends the whole day in the pool, and now he sits in his bath, gurgling, patting the water ecstatically. Helen moves her suddenly large hands over and over Will, caressing as much as cleaning him, watching out the window as Ted and Mark roll together on the grass. This is all so perfect, she thinks. This is perfect.

Ted is lying on the couch reading one of Will's books. He is reading about a pig that builds a house. A busload of bunny rabbits moves into the house. They will be happy there. Will is sleeping and Helen is reading in bed. Mark is lying on the living-room floor, watching MTV. Ted sits on the couch, his bare feet resting lightly on Mark's back. "What did you do today?" he asks.

"Nothing," Mark says. "Played."

"What did you play?"

"Games," says Mark. He doesn't look up. He is looking at the TV. On it, people eat a huge banquet with their hands while a cat stalks down the middle of the table. Ted can't understand the words to the song. He starts to massage Mark's back with his feet.

"Does that feel good?" he asks.

"A little."

"Was Mommy here today?"

"Yes," says Mark.

"Isn't there a movie on?"

"I don't know," says Mark. "Probably."

"This is weird," says Ted. "Do you like this?"

"Not really," says Mark. "Their mouths aren't even right. Look."

Ted looks at the TV. The singer is a beat behind the music. He is obviously lip-synching to a pre-recorded soundtrack. "Tell me something," says Ted.

"What?"

"I don't know. Just something."

Mark turns his head away from the TV and rests his

cheek on the floor, so he is looking at Ted. His eyes are closed. "Mommy left her sunglasses here," Mark says. "I found them. They're hidden in the laundry room."

"Oh," says Ted. "Are you tired?"

"A little."

"I am," says Ted. "I'm very tired."

"Go to bed, then," says Mark.

"I will," says Ted. "I'm going to. But not before you."

"I can put myself to bed," says Mark.

"Can you?"

"Yes."

Ted stands up and turns the TV off. The picture quickly shrinks and then disappears. Ted looks at the blank screen for a second, as if the picture might reappear. He cannot believe it was gotten rid of that easily. "Where in the laundry room?" he asks.

"What?" says Mark.

"Where did you hide Mommy's sunglasses? Where in the laundry room?"

Mark looks up at Ted. One of his cheeks is scarred from the carpeting. "It's a secret," he says.

On his way to the bedroom, Ted checks on Will. He stands by the crib and watches Will sleep. Is Will dreaming? When Ted was little, he had a dog that whimpered and shivered in her sleep, and Ted's mother always said it was because she was dreaming of chasing rabbits. Ted never knew what to make of this theory. The dog never chased rabbits when it was awake, so how could she dream about it? He watches Will sleep for a long time, half expecting him to whimper, or shiver.

Brushing his teeth, Ted wishes he had his beard back. He should have held out a little longer. That afternoon, he didn't know what to do with the hair that collected in his friend's sink. He was afraid to wash it down the drain, and he didn't want his friend to find it in the wastepaper basket. Finally, he wrapped it carefully in newspaper, took it out with him, and threw it surreptitiously into a garbage can, like something stolen or explosive. Ted can't understand why, given the fact he's seriously looking for a job, stopped seeing Diane, realized he truly loves Helen, why then doesn't he feel better about himself? He still must be doing something wrong. He looks in the mirror at his newly shaved face. He has trouble recognizing himself.

In the bedroom, Helen lowers her book and watches him undress. She smiles, leans forward. If Ted could only think of what it is he's doing wrong, he would change it, at once, so everything would be O.K. again. He wishes music would begin, so he could move his lips, and explain this, and everything else, to Helen.

The Secret Dog

When my wife, Miranda, finally falls asleep, I get out of bed and stand for a moment in the darkness, making sure she won't awaken. Miranda is a sound sleeper: Life exhausts her. She lies in bed, her arms thrown back up over her head, someone floating down a river. I watch her for a moment and then I go downstairs to the closet where I keep my dog. On the door is a sign that says "Miranda: Keep Out."

Miranda is allergic to dogs, and will not allow them in the house. So I have a secret dog.

I open the door to the closet without turning on any lights. Dog is sleeping and wakes up when she hears me. I have trained her to sleep all day and never to bark. She is very smart. In fact she is remarkable. I kneel in the hall, and Dog walks over and presses her head into my stomach. I hold it gently. The only sound is Dog's tail wagging, but it is a very quiet sound, and I know it will not wake Miranda. This is a moment I look forward to all day.

Dog and I go out to the car. I purposely park down the street so Miranda won't hear the car start. I tell her I can never find a space in front of the house. She suspects nothing. Once Dog and I are in the car, I feed her. I keep her food in the glove compartment. I keep the glove compartment locked. Dog stands on the front seat next to me and eats her dinner. I stroke her back while she is eating. Every few bites she looks up and smiles at me.

When she is done eating I start the car. I drive about a mile to an A & P that is open all night. As I drive, Dog stands with her nose out the window. I open the window only a crack because I am afraid Dog might jump out.

At the A & P we get out. First I take her behind the store to a grassy bank beside the railroad tracks where she can relieve herself. Every few days she does this in the closet, but usually she is very good about waiting till we get out. She hops about the tracks, sniffing and wagging her tail. She is a joy to watch. She squats, and I look the other way.

Then we go back to the parking lot, which is usually empty. Every now and then a car pulls in and someone jumps out and runs into the A & P. We have plenty of room. This is when I train Dog. I have a book, which I also keep locked in the glove compartment, called *How to Train Your Schnauzer*. Dog is not a schnauzer, but it seems to be working well. We are on week nine, although we've only been working for four weeks. That is how smart Dog is.

I have to give Dog plenty of exercise so she will sleep all day. We begin running. Dog runs right beside me. We run a mile or two through the deserted streets of the sleeping town and then walk back to the car. Dog trots beside me, panting. Her long pink tongue hangs out one side of her mouth. She stops and sniffs at discarded papers that flutter on the sidewalk.

We do this every night.

One night when I come in, there is a light on in the kitchen. This has never happened before. I put Dog in her closet and quietly close the door. I walk slowly up to the kitchen. Miranda is standing by the table in her bathrobe. She is slicing a banana into a bowl of cereal. She won't look at me. Her hair is loose and hangs down over her face, which is bowed above the banana. I cannot see her face. I sit down and still she will not look at me. Miranda, I often think, looks more beautiful when wakened from sleep than during the day.

Suddenly the knife slits her finger, but Miranda does not acknowledge this wound. She continues to slice the banana. I realize she is crying.

"You cut yourself," I say, quietly. I think I can hear Dog plopping down on the floor in the closet.

Miranda raises her cut finger to her mouth. She sucks on it, then wraps it in a napkin. She tucks her hair behind her ears and sits down. Then she looks up at me. "Where have you been?" she whispers. There are two pink spots, high on her white cheeks. There is also a little blood on her lips. She has stopped crying. "Where have you been?" she repeats.

I watch the napkin she wrapped her finger in turn red, slowly. I cannot speak. Miranda stands up. She runs her finger under the faucet, and looks at it. She wraps it in a clean napkin. She is facing away from me, toward the sink. "Who are you seeing?" she says. "Do I know her?"

It has never occurred to me that Miranda might think I am having an affair. This is a great relief, for if she believes this she must not suspect Dog. "I'm not having an affair," I say. "I haven't seen anyone."

Miranda looks over at me. "Really?" she says.

"Yes," I say. "Really."

"Where have you been?" asks Miranda.

I think for a moment. "I can't tell you."

Miranda looks down at her injured finger. "Why can't you tell me?"

"It's a secret," I say. "I can't tell you because it's a secret. But I'm not having an affair. Do you understand?"

For a few seconds Miranda says nothing. She glances above my head at her reflection in the window. I, too, turn and watch her in the window. She looks very beautiful. I see her mouth move against the night. "Yes," she says. "I understand."

The next day at work I find I am very tired. I have been sleeping very little since I got Dog. Suddenly I wake up. Joyce, my boss, is standing in front of my desk. She smiles at me. "You've been sleeping," she says. "That isn't allowed."

I sit up straight and open my top desk drawer as if I'm looking for something. Then I close it. I look up at Joyce. She just stands there. "Why are you sleeping?" she asks. "Are you tired?"

"I'm exhausted," I say.

"Why?" asks Joyce.

"My wife just had a baby," I lie. "It's been very sick, and I have to stay up all night with it. That's why I'm tired." This is a very bad lie. Miranda and I can't have a baby.

"When did Miranda have a baby?" Joyce smiles. She sits down in my customer chair. "I didn't even know she was pregnant."

"A month ago," I say. "I thought I told you. I guess I've been too tired."

"How wonderful!" says Joyce. "Lucky you! What is it?"

"What do you mean?" I say.

"A boy or a girl?" asks Joyce. She is so nice.

"It's a girl."

"What's her name?"

I think for a second. "Dorothy," I say.

"Well," says Joyce, "congratulations." She stands up, and winks at me. "Just try to stay awake," she says. "But I understand."

The next night when I get home there is a big bouquet on the kitchen table. Miranda is sitting at the table, smoking. Miranda quit smoking years ago, although sometimes I find a pack beneath the seat of the car. What I do then is take them all out but one. I leave one for her to smoke, and toss the rest.

Miranda points to the flowers with her cigarette. Then she hands me a little card. A stork flies across the top, carrying a baby wrapped in a diaper. Pink ribbons from the words "Congratulations on the New Arrival!" and underneath that is written "Welcome Dorothy! Love, Joyce." The *o* in Joyce contains two little eyes and a big smile.

Miranda stubs her cigarette in the ashtray. "Who," she says, "is Dorothy?"

"I don't know," I say.

"If this is Joyce's idea of a joke," cries Miranda, "I think she must be pretty sick." She stands up and looks at the flowers. They are irises and tulips and a shriveled pink balloon on a stick. Miranda popped the balloon. Maybe she did it with her cigarette. "She must be pretty sick," Miranda repeats. "Since when do we have a baby? Did you tell Joyce we had a baby?" Miranda looks at me. "Did you?"

I don't know what to say. I never thought Joyce would send us flowers. I didn't think she was that nice. "Yes," I say, finally.

"You did?" Miranda is screaming, and it occurs to me that she is probably hysterical. "How could you? Why?"

"I fell asleep at work," I say. "It was just an excuse. I told Joyce I had to stay up nights with our baby. With Dorothy. I said Dorothy was very sick and I had to stay up nights with her."

"You're awful," says Miranda. "You're a moron. I don't understand what's happened to you. What's happened to you? I bet you are having an affair."

"Calm down," I say. "That's not true. You know that's not true. You said you understood. Remember?"

"But I don't understand," says Miranda. "I don't understand anymore. Where do you go at night?"

"It's a secret," I say. "I told you it was a secret."

"You can't have a secret like that," says Miranda. "I can't—Why can't you tell me? What could be so bad that you couldn't tell me?"

"It isn't bad," I say.

"Then why can't you tell me?"

"It's just private," I say.

"But I'm your wife," says Miranda.

"I know you're my wife," I say. "I love you."

"Do you?" asks Miranda.

"Yes," I say.

"And you don't love someone else?"

Dog isn't really a someone. She's a something. I love something else. I love Dog and I love Miranda. If Miranda weren't allergic it would all be fine. "No," I say.

Miranda stands up. "I'm going to bed," she says. "I don't feel well." She walks past me, toward the door, then she turns around. "Please get rid of the flowers," she says.

That night I wait a long time before I go down to Dog. I want to make sure Miranda is fast asleep. Finally I am satisfied. Miranda's face is turned away from mine on the pillow and her cheeks move in and out a little and the blankets rise and fall across her breasts, but besides that she is perfectly still. The lights from passing cars flit across her face, and she almost looks dead, she is so still.

I go down to get Dog. It is wonderful to see her. She comes out of the closet and whines a little, very quietly. Then she rubs her head against my chest. I am very sad tonight, and even Dog cannot cheer me up. Patting her, kissing her between her eyes, only makes me sadder. Dog senses this, and lies down close beside me on the car seat.

At the A & P I almost lose Dog. She runs between two huge trucks that are parked behind the store, and disappears.

It is dark back here and quiet. There is no one about. I think I can hear Dog's tags and collar jingling, but it sounds very far away, on the other side of the tracks. I am afraid to call her, it is so quiet. The moon is out and broken glass glints on the pavement. I whistle softly, and finally Dog comes. I hear her coming across the tracks and back between the trucks. She runs across the parking lot, in and out of the shadows, like a ghost. I put out my hand to touch her, and she is there.

I go into the A & P to buy dog food. Dog is afraid of the automatic door and shies when it swings open of its own accord. I pick her up.

"You can't bring the dog in here," says the checkout girl. "Unless he's a Seeing Eye dog. Are you blind?"

Since I am carrying Dog, I can hardly claim I am blind. "No," I say. I put Dog down.

"Well, then he can't come in. Sorry."

I pick up Dog and go back out. Dog is tired; her body is limp and warm in my arms. I carry her like a baby, her head against my shoulder. I put her in the car, lock the door, and go back in the store.

I walk up and down the aisles enjoying myself. Pet food is always in the middle aisle, regardless of the store. This fact fascinates me. The only other person in the store is in pet food. She's wearing a long green dress, sandals, and a pink scarf. Her red hair sticks out from under the scarf in all directions. She stares at me as I walk down the aisle. She is waiting to tell me something, I can tell.

"I read palms," she whispers, as I reach out for the dog food. "I tell fortunes."

I say nothing. I read the box. "Complete as a meal in a can," it says. "Without any of the mess."

"Do me a favor," the woman says. She reaches out and touches my arm.

"What?" I say.

"Escort me up and down the aisles," she says. "I'll read your palm when we're done."

"Why?" I say.

"Why what?" Before I can answer she says, "Why not? I'm lonely. Please."

"O.K.," I say. I hope this won't take too long.

We walk toward the front of the store. The woman consults her shopping list. "My name is Jane," she says, as if this is written on her list. "Just Jane. Soda. Will you do me another favor?" She looks up at me.

"What?" I say.

She touches my arm again. "Pretend you're my husband," she says. "Pretend we're married and we're shopping. Will you do that?"

"Why?" I ask.

Once again she looks at her list, as if the answer is there. "Soda," she mumbles. "What kind of soda do you like?" She hesitates. "Dear."

We are in the beverage aisle, and all the bottles gleam around us. "I like Seven-Up," I say, because that is the first kind I see.

"The un-cola," says Jane. "I don't like it. I like Coke. But we'll get Seven-Up for you." She puts a large plastic bottle of Seven-Up in the cart. We proceed.

"Please don't get that for me." I feel very foolish. "If you like Coke, get Coke. I like Coke fine."

She stops. "Do you?" she says. "Do you like Coke fine?"

"Yes."

"But which do you like better?"

"Please get whatever you want," I say. "This is silly."

Jane puts the Seven-Up back on the wrong shelf. "Do you like birch beer?" she asks.

"Yes," I say.

"Fine, then." Jane reaches for some birch beer. "We'll get that."

We continue through the store like this, disagreeing about yogurt, deodorant, bread, juice, and ice cream. The checkout girl rings up my dog food first. Then she does Jane's groceries. I help her carry them out to her car. It is the only other one in the parking lot. I can see Dog, with her front paws poised on the dashboard, watching me. "Good night," I say to Jane. I'm glad this is over.

"Wait," says Jane. "I promised to tell your fortune. Give me your palm."

I hold out my hand and Jane takes it. Her hand is warm and wet. "Move." She pushes me back toward my car, under the light. She opens my palm and holds it flat. She wipes it off with her scarf. The light makes it look very white. For a long time she says nothing. I can hear Dog whine in the car.

When Jane speaks, she addresses my palm and not me. "I see blue lights. I see swimmers. I see rhododendrons. You will live a long time." She pauses. "You will always feel like this." She slowly rolls my fingers toward my palm, making a fist. She looks up at me.

"Like what?" I ask.

Jane lets go of my hand, and makes a vague gesture with her own, indicating the A & P, the parking lot, my car with Dog in it. "Like this," she repeats, softly. "You will always feel like this."

Joyce is there, standing above me. "Perhaps you should take some sick time," she says. "You can't keep falling asleep at work."

I feel very tired. I just want to go back to sleep. I don't know what to say.

"Do you have any comp time coming?" says Joyce. "Perhaps you should take it now."

"I'm tired," I say. Joyce is a little out of focus, on account of I just woke up.

"I know you're tired," says Joyce. She seems to be talking very loudly. Joyce sent us flowers. She is nice. "You look very tired. That's why I think you should take some time off. Don't you think that would be a good idea? Do you understand?"

"I guess so," I say.

"Well, think about it," says Joyce. "Think about it, and let me know. Things can't go on like this."

"I know," I say.

"Good," says Joyce. Then she leaves.

When I get home that night things are fine. Miranda suggests we go out to dinner, and we do. It is very nice. We drink a lot of wine and eat and eat and then we drive home. We watch the news on TV. It is terrible news; even the local news is terrible. Miranda yawns and goes into the bathroom. I can hear her in there: the water flowing, the toilet flushing. It all sounds so lovely, so safe. I can hear Miranda setting the alarm in the bedroom, and the radio playing softly.

"Are you coming?" she calls down the hall. "Come to bed."

I get in bed with Miranda and pretend to go to sleep. It is windy and cold outside, and the trees rattle against the windows. It is hard to stay awake. My head is spinning with all the wine I drank, and I am so tired. But I stay awake until Miranda falls asleep. I get up and go down to Dog.

When I open the closet, Dog is not there. The closet is empty. I call Dog softly, thinking she has got out somehow. I call and call, in little whispers, but she doesn't come.

I stand in the hall for a long while thinking I must have fallen asleep. Maybe I am dreaming. I do not understand what is happening, and I begin to cry a little. I go back upstairs and into the bathroom and close the door. When I stop crying

I come out and stand in the bedroom. Moonlight falls through the window and onto the bed; onto the part where I am not sleeping, onto the empty spot beside Miranda, who sleeps against the wall, in shadow. The first time I saw Miranda was in a hotel in Florida. She was coming out of her room with a folding beach chair. She asked me to hold it while she answered the telephone, which was ringing in her room. I stood in the corridor and held the chair for what seemed to be a very long time. I could hear Miranda talking in her room, but I couldn't make out what she was saying.

Miranda wakes up. She turns over, into the moonlight, and looks up at me. "What are you doing?" she says, sleepily. "Why aren't you in bed? Are you crying?"

I realize I am still crying a little. Miranda sits up in bed, very beautiful, the light pale on her face. "Why are you crying?" she asks.

I don't know what to say. The wind blows and the bedroom seems to shake. I can hardly speak. "Where is Dog?" I finally say. "What did you do with Dog?"

"Dog?" says Miranda. "What dog?" She leans forward, across the bed, toward me. "There never was any dog."

Jump or Dive

Jason, my uncle's lover, sat in the dark kitchen eating what sounded like a bowl of cereal. He had some disease that made him hungry every few hours—something about not enough sugar in his blood. Every night, he got up at about three o'clock and fixed himself a snack. Since I was sleeping on the living-room couch, I could hear him.

My parents and I had driven down from Oregon to visit my Uncle Walter, who lived in Arizona. He was my father's younger brother. My sister Jackie got to stay home, on account of having just graduated from high school and having a job at the Lob-Steer Restaurant. But there was no way my parents were letting me stay home: I had just finished ninth grade and I was unemployed.

My parents slept in the guest room. Jason and Uncle Walter slept together in the master bedroom. The first morning, when I went into the bathroom, I saw Jason sitting on the edge of the big unmade bed in his jockey shorts. Jason was very tan, but it was an odd tan: his face and the bottom three-quarters of his arms were much darker than his chest. It looked as if he was wearing a T-shirt.

The living-room couch was made of leather and had little metal nubs stuck all over it. It was almost impossible to sleep on. I lay there listening to Jason crunch. The only other noise was the air-conditioner, which turned itself off and on constantly to maintain the same, ideal temperature. When it went off, you could hear the insects outside. A small square of light from the opened refrigerator appeared on the dining-room wall. Jason was putting the milk away. The faucet ran for a second, and then Jason walked through the living room, his white underwear bright against his body. I pretended I was asleep.

After a while, the air-conditioner went off, but I didn't hear the insects. At some point in the night—the point that seems closer to morning than to evening—they stopped their drone, as though they were unionized and paid to sing only so long. The house was very quiet. In the master bedroom, I could hear bodies moving, and murmuring, but I couldn't tell if it was people making love or turning over and over, trying to get comfortable. It went on for a few minutes, and then it stopped.

We were staying at Uncle Walter's for a week, and every hour of every day was planned. We always had a morning activity and an afternoon activity. Then we had cocktail hour, then dinner, then some card game. Usually hearts, with the teams switching: some nights Jason and Walter versus my parents, some nights the brothers challenging Jason and my mother. I never played. I watched TV, or rode Jason's moped around the deserted roads of Gretna Green, which was the name of Uncle Walter's condominium village. The houses in Gretna Green were called villas, and they all had different names— some for gems, some for colors, and some for animals. Uncle Walter and Jason lived in Villa Indigo.

We started each morning on the patio, where we'd eat breakfast and "plan the day." The adults took a long time planning the day so there would be less day to spend. All the other villa inhabitants ate breakfast on their patios, too. The patios were separated by lawn and rock gardens and pine trees, but there wasn't much privacy: everyone could see everyone else sitting under uniformly striped umbrellas, but everyone pretended he couldn't. They were mostly old people, retired people. Children were allowed only as guests. Everyone looked at me as if I was a freak.

Wednesday morning, Uncle Walter was inside making coffee in the new coffee machine my parents had brought him. My mother told me that whenever you're invited to someone's house overnight you should bring something—a hostess gift. Or a host gift, she added. She was helping Uncle Walter make breakfast. Jason was lying on a chaise in the sun, trying to even out his tan. My father was reading the *Wall Street Journal*. He got up early every morning and drove into town and bought it, so he could "stay in touch." My mother made him throw it away right after he read it so it wouldn't interfere with the rest of the day.

Jason had his eyes closed, but he was talking. He was listing the things we could do that day. I was sitting on the edge of a big planter filled with pachysandra and broken statuary that Leonard, my uncle's ex-boyfriend, had dug up somewhere. Leonard was an archeologist. He used to teach paleontology at Northern Arizona University, but he didn't get tenure, so he took a job with an oil company in South America, making sure the engineers didn't drill in sacred spots. The day before, I'd seen a tiny, purple-throated lizard in the vines, and I was trying to find him again. I wanted to catch him and take him back to Oregon.

Jason paused in his list, and my father said, "Uh-huh." That's what he always says when he's reading the newspaper and you talk to him.

"We could go to the dinosaur museum," Jason said.

"What's that?" I said.

Jason sat up and looked at me. That was the first thing I'd said to him, I think. I'd been ignoring him.

"Well, I've never been there," he said. Even though it was early in the morning, his brown forehead was already beaded with sweat. "It has some reconstructed dinosaurs and footprints and stuff."

"Let's go there," I said. "I like dinosaurs."

"Uh-huh," said my father.

My mother came through the sliding glass doors carrying a platter of scrambled eggs. Uncle Walter followed with the coffee.

"We're going to go to the dinosaur museum this morning," Jason said.

"Please, not that pit," Uncle Walter said.

"But Evan wants to go," Jason said. "It's about time we did something he liked."

Everyone looked at me. "It doesn't matter," I said.

"Oh, no," Uncle Walter said. "Actually, it's fascinating. It just brings back bad memories."

As it turned out, Uncle Walter and my father stayed home to discuss their finances. My grandmother had left them her money jointly, and they're always arguing about how to invest it. Jason drove my mother and me out to the dinosaur museum. I think my mother came just because she didn't want to leave me alone with Jason. She doesn't trust Uncle Walter's friends, but she doesn't let on. My father thinks it's very important we all treat Uncle Walter normally. Once he hit Jackie because she called Uncle Walter a fag. That's the only time he's ever hit either of us.

The dinosaur museum looked like an airplane hangar in the middle of the desert. Inside, trenches were dug into the earth and bones stuck out of their walls. They were still exhuming some of the skeletons. The sand felt oddly damp. My mother took off her sandals and carried them; Jason looked around quickly, and then went outside and sat on the hood of the car, smoking, with his shirt off. At the gift stand, I bought a small bag of dinosaur bone chips. My mother bought a 3-D panoramic postcard. When you held it one way, a dinosaur stood with a creature in its toothy mouth. When you tilted it, the creature disappeared. Swallowed.

On the way home, we stopped at a Safeway to do some grocery shopping. Both Jason and my mother seemed reluctant to push the shopping cart, so I did. In the produce aisle, Jason picked up cantaloupes and shook them next to his ear. A few feet away, my mother folded back the husks to get a good look at the kernels on the corncobs. It seemed as if everyone was pawing at the food. It made me nervous, because once, when I was little, I opened up a box of chocolate Ding Dongs in the grocery store and started eating one, and the manager came over and yelled at me. The only good thing about that was that my mother was forced to buy the Ding Dongs, but every time I ate one I felt sick.

A man in Bermuda shorts and a yellow cardigan sweater started talking to Jason. My mother returned with six apparently decent ears of corn. She dumped them into the cart. "Who's that?" she asked me, meaning the man Jason was talking to.

"I don't know," I said. The man made a practice golf swing, right there in the produce aisle. Jason watched him. Jason was a golf pro at a country club. He used to be part of the golf tour you see on television on weekend afternoons, but he quit. Now he gave lessons at the country club. Uncle Walter had been one of his pupils. That's how they met.

"It's hard to tell," Jason was saying. "I'd try opening up your stance a little more." He put a cantaloupe in our shopping cart.

"Hi," the man said to us.

"Mr. Baird, I'd like you to meet my wife, Ann," Jason said.

Mr. Baird shook my mother's hand. "How come we never see you down the club?"

"Oh . . ." my mother said.

"Ann hates golf," Jason said.

"And how 'bout you?" The man looked at me. "Do you like golf?"

"Sure," I said.

"Well, we'll have to get you out on the links. Can you beat your dad?"

"Not yet," I said.

"It won't be long," Mr. Baird said. He patted Jason on the shoulder. "Nice to see you, Jason. Nice to meet you, Mrs. Jerome."

He walked down the aisle and disappeared into the bakery section. My mother and I both looked at Jason. Even though it was cold in the produce aisle, he was sweating. No one said anything for a few seconds. Then my mother said, "Evan, why don't you go find some Doritos? And some Gatorade, too, if you want."

Back at Villa Indigo, my father and Uncle Walter were playing cribbage. Jason kissed Uncle Walter on the top of his semi-bald head. My father watched and then stood up and kissed my mother. I didn't kiss anyone.

Thursday, my mother and I went into Flagstaff to buy new school clothes. Back in Portland, when we go into malls we separate and make plans to meet at a specified time and place, but this was different: it was a strange mall, and since it was school clothes, my mother would pay for them, and therefore she could help pick them out. So we shopped together, which we hadn't done in a while. It was awkward. She pulled things off the rack which I had ignored, and when I started looking at the Right Now for Young Men stuff she entered the Traditional Shoppe. We finally bought some underwear, and some orange and yellow socks, which my mother said were "fun."

Then we went to the shoe store. I hate trying on shoes. I wish the salespeople would just give you the box and let you try them on yourself. There's something about someone else doing it all—especially touching your feet—that embarrasses me. It's as if the person was your servant or something. And in this case the salesperson was a girl about my age, and I could tell she thought I was weird, shopping with my mother. My mother sat in the chair beside me, her pocketbook in her lap. She was wearing sneakers with little bunny-rabbit tails sticking out the back from her socks.

"Stand up," the girl said.

I stood up.

"How do they feel?" my mother asked.

"O.K.," I said.

"Walk around," my mother commanded.

I walked up the aisle, feeling everyone watching me. Then I walked back and sat down. I bent over and unlaced the shoes.

"So what do you think?" my mother asked.

The girl stood there, picking her nails. "They look very nice," she said.

I just wanted to get out of there. "I like them," I said. We bought the shoes.

On the way home, we pulled into a gas station/bar in the desert. "I can't face Villa Indigo without a drink," my mother said.

"What do you mean?" I asked.

"Nothing," she said. "Are you having a good time?"

"Now?"

"No. On this trip. At Uncle Walter's."

"I guess so," I said.

"Do you like Jason?"

"Better than Leonard."

"Leonard was strange," my mother said. "I never warmed to Leonard."

We got out of the car and walked into the bar. It was dark inside, and empty. A fat woman sat behind the bar, making something out of papier-mâché. It looked like one of those statues of the Virgin Mary people have in their front yards. "Hiya," she said. "What can I get you?"

My mother asked for a beer and I asked for some cranberry juice. They didn't have any, so I ordered a Coke. The woman got my mother's beer from a portable cooler like the ones you take to football games. It seemed very unprofessional. Then she sprayed Coke into a glass with one of those showerhead things. My mother and I sat at a table in the sun, but it wasn't hot, it was cold. Above us, the air-conditioner dripped.

My mother drank her beer from the long-necked green bottle. "What do you think your sister's doing right now?" she asked.

"What time is it?"

"Four."

"Probably getting ready to go to work. Taking a shower."

My mother nodded. "Maybe we'll call her tonight."

I laughed, because my mother called her every night. She would always make Jackie explain all the noises in the background. "It sounds like a party to me," she kept repeating.

My Coke was flat. It tasted weird, too. I watched the woman at the bar. She was poking at her statue with a swizzlestick—putting in eyes, I thought.

"How would you like to go see the Petrified Forest?" my mother asked.

"We're going to another national park?" On the way to Uncle Walter's, we had stopped at the Grand Canyon and taken a mule ride down to the river. Halfway down, my mother got hysterical, fell off her mule, and wouldn't get back on. A helicopter had to fly into the canyon and rescue her. It was horrible to see her like that.

"This one's perfectly flat," she said. "And no mules."

"When?" I said.

"We'd go down on Saturday and come back to Walter's on Monday. And leave for home Tuesday."

The bar woman brought us a second round of drinks. We had not asked for them. My Coke glass was still full. My mother drained her beer bottle and looked at the new one. "Oh dear," she said. "I guess we look like we need it."

The next night, at six-thirty, as my parents left for their special anniversary dinner in Flagstaff, the automatic lawn sprinklers went on. They were activated every evening. Jason explained that if the lawns were watered during the day the beads of moisture would magnify the sun's rays and burn the grass. My parents walked through the whirling water, got in their car, and drove away.

Jason and Uncle Walter were making dinner for me—steaks, on their new electric barbecue. I think they thought steak was a good, masculine food. Instead of charcoal, their grill had little lava rocks on the bottom. They reminded me of my dinosaur bone chips.

The steaks came in packs of two, so Uncle Walter was cooking up four. The fourth steak worried me. Who was it for? Would we split it? Was someone else coming to dinner?

"You're being awfully quiet," Uncle Walter said. For a minute, I hoped he was talking to the steaks—they weren't sizzling—so I didn't answer.

Then Uncle Walter looked over at me. "Cat got your tongue?" he asked.

"What cat?" I said.

"The cat," he said. "The proverbial cat. The big cat in the sky."

"No," I said.

"Then talk to me."

"I don't talk on demand," I said.

Uncle Walter smiled down at his steaks, lightly piercing

them with his chef's fork. "Are you a freshman?" he asked.

"Well, a sophomore now," I said.

"How do you like being a sophomore?"

My lizard appeared from beneath a crimson leaf and clicked his eyes in all directions, checking out the evening.

"It's not something you like or dislike," I said. "It's something you are."

"Ah," Uncle Walter said. "So you're a fatalist?"

I didn't answer. I slowly reached out my hand toward the lizard, even though I was too far away to touch it. He clicked his eyes toward me but didn't move. I think he recognized me. My arm looked white and disembodied in the evening light.

Jason slid open the terrace doors, and the music from the stereo was suddenly loud. The lizard darted back under the foliage.

"I need a prep chef," Jason said. "Get in here, Evan."

I followed Jason into the kitchen. On the table was a wooden board, and on that was a tomato, an avocado, and an apple. Jason handed me a knife. "Chop those up," he said.

I picked up the avocado. "Should I peel this?" I asked. "Or what?"

Jason took the avocado and sliced it in half. One half held the pit and the other half held nothing. Then he pulled the warty skin off in two curved pieces and handed the naked globes back to me. "Now chop it."

I started chopping the stuff. Jason took three baked potatoes out of the oven. I could tell they were hot by the way he tossed them onto the counter. He made slits in them and forked the white stuffing into a bowl.

"What are you doing?" I asked.

"Making baked potatoes," he said. He sliced butter into the bowl.

"But why are you taking the potato out of the skin?"

"Because these are stuffed potatoes. You take the potato out and doctor it up and then put it back in. Do you like cheese?"

"Yes," I said.

"Do you like chives?"

"I don't know," I said. "I've never had them."

"You've never had chives?"

"My mother makes normal food," I said. "She leaves the potato in the skin."

"That figures," Jason said.

After dinner, we went to the driving range. Jason bought two large buckets and we followed him upstairs to the second level. I sat on a bench and watched Jason and my uncle hit ball after ball out into the floodlit night. Sometimes the balls arched up into the darkness, then reappeared as they fell.

Uncle Walter wasn't too good. A few times, he topped the ball and it dribbled over the edge and fell on the grass right below us. When that happened, he looked around to see who noticed, and winked at me.

"Do you want to hit some?" he asked me, offering his club.

"Sure," I said. I was on the golf team last fall, but this spring I played baseball. I think golf is an élitist sport. Baseball is more democratic.

I teed up a ball and took a practice swing, because my father, who taught me to play golf, told me always to take a practice swing. Always. My first shot was pretty good. It didn't go too far, but it went straight out and bounced a ways before I lost track of it in the shadows. I hit another.

Jason, who was in the next cubicle, put down his club and watched me. "You have a great natural swing," he said.

His attention bothered me, and I almost missed my next ball. It rolled off the tee. I picked it up and re-teed it.

"Wait," Jason said. He walked over and stood behind me.

"You're swinging much too hard." He leaned over me so that he was embracing me from behind, his large tan hands on top of mine, holding the club. "Now, just relax," he said, his voice right beside my cheek.

I tried to relax, but I couldn't. I suddenly felt very hot.

"O.K.," Jason said, "nice and easy. Keep the left arm straight." He raised his arms, and with them the club. Then we swung through, and he held the club still in the air, pointed out into the night. He let go of the club and ran his hand along my left arm, from my wrist up to my shoulder. "Straight," he said. "Keep it nice and straight." Then he stepped back and told me to try another swing by myself.

I did.

"Looking good," Jason said.

"Why don't you finish the bucket?" my uncle said. "I'm going down to get a beer."

Jason returned to his stall and resumed his practice. I teed up another ball, hit it, then another, and another, till I'd established a rhythm, whacking ball after ball, and all around me clubs were cutting the night, filling the sky with tiny white meteorites.

Back at Villa Indigo, the sprinklers had stopped, but the insects were making their strange noise in the trees. Jason and I went for a swim while my uncle watched TV. Jason wore a bathing suit like the swimmers in the Olympics: red-white-and-blue, and shaped like underwear. We walked out the terrace doors and across the wet lawn toward the pool, which was deserted and glowed bright blue. Jason dived in and swam some laps. I practiced diving off the board into the deep end, timing my dives so they wouldn't interfere with him. After about ten laps, he started treading water in the deep end and looked up at me. I was bouncing on the diving board.

"Want to play a game?" he said.

"What?"

Jason swam to the side and pulled himself out of the pool. "Jump or Dive," he said. "We'll play for money."

"How do you play?"

"Don't you know anything?" Jason said. "What do you do in Ohio?"

"It's Oregon," I said. "Not much."

"I can believe it. This is a very simple game. One person jumps off the diving board—jumps high—and when he's at the very highest the other person yells either 'Jump' or 'Dive,' and the person has to dive if the other person yells 'Dive' and jump if he yells 'Jump.' If you do the wrong thing, you owe the guy a quarter. O.K.?"

"O.K.," I said. "You go first."

I stepped off the diving board and Jason climbed on. "The higher you jump, the more time you have to twist," he said.

"Go," I said. "I'm ready."

Jason took three steps and sprang, and I yelled, "Dive." He did.

He got out of the pool, grinning. "O.K.," he said. "Your turn."

I sprang off the board and heard Jason yell, "Jump," but I was already falling forward head first. I tried to twist backward, but it was still a dive.

"You owe me a quarter," Jason said when I surfaced. He was standing on the diving board, bouncing. I swam to the side. "Here I go," he said.

I waited till he was coming straight down toward the water, feet first, before I yelled, "Dive," but somehow Jason somersaulted forward and dived into the pool.

We played for about fifteen minutes, until I owed Jason two dollars and twenty-five cents and my body was covered with red welts from smacking the water at bad angles. Suddenly the lights in the pool went off.

"It must be ten o'clock," Jason said. "Time for the geriatrics to go to bed."

The black water looked cold and scary. I got out and sat in a chair. We hadn't brought towels with us, and I shivered. Jason stayed in the pool.

"It's warmer in the water," he said.

I didn't say anything. With the lights off in the pool, the stars appeared brighter in the sky. I leaned my head back and looked up at them.

Something landed with a splat on the concrete beside me. It was Jason's bathing suit. I could hear him in the pool. He was swimming slowly underwater, coming up for a breath and then disappearing again. I knew that at some point he'd get out of the water and be naked, so I walked across the lawn toward Villa Indigo. Inside, I could see Uncle Walter lying on the couch, watching TV.

Later that night, I woke up hearing noises in the kitchen. I assumed it was Jason, but then I heard talking, and realized it was my parents, back from their anniversary dinner.

I got up off the couch and went into the kitchen. My mother was leaning against the counter, drinking a glass of seltzer. My father was sitting on one of the barstools, smoking a cigarette. He put it out when I came in. He's not supposed to smoke anymore. We made a deal in our family last year involving his quitting: my mother would lose fifteen pounds, my sister would take Science Honors (and pass), and I was supposed to brush Princess Leia, our dog, every day without having to be told.

"Our little baby," my mother said. "Did we wake you up?"

"Yes," I said.

"This is the first one I've had in months," my father said. "Honest. I just found it lying here."

"I told him he could smoke it," my mother said. "As a special anniversary treat."

"How was dinner?" I asked.

"O.K.," my mother said. "The restaurant didn't turn around, though. It was broken."

"That's funny," my father said. "I could have sworn it was revolving."

"You were just drunk," my mother said.

"Oh, no," my father said. "It was the stars in my eyes." He leaned forward and kissed my mother.

She finished her seltzer, rinsed the glass, and put it in the sink. "I'm going to bed," she said. "Good night."

My father and I both said good night, and my mother walked down the hall. My father picked up his cigarette. "It wasn't even very good," he said. He looked at it, then held it under his nose and smelled it. "I think it was stale. Just my luck."

I took the cigarette butt out of his hands and threw it away. When I turned around, he was standing by the terrace doors, looking out at the dark trees. It was windy.

"Have you made up your mind?" he asked.

"About what?"

"The trip."

"What trip?"

My father turned away from the terrace. "Didn't Mom tell you? Uncle Walter said you could stay here while Mom and I went down to see the Petrified Forest. If you want to. You can come with us otherwise."

"Oh," I said.

"I think Uncle Walter would like it if he had some time alone with you. I don't think he feels very close to you anymore. And he feels bad Jackie didn't come."

"Oh," I said. "I don't know."

"Is it because of Jason?"

"No," I said.

"Because I'd understand if it was."

"No," I said, "it's not that. I like Jason. I just don't know if I want to stay here. . . ."

"Well, it's no big deal. Just two days." My father reached up and turned off the light. It was a dual overhead light and fan, and the fan spun around some in the darkness, each spin slower. My father put his hands on my shoulders and half pushed, half guided me back to the couch. "It's late," he said. "See you tomorrow."

I lay on the couch. I couldn't fall asleep, because I knew that in a while Jason would be up for his snack. That kept me awake, and the decision about what to do. For some reason, it did seem like a big deal: going or staying. I could still picture my mother, backed up against the wall of the Grand Canyon, as far from the cliff as possible, crying, her mule braying, the helicopter whirring in the sky above us. It seemed like a choice between that and Jason swimming in the dark water, slowly and nakedly. I didn't want to be there for either.

The thing was, after I sprang off the diving board I did hear Jason shout, but my brain didn't make any sense of it. I could just feel myself hanging there, above the horrible bright-blue water, but I couldn't make my body turn, even though I was dropping dangerously, and much too fast.

The Winter Bazaar

When Bertha Knox died, Knox Farm was developed with "luxury" homes and renamed Norwell Estates. They were the first split-level houses in that part of Indiana, and for a while it was a big deal to visit someone in the Estates to see how the kitchen and living room and bedroom were all on different levels. All that remained of the farm was the house and a couple of acres of cornfields, which belonged to the Methodist Church. Bertha Knox had been a Presbyterian, but the Presbyterians had hired a woman minister, so Mrs. Knox left her house to the Methodists, after her lawyer told her she couldn't leave it to her dog, Mr. Jim.

A man from Gaitlinburg eventually bought the farmhouse and the fields fronting the Range Road from the Methodist Church. His plan was to get the zoning changed and open a Dairy Freeze, but when the selectmen proved uncooperative, he stopped paying his mortgage. The Norwell Valley Savings Bank (the only bank in town) was forced to foreclose on the property. The furnishings of the house had remained in Methodist ownership, and anything that wasn't junk was being sold at the Winter Bazaar.

One morning in early October, Walter Doyle, who was the president of the Norwell Valley Savings Bank, stopped at the farmhouse on his way to the Rotary lunch at McGooley's Tavern, over in Hempel. He only intended to have a quick look around, but something about the abandoned, sunlit rooms entranced him. He went upstairs. The bedrooms were tidy and poised, as if awaiting guests. He couldn't remember when he was last in such a quiet, peaceful place, and the thought of lunch in the basement of McGooley's—the smoke, the sticky floors, the gelatinous beef stew—repulsed him. So he took a bath, a decadently long bath, in the large porcelain bathtub, and then he lay down on one of the beds in his boxer shorts and T-shirt.

When he woke up the sun had passed from the window. For a moment he didn't remember who or where he was. This feeling of disorientation was so rich and transporting he lay still and let it linger. But slowly it faded; his life filtered back into place, familiar and intact. He got dressed and went downstairs.

Mrs. Topsy Hatter, the chairman of the Winter Bazaar Committee, was standing in the kitchen with a carving knife poised in front her. When she saw it was Walter Doyle coming down the stairs, she said, "Jesus, Walter, you scared me."

"Sorry," Walter said.

"How long have you been here?" Topsy put the knife back in a drawer.

She was wrapping glasses in yellowed newspaper. All the cabinet doors were open, arms reaching into the room. The kitchen table was crowded with stemware.

"I fell asleep upstairs," Walter said. "I just stopped by to check things, and I fell asleep. I don't know what's wrong with me."

"You're probably just tired."

Walter didn't know Mrs. Hatter very well, but he had always been a little bit in love with her. He had baby-sat for her kids, Ellen and Knight, twenty-five years ago. Mr. Hatter had died sometime after that. Mrs. Hatter had worked for the phone company, and brought up Ellen's two kids after Ellen fell apart, but they were pretty much grown up now. She still lived in her big old house out on Cobble Road. She was active in the town, but she didn't really fit in with the other ladies. There had always been something competent and independent about her, a way of dismissing things she found irrelevant, that frightened people. Topsy Hatter did things like wear pants and let her black, black hair hang long and loose, back when other women were wearing dresses and getting what they called hairdos at Joanie's every week. Walter was sure Mrs. Hatter had never set a foot inside of Joanie's.

"Are you taking those for the bazaar?" he asked.

"Yes," she said. "You know, Bertha Knox had some nice things. It's kind of sad, her not having anyone to give them to. A stupid dog."

"Can I help?"

"Oh, no," said Topsy. "This is my job. Shouldn't you be at work?"

"They will survive without me." Walter sat down at the kitchen table. He picked up one of the glasses, got up, and filled it at the tap. The water was rusty, but he let it run till it turned clear. It tasted fresher and sweeter than the water at home. It must be well water, he thought.

"You're doing this all yourself?" He sat back down. "Don't you have any helpers?"

"No," said Topsy. "I like it, coming out here. It's nice and quiet. I'll let the ladies take care of the rest, but I like being out here alone."

"It doesn't scare you?"

Topsy laughed. "No," she said. "It doesn't scare me."

"I like being here, too," Walter said.

He watched her swaddle a glass. Her dark hair was gray now, but he couldn't tell how long, since it was in a bun. "You used to have such long hair," he said. "It was beautiful. Is it still?"

"It's still long," she said, "but I don't think it was ever beautiful."

"Can I see it?"

"No," she said.

"Why not?" he asked.

"Because."

He picked up a sheet of the newspaper. It was the *Norwell Bulletin*, ten years old. "Old news," he said.

"I found it in the basement. There are stacks and stacks of them."

"You went down into the basement?" That was where Bertha Knox and Mr. Jim's bodies had been found.

"Apparently."

"You weren't scared?"

"Of what?"

"I don't know. Scared to go down there?"

"No," said Topsy. "I wasn't. I don't scare easy."

The next day he was there when she arrived. She recognized his car behind the hedge and she thought about backing up and leaving, but she didn't. She parked beside it and went inside. He was packing the glasses she had wrapped in a cardboard box.

"What are you doing here?" she asked.

"I'm not here," he said. He smiled. "I'm in Gaitlinburg. I'm meeting with Mr. Angelo Carmichael in Gaitlinburg."

"Who's Mr. Angelo Carmichael?"

"The Dairy Freeze man. We're having lunch."

For a moment Topsy just stood there. She was trying to think things out, think of everything, be logical. But she had trouble concentrating. Walter stood up. He was a handsome man. He opened the refrigerator. From the back he was a large handsome man. The only thing in the fridge was a bottle of wine. He took it out and looked at it as if he were surprised to find it there.

"Would you like a glass of wine?" he asked. He held the bottle out to her, like a waiter in a restaurant, so she could see the label. Only she couldn't see it; she had trouble seeing anything. She sat down.

"Some wine?" Walter asked.

"Don't you think it's a little early for wine?"

Walter looked disappointed. He shrugged. "I guess so," he said. "Maybe later."

"Maybe," Topsy said.

"Do you mind that I'm here?" he asked. He sat down beside her.

Topsy didn't answer.

"Do you want me to leave?"

"Maybe I will have a little wine," Topsy said. "Just a touch."

The next day his car was there, and she turned around and drove home, but when she got there she realized she wanted to see him, so she drove back to the farmhouse. But his car was gone.

She didn't think he'd be there the next day, and she was right. She started to sort through the pots and pans. After about half an hour she heard a noise upstairs. It sounded like a bird. She stopped and listened, but she didn't hear anything.

"Walter?" she called.

The noise again: an owl.

She went upstairs and found Walter in the back bedroom, in bed, apparently naked. She stood in the doorway.

"What in God's name are you doing?" she asked.

"Waiting for you?"

"You're a married man, Walter," she said. "What would your wife think of you now?"

"I don't think Virginia is thinking of me now."

"What if she were?"

He looked down at the sheet sloped over his stomach and legs. "She'd think I looked silly," he said.

"She'd be right," Topsy said. She went downstairs.

In a little while he came down. She had spread the pots and pans all across the kitchen floor, and he stopped at the door, looking at the display.

"I'm sorry," he said. "I didn't mean to embarrass you."

"You didn't embarrass me," said Topsy. "You embarrassed yourself."

"You think so?"

"Yes," said Topsy. "I do."

He picked his way through the maze of pots and sat at the table. "I've never been unfaithful," he said.

"Do you want a medal?"

"No," he said. "Just so you know. I mean, I'm not a Don Juan."

Topsy smiled. "I didn't think you were."

"Have you ever been unfaithful?"

"I'm not married," said Topsy.

"I mean when you were."

"It's none of your business," said Topsy.

"That means yes," said Walter. "What about since . . . well, since he died? Have you had . . . affairs?"

"I don't think one has affairs in Norwell."

"You'd be surprised."

"I'm sure I would."

Walter stood up. "Well, I guess I better go."

"I suppose so," said Topsy.

"I guess I shouldn't come back, either."

"It would probably be better."

"O.K.," said Walter. He put his topcoat on, picked up his keys. "Good-bye," he said.

Topsy nodded good-bye.

He got his car out of the garage and drove away. Topsy returned to the pots and pans, scrubbing their heat-stained copper bottoms, but after a while she went upstairs, up into the room. He had made the bed, but badly. Men can't make beds, Topsy thought. She started to remake it, and realized the sheets were still warm from him. She put her hand, palm down, on the bottom sheet. She felt as if she were doing something dangerous. She was standing like that, touching the warm spot, when she heard a car in the driveway. She looked out the window and saw Walter come in the back door. He made owl noises. She stayed still, knowing he would find her.

He did. She stood by the bed, and he stood in the doorway.

"I'm back," he said.

"I see," she said. "I was just . . . making the bed." But she wasn't making the bed. She was standing there, looking at him.

"Are you glad I came back?" he asked.

Topsy waited a moment. She couldn't speak, so she nodded yes.

"Good," he said. He came closer, touched her hair. "Well?" he said.

"Wait," said Topsy. "There have got to be rules."

He took his hand away. "Of course," he said. "Rules. What rules? Tell me."

Topsy tried to think of rules. What would good rules be? "Well," she began. "We can stop whenever we want. Either of us. We can just say 'Stop' and it will be over."

"O.K.," said Walter. "Sure."

"And we both have to remember that you're married. That that comes first. That I don't want you to leave your wife. Is that understood?"

Walter nodded.

"And this is between us. Just us. This is private."

"Of course," said Walter. He sat down on the bed. "Sit down," he said.

"Wait," said Topsy. "I'm still thinking." For a moment neither of them said anything. "I guess that's all," said Topsy. "Can you think of anything else?"

Walter shook his head. "I can't think of anything," he said.

They never made plans. They never called each other. They'd just go, and if the other person showed—well, then. Whoever got there first turned on the electric space heater and waited. If it was Topsy waiting, she continued her bazaar work: cleaning out closets, washing sheets, rummaging in the bookshelves.

They made love and ate sandwiches and drank coffee or wine and talked. As it got colder, they spent more time in bed and less in the kitchen. They listened to squirrels in the attic. They made love.

Walter often fell asleep, and if he did it was Topsy's responsibility to wake him at three o'clock. One afternoon she was lying in bed between warmth from the space heater and warmth from Walter. She had her eyes closed and was making an effort to stay awake, although she wanted very much to sleep simultaneously with Walter. She could feel him dreaming, his big body pressed against her, his mouth wet at the back of her neck, and she felt that if she slipped into sleep she would find herself in his dream: something about a beach, hot sand, hot sun, water, sky, and birds clamoring in trees. After a while she felt the pressure of his body relax, and she knew he was awake.

"Did you have a good sleep?" she asked.

He answered by pulling her closer. She could feel sweat along her back where his stomach had rested, sweat their bodies had created together. She leaned out of the bed and turned down the space heater. She watched its coils fade from orange to red, heard its *ping ping ping*, and felt a sudden tremor of happiness, of the world stretching out all around her, curved and occurring.

"I'm all hot," she said.

He wasn't talking yet. She tried to turn toward him, but he pressed himself harder against her. He wrapped his arms around her, and moved against her, slowly.

"I'm sweating," she said.

He kissed her back, and licked her spine. His tongue felt cool. She tried again to turn and this time he let her. The blankets slipped away from her and he tried to cover her again but she said, "No. I'm hot."

Even the windows were sweating. Topsy got out of bed and opened one. She turned the heater off. She stood looking out, feeling the cold air on her face. She watched the cornstalks rearrange themselves as something—a dog?—walked through them. Darkness was spilling into the sky from some rip near the horizon.

"Come back to bed," Walter said.

"It's late," she said. "You should go."

"Come back," he said. "I have time."

"Where are you today?" she asked. "What's your excuse for not being at work?"

"You," he said. "Come here. Please."

"Is that what you told Gladys?" Gladys was Walter's secretary.

"Yes," said Walter. "And I told Virginia I wouldn't be home for dinner because I'd be in bed with you."

"What did Virginia say?"

Walter didn't answer. Topsy turned away from the window. He was looking at the ceiling. "What would Virginia think of that?" she asked.

"She wouldn't like it," he said. He looked at her. "Virginia . . . loves me."

"Do you love her?"

"In a way," he said. "In our way, yes."

"What way is that?"

"It's hard to describe," he said.

She came and sat on the bed.

"I'm cold," he said.

She went back over and closed the window. The thing was a dog—she saw it emerge from the corn and run through the trees toward Norwell Estates. Someone was calling it. Dinnertime.

"Did you love . . . what was his name?" Walter asked.

"Who?"

"Your husband."

"Karl," she said. "For a while, yes. And then, no."

"Did you hate him?"

"No," she said.

"That's good," he said. "Sometimes I think Virginia hates me."

"Sometimes she probably does."

"I never hate her. I feel sorry for her, but I don't hate her."

"Why do you feel sorry for her?"

Walter thought for a moment. "Because," he said. "It's a little pathetic. I mean all her good deeds. The Foodmobile and the Morning Doves—"

"What are the Morning Doves?"

"They call up senior citizens every morning to make sure they didn't die overnight. Because of what happened with Bertha Knox." Bertha Knox had been dead for quite a while when the gas man found her in the basement.

"What's pathetic about good deeds?"

"Nothing. I mean, I think it's great how much she does. I'm very proud of her."

"But you said it was pathetic."

"Oh, forget it," said Walter. "I don't want to talk about it."

Topsy came back and sat on the bed. "Sometimes I forget I was married. Isn't that terrible?"

"What do you mean, forget?"

"I just forget. I forget all about Karl. Like it never happened. It's very important when it's happening, but when it's over, it's surprising how little . . . effect it has."

"Did you like being married?"

"Of course. I mean, it was nice, raising a family."

"That would be nice," said Walter.

"Why don't . . . you and Virginia?"

"We've tried," said Walter. "It's very difficult. Both times Virginia got pregnant she miscarried. And I guess we feel a little too old for it now."

"How old are you?"

"Forty-two," said Walter. "Virginia is thirty-eight."

"That's not too old," said Topsy. "I was forty-two when I got Kittery and Dominick."

"But you didn't give birth to them," said Walter.

"No," said Topsy. "Ellen did that." They were quiet a moment, and then Topsy stood up and turned on the light.

"Turn it off," Walter said. "Lie down with me."

"No," said Topsy. "It's time to go home."

"Come lie down. For just a little while. I'm sad."

Topsy turned off the light. In the wake of illumination the room seemed darker than it had before. "Why are you sad?" she asked.

Walter thought for a moment. "I don't know," he said.

Tiny Peterson, the junk man, came with his truck and moved everything Topsy had deemed salable to the Sunnipee Hall. Then he came back and took away what was left: That was the junk. There had been a lot of it, and Topsy knew there was no reason to save it for the rummage sale in May. She had learned from experience that there are some things no one will buy, things in this world—often fine things—that are superfluous. That make the mistake of becoming un-owned.

A few nights later she and Walter had dinner together in the emptied farmhouse. Virginia was visiting her niece in Dayton. In the darkness of the kitchen everything was black and white except for the red sheen of wine in the glasses on the table.

"This was a bad idea," Topsy said. "I've been meaning to tell you something."

"What?"

"Well, I feel funny about coming here now," Topsy said. She picked up a wineglass and looked at it. "Now that there's no work to do."

"There's still work to do," Walter said. "Our private work."

"No," said Topsy. "I don't feel right about it anymore."

"You mean, it's all right to have an affair if it's accom-panied by church-work and not O.K. if it's not?"

"No," said Topsy. "I just mean being here."

"But this is the perfect place. You know it is."

"Well, we can't come here forever. Eventually someone will buy it, won't they?"

"Not if I can help it," said Walter.

"Well, I didn't really mean the place, anyway," Topsy said.

"What did you mean?" Walter stood up. He took the glass of wine from her and drank from it.

"I meant . . . us. I think we should think about ending it."

"Why?"

"What do you think? What do you think about ending it?"

"I don't want to end it," said Walter. He leaned against the sink. "Do you?"

"I think it might be a good idea."

"Why?"

"Well, because. Because I'm starting to depend on it. I'm starting to depend on you."

"What's wrong with that?"

"I don't like it. It's not what I wanted. I didn't want to get attached."

"Are you?"

Topsy looked across the kitchen at him. He was just a dark figure in the shadows, but she could picture him. "I think I am," she said.

"So am I," he said.

"Then we should end it," she said. "Remember the rule?"

"What rule?"

"That you're married. That we wouldn't . . . get fond of each other."

"But we were always fond of each other. Right from the start. At least I was of you." He drank the rest of the wine and put the glass in the sink, then came over and sat next to her. "Why can't we just keep going and see what happens?"

"No," she said. "It will only get worse."

"So let it get worse."

"I don't want it to get worse," Topsy said. "I want to end it now."

He stood up. "I thought you weren't scared. You told me you weren't easily scared."

Topsy shrugged. "I guess I was wrong," she said.

Two weeks later, Topsy stood behind the cashier's table at the Winter Bazaar and watched Walter Doyle walk up and down the aisles. He arrived at the cashier's with a tackle box full of lures and weights.

"Those are twenty-five cents apiece," Topsy said.

"Do I get a discount if I buy them all?"

"I guess so," said Topsy.

"How about five dollars?"

"You want the box, too?"

"Of course," said Walter.

"Five dollars for the contents, and five dollars for the box. Ten for it all."

"This box isn't worth five dollars," said Walter. "Not even brand-new."

"Eight dollars, then," Topsy said. "For everything."

"O.K.," said Walter. He gave her a ten-dollar bill.

"Do you want your change? Any amount over your purchase price is a tax-deductible contribution."

"I'll take my change," said Walter.

Topsy gave him two tired dollar bills.

"You've got quite a crowd," he said. "How's it going?"

"We need buyers."

"Virginia's coming this afternoon. She's a buyer. Is that coffee free?"

"A nickel."

"What about a free cup for purchases eight dollars and over?"

"It's a nickel, Walter."

Walter extracted a dime from his pants pocket. "Keep the change," he said. "That's tax-deductible, right?"

Topsy poured him a cup of coffee.

"Are cream and sugar extra?" he asked.

"Help yourself," said Topsy.

Walter drank his coffee and watched Topsy fill a tray of paper cups with juice. She arranged all the cups with their edges touching, and then poured the juice down the rows in one long swoop, filling each cup perfectly, spilling none.

"Looks like you've done that before," Walter said.

"Just one of my many talents," said Topsy.

"Do you have a lost-and-found?" asked Walter.

"What did you lose?"

"A . . . glove."

"There's a box in the kitchen," Topsy said. "But I haven't seen any men's gloves."

"Could we look?"

"It's in the kitchen. Go ahead."

"Come with me."

"I have to stay here."

"You could get someone to cover for you, couldn't you?"

"I don't see the point. I'm sure you can find your own glove. If you did, indeed, lose it."

" 'Indeed'?"

"What?"

"Since when do you say, 'did, indeed'?"

Topsy shrugged. She drank a glass of juice. "Since now," she said.

"As a matter fact, I didn't, indeed, lose a glove."

"I thought not."

"You thought not?"

"Stop it, Walter."

"Well, why are you talking like that?"

"Like what?"

"Like . . . you don't like me."

"I'm not. I don't."

"Don't what?"

"Don't not like you."

"I don't not like you either."

A child interrupted them to buy a deflated beach ball and a transistor radio shaped like a frog.

"I miss you," said Walter, when the transaction had been completed. "Do you miss me?"

"I try not to," said Topsy.

"But you do?"

"A little."

"How much?"

"I told you: a little."

"Don't lie."

"I'm not lying. I don't lie."

Walter felt like saying, yeah, you don't get scared, either, but he didn't. Instead he said, "Are you sure?"

"Walter, stop it. Please. I'm not going to discuss this in the church hall."

"Will you discuss it somewhere else?"

"No. It's pointless."

Walter threw his empty coffee cup into the garbage can. He picked up his tackle box. "Here," he said. "I don't really want this." He put the box down on the table.

"Take it," said Topsy. "You paid for it."

"I don't want it. I don't fish."

"Well, then, let me give you your money back." She took eight dollars out of the box and held them out, but Walter was walking toward the door. She looked at the money in her hand, then put it back in the cash box.

When Virginia Doyle came in later that afternoon, Topsy deducted eight dollars from her grand total. When Virginia asked why, Topsy said they were just giving discounts to good customers. Virginia looked at her as if she were crazy. She told her that was no way to run a church bazaar.

For a while after Topsy stopped seeing Walter, she avoided driving past Knox Farm. If she were going over to Hempel she took the long way, out to the end of Cobble Road and back around through Gaitlinburg. But one day—the first day it was warm enough to drive with the windows open—she found that she had forgotten to take the long way; that she was on the Range Road, and the next thing she knew she was driving up the dirt road to the farmhouse. For a few minutes she just sat in the car, not knowing what she wanted to do. She had tried to park out of sight and when she opened the windows wider an overgrown arm of forsythia unfurled into the car. The thin stalk was speckled with wartlike, pale green buds; it bobbed in front of her face. She opened her mouth and set her lips to it. She bit a little so she could taste its bitterness. She closed her eyes. She thought about her life and how things happened in it, how you couldn't stop things from happening or control them. It was as if you and all the things that could possibly happen in your life were floating in a pool the size of an ocean and you only touched some of them, and it was all accidental, and the things you wanted were as slim and slippery as fish. Fish swam between your fingers and legs and brushed against your sides; silver-sided fish nibbled at your toes; shy, skittish fish flitted to the surface and then flipped away, no matter how still you stood, no matter how quiet you were, for they could sense your desire: It pulsed from you like sonar—*come to me, come to me, come to me*—driving the swarms of swimming things far away.

In early summer, when the days were like balm, Topsy drove to the Norwell Valley Savings Bank and climbed the stairs to Walter's office. Gladys Wallace was feeding a pencil to an electric sharpener.

"Hello, Gladys," Topsy said.

"Well, hi, Mrs. Hatter. What can we do for you?"

"Is Walter in?"

"Mr. Doyle? He's in a meeting at the moment. Did you have an appointment?"

"No, I don't. But maybe you could tell Walter—Mr. Doyle—that I'm here. He told me to stop by anytime."

"O.K., I'll let him know. Will you excuse me?"

"I sure will," said Topsy. She sat in an easy chair and picked up a copy of *Colonial Homes*.

Gladys reappeared shortly, closing the door behind her as if she had just got a baby down inside. "He says he'll see you now," she said. "You can go right in."

"Thanks," said Topsy. She went in Walter's office and

closed the door, a little less quietly than Gladys had. "Hello, Walter," she said.

Walter nodded. He looked a little stunned.

"They climb out the window?" Topsy asked.

"Who?" asked Walter.

"The folks you were meeting with. Gladys told me you were in a meeting."

"I wasn't," said Walter.

"I guessed not," said Topsy.

"I'm in a meeting sometimes," said Walter.

"I'm sure you are," said Topsy. She sat down. For a moment neither of them said anything. They heard Gladys resume her pencil-sharpening. "Don't you want to know why I'm here?" Topsy asked.

"I was wondering," said Walter. "Although it's nice to see you."

Topsy snorted. "I'm here on business," she said. "I want to buy Knox Farm. I'm going to sell my house."

"Why?" asked Walter.

"Why what?"

"Why are you going to sell your house?"

"It's too big."

"Knox Farm isn't small."

Topsy smiled. "This is business, Walter," she said. "I just want to buy a house your bank happens to own."

"Well, how much are you offering?"

"I'd like to see it," said Topsy.

"I thought you had."

"I'd like to see it again. Before I make an offer."

"Oh," said Walter. "I guess that seems fair."

"Maybe you'd drive out there with me? Show it to me?"

They looked at each other for a moment. Then Walter stood up and put on his jacket. "Certainly," he said. "I don't see why not."

———

Walter opened the back door with a key that was hidden in the milk box. They went into the kitchen. The only thing in it was sunlight.

"This is the kitchen," Walter said. He turned on the faucet; rusty water flowed into the sink. "Running water," he announced.

"Stop it," said Topsy.

Walter turned off the water and shrugged. "What do you want?" he asked. "What are we doing here?"

"I just wanted to talk to you," Topsy said.

"Oh," said Walter.

"I'm lonely," said Topsy.

Walter didn't respond. He didn't want to look at her so he opened a silverware drawer, looked in at its emptiness.

"I can't stand . . . being lonely like this," he heard her say. "I mean, I was lonely before you, but I never realized. It wasn't till we were together—well, after, when we stopped—that I realized . . ."

Inside the drawer an ant walked across a field of green felt. It climbed over a cork and paused at the summit. Walter decided to pretend he hadn't heard what Topsy had said. Once decided, it was easy.

After a moment, he said, "Did you really want to buy the house?"

"No," said Topsy. "Well, maybe for a minute. It was just an idea. A dumb idea."

"It's not a bad house," Walter said. He closed the drawer and wiped his hands together. He stood up straighter. "Well, then," he said. "I guess we should be going." He jiggled his car keys.

Topsy didn't move. "You go," she said. "It's O.K. I want to stay for a while."

"How will you get home?"

"I'll walk. Go."

He looked around the kitchen as if instructions for how

to act might be displayed somewhere, like a choking poster. "I'm sorry," he said. "It's not that I don't want to stay . . ."

"I didn't expect you to stay. I don't know what I thought. Please, go."

"No. I mean, I still feel the—I still feel for you. I do. It's just that, well, things are better with Virginia. We've worked some things out. I mean, we're trying. And I don't think I should—"

"It's all right." She looked up at him and smiled. "That's good for you. I'm happy."

Walter studied his keys as if they were unfamiliar to him. "Are you sure you don't want a ride?"

"It's a nice day to walk," she said.

"O.K., then," he said. He moved toward her, as if he might embrace her, but then walked around her, out the door. She waited till his car had pulled away, till the sound of it was gone, before she moved. She went upstairs and walked through the rooms, looked out the bedroom window. The same cornstalks were still standing patiently in the field. She didn't feel particularly sad. She felt numb.

Eventually she went back downstairs. Walter had left the key in the door. She thought about taking it as a souvenir, but then she realized she didn't want one. She locked the door and tossed the key into the milk box, kicked the lid shut with her foot, and started walking home.

Fast Forward

Maureen, the new receptionist, told me I had a call on 2, but when I picked up 2 it was Mrs. LaRossa, wanting to know if Kenny had come back from lunch. I told her no, and that I would have him call when he did. Then I picked up 3, which was also blinking. "Hello?" I said.

"Patrick? This is me." It was my friend Alison.

"Hi," I said. "What's happening?"

"Well," said Alison, "it depends what you're doing this weekend. What are you doing this weekend?"

"Nothing," I said.

"Then do you want to come up to Maine with me? I have to visit my mother."

"How is she?" I asked.

"Not too good. That's why I'm going." Alison's mother had some disease. She had been dying, on and off, for years.

"Oh," I said. "That's too bad."

"Can you come? I'm driving up Friday night after work." Alison worked as a projectionist in a movie theater in Cambridge.

"I guess so," I said. "Sure."

"That's great," said Alison. "I really appreciate it. I hate going up there alone. I can't deal with it."

"What time are you leaving?"

"Oh," said Alison. "About midnight. The last show is at ten."

"What is it?"

"*My Fair Lady*," Alison said. "If you can believe it."

The first time I met Alison's mother I didn't know that she was sick, or that she was dying, although in fact she was.

Alison and I went to college together in Maine, and Mrs. Arbinger, Alison's mother, used to come visit. She'd drive up in her champagne-colored Peugeot and take us out to dinner—Alison and her roommate and anyone else who happened to be around. Since I lived in the same suite, I was usually invited.

The first time I began to realize that Mrs. Arbinger was ill was at graduation. It was held outside, and after it was over I was enduring the photographic zeal of my parents when Alison appeared, looking for her mother. As the sea of chairs slowly emptied, we saw her sitting alone, making no move to get up. Alison ran over; I followed. Mrs. Arbinger was sitting very still. She had recently had some sort of operation on her throat and had wrapped long silk scarves around it.

"What's wrong?" Alison said, panting, although she had not run far.

Mrs. Arbinger smiled. "Nothing," she said. "I just can't stand up. If I stand up I know I'll fall over. I didn't want to make a scene."

"Oh, God," said Alison.

Mrs. Arbinger looked at me. "Patrick," she said. "Congratulations."

On Friday night, I came home from work and ate a tuna melt. I drank two beers, then fell asleep. When I woke up, it was nine-thirty and I could still taste the tuna melt. I brushed my teeth, and decided to go to the movies.

It wasn't crowded, and I got a good seat and hung my legs over the chair in front of me. I looked back up at the projection booth and saw Alison threading the first reel. I waved, but she didn't see me.

For some reason I'd gotten *My Fair Lady* mixed up with *Hello, Dolly!* I kept waiting for Eliza Doolittle to come into a restaurant and everyone to go crazy, and it was a while—after the scene at Ascot—until I realized it wasn't going to happen. I watched the rest of the movie feeling a little cheated.

When the lights came up, I went into the lobby and up the secret staircase into the booth. Alison was furiously rewinding one reel on the projector and another on the manual rewind. "You won't believe this," she shouted.

"What?" I said.

"There's a midnight show. I've got to show it again."

"*My Fair Lady?*" I said. "At midnight?"

"Maybe no one will come. If no one shows up, we can leave."

I looked down into the theater. Ten people had already come in. "There are some fools down there," I said.

"Christ," said Alison. "I hate when they do this to me. Could you wind this? I have to splice the second reel. For the third time tonight."

We started the first reel about ten past twelve. Alison turned the sound off in the projection booth and we watched a silent *My Fair Lady.* Alison, who knew all the words by heart, dubbed for Audrey Hepburn. She was almost as good as Marni Nixon. It was a quarter past three by the time we left Boston in Alison's burgundy Peugeot. The Arbingers buy them by the half dozen, I think. I was going through Alison's extensive collection of tapes, playing the one or two songs I liked from each tape. This meant I was spending most of the time fast-forwarding.

"Can't you play just one tape from beginning to end?"

Alison asked. She rolled down her window and flicked her cigarette into the night. I watched the sparks fly away. Judy Collins began singing "Who Knows Where the Time Goes?" and it sounded perfect, so I didn't bother to respond.

"Actually," Alison said, rolling up her window, "I have to tell you something."

"What?"

Alison turned the tape down a notch and hung her wrist over the steering wheel. She was going seventy-five. "You're here under false pretenses."

"What? Where?"

"Here," Alison said. "With me. Going to Maine."

"What's false about them?"

Alison looked over at me, then looked back out at the road. "Well, you're my fiancé. We're engaged, and we're getting married in the spring. My mother wants to see you one more time before she dies. She's dying. That's the only reason why I'm subjecting you to this."

"Why?" I asked. "Why did you tell her we were engaged?"

"I don't know. I forget how it all started. For a while she's had this thing about me—about how important it is for me to be married and happy and pregnant and all before she dies. It started very subtly, but as she's got sicker she's kind of latched onto the idea. She wouldn't give it up. And she's always, always liked you—right from the start. She always asks about you, and since we were together at school—at least whenever she came up—it was easy to invent a romance."

"But how did we get engaged?"

"God, it's been going on for so long. If you knew, you would kill me. I mean, you would. I've been awful. We live together in Boston. We're getting married in June, in Maine. I'm wearing my mother's wedding dress." Alison paused. I didn't say anything. "I'm sorry," she said.

I couldn't think what to say. Alison slowed down and

pulled over onto the shoulder. The highway was deserted. No cars passed us. It was dark. Judy Collins was singing the whale song. "You don't have to do this," Alison said. "We can turn around."

Alison had always referred to the house in Maine as the Abbey, but it didn't look like one. It looked like a picture I remember of the House of the Seven Gables in a Classics comic book I read in sixth grade: it was all peaky roofs and thin, arched windows.

I didn't really get a good look at it Friday night. I had fallen asleep, and I woke up in the garage. We were parked between two sleeping Peugeots.

"We're here," Alison said.

"What time is it?"

Alison flicked the keys so that the dashboard lights went back on. The digital clock read 5:15. "In a while the sun will come up," she said. "It's just starting to get light."

"Aren't you tired?" I asked.

"No," said Alison.

Upstairs, there was a long hall of closed doors. Alison opened one. "You can sleep in here," she said. "There's a bathroom attached. Sleep as late as you want."

If I had been more awake, I would have asked her what the plan was, but I just nodded. Alison smiled and closed the door.

There was a huge bed in the middle of the room. It looked like a canopy bed, except it had no canopy—just tall posts that ended in carved pineapples. The blankets had been turned back.

I undressed and got into the bed. I thought I would fall asleep right away, but I couldn't. Every time I closed my eyes, I could see Audrey Hepburn running around in her night-gown, singing "I Could Have Danced All Night." It was something about the bed. I got out and sat in a leather chair. Outside the leaded-glass windows, trees appeared.

When I woke up I was back in the bed. I couldn't remember moving. Someone was knocking on the door.

"Yes?" I said.

"Are you decent?" a woman's voice called.

It sounded as if it might have been a moral question, but I figured it wasn't. "Yes," I said. "Come in."

The door opened, and a middle-aged woman stood there in a dress and high heels. "Patrick?" she said. "I'm Mrs. Hawks, Alison's aunt. I just wanted you to know that breakfast is about to be taken away, so if you're hungry you should come down."

She disappeared but left the door open. I thought I could still hear her in the hall, and I tried to figure out how to get out of the bed without being seen in my underwear. Finally, I kind of rolled out and crawled into the bathroom.

When I came downstairs—it took me a while to find the stairs—Mrs. Hawks was standing in the front hall going through mail. "You might find something nourishing in the dining room," she said, pointing across the hall.

"Is Alison up?" I asked.

"Goodness, yes. She's in with her mother."

I was eating a charred apple when Alison came into the dining room. She was wearing a kilt and a white blouse with ruffles. It looked a little like a national costume. "Why are you dressed like that?" I asked.

"My mother ordered them for me. I was just trying them on."

"Are they part of your trousseau?" I asked.

"Will you shut up," Alison said. "Now, you have a choice."

"I thought we decided to go through with it."

"No, not the wedding story," Alison said. "The dentist."

"I have to go to the dentist?"

"No. I do. Do you want to come? That's your choice. Do you want to come?"

"What's the alternative?" I asked.

"Staying here," said Alison.

The dentist was really the dentist's daughter. He had died, and she had inherited his practice. The office was in the garage of their house, and while Alison visited with the dentist I sat in the living room. The dentist's mother was the receptionist. She got me a cup of coffee. "Are you a friend of Alison's?" she asked.

"Yes," I said. "We went to school together."

"I hear Alison's engaged."

"Did you? I thought it was a secret."

"Oh," she said. "Well, Mrs. Hawks told me. She had her gums scraped. She didn't say it was a secret."

"It is," I said.

"Are you the lucky man?"

"No," I said.

"Alison's a nice girl. It's just too bad she can't find something to do with her life. Patty's always known she wanted to be a dentist. It's easier for the girls who are like that, I suppose. Is Alison still working in that movie house?"

"Yes. She's the manager now," I lied.

"Is she really? Well, good for her." The phone rang and the woman answered it.

A few minutes later, Alison came out of the garage looking angry. "Let's get out of here," she said.

"Don't you have to pay?"

"No," said Alison. "This is Maine. They bill me."

Once we had turned the corner and the dentist's house had disappeared Alison said, "I never did like her. She told me I have gum disease. I don't have gum disease. My gums are fine. She just wants to get back at me."

"For what?"

"I don't know," Alison said. "For being popular, I suppose. Patty was kind of a drip in high school."

"Maybe you do have gum disease. Do you floss?"

"Patrick," Alison said. "Lay off."

After a few minutes Alison seemed to relax. At least we slowed down a little.

"How's your mother?" I asked.

"She seems O.K.," Alison said. "It's hard to tell."

"Why isn't she in a hospital?"

"She's a Christian Scientist. Plus she's past that point."

"What point?"

"The point where you stay at the hospital. She'd have been sent home. We have a special nurse there." Alison pulled into the parking lot of a supermarket. "Do you want to get some real food? The macrobiotic diet at the Abbey is enough to kill you."

"Is that what it is? I think I had a baked apple for breakfast."

Alison opened the door. "Wait till you see lunch."

We went into the supermarket and bought onion bagels, Doritos, Pepperidge Farm cookies, and a six-pack of Busch beer.

When we got back in the car, Alison said, "She wants to see you this afternoon. She's usually pretty good in the afternoon, but you don't have to go. I can say you went fishing."

"It's raining," I said.

"Isn't that when people fish?"

"I'll see her," I said. "I might as well."

"Then there's just one thing I have to tell you."

"What?"

"Well, in addition to marrying me, you're also going to law school."

"Law school! Alison, that's cruel." I had applied and been denied admission to almost every decent law school in the eastern United States.

"Well, it made my mother very happy," she said. "For you and for me."

"Where am I going?"

"BU," said Alison. "I thought Harvard was stretching it."

After lunch (brown rice, seaweed, and beet juice) Alison and I went up to see Mrs. Arbinger. She lay in a big bed like the one I had slept in the night before, only this one had a canopy. Her face was very thin and pale, but her eyes were bright. She had so much lipstick on that it looked as if her mouth had come off and been clumsily reattached. The nurse, who was dressed in a caftan, sat on a window seat, knitting. Alison sat on the bed, and I stood beside it.

Mrs. Arbinger looked around at all of us for a moment. "It's like a party," she said. No one answered. "Look what I found," she continued, undaunted. "My wedding album." She indicated a white book on the bed beside her. She opened the album to a picture of her and Mr. Arbinger cutting a many-tiered wedding cake. They stood side by side, clasping hands on a cake knife that was pointed at the marzipan bride and groom. They were divorced soon after Alison was born. Mr. Arbinger lived in Italy now. I'd never met him. Mrs. Arbinger turned the page to a picture of her standing at the top of a curved staircase in her wedding gown, her bouquet dripping vines over the bannister.

"I was a beautiful bride," Mrs. Arbinger said, more to the picture than to any of us. She closed the book. "You'll be beautiful, too," she said to Alison. "I hope the dress fits. Have you tried it on?"

"Not yet," said Alison.

"You must. It will have to be altered. That kind of dress must fit perfectly; otherwise it looks cheap."

"Let's not talk about the wedding," Alison said. "It makes me nervous." She stood up. As if on cue, the nurse stopped her knitting and stood up, too.

"Do you think I could talk to Patrick alone?" Mrs. Arbinger said to no one in particular.

"I was just going down to get your juice," the nurse said.

"I'll come, too," said Alison. They both left.

Mrs. Arbinger waited a moment. I thought she had forgotten about me. Then she patted the bed beside her. Her fingers were very thin and her rings twisted around below her knuckles. "Sit down," she said. "Please."

The comforter was so puffy and Mrs. Arbinger was so thin that I couldn't really tell where her body began. I perched on the foot of the bed, and Mrs. Arbinger patted a spot nearer to her. The patting seemed to exhaust her. "A little closer," she said.

I moved up the bed. She took one of my hands in hers. For a moment I thought she was going to read my palm, but she just looked at it, then put it back on the bed and patted it. She smiled at me. I noticed that her teeth were very white. They looked like the only healthy part of her left. I wondered if they were dentures.

"It's so nice to see you," Mrs. Arbinger said. "It was nice of you to come up."

I just nodded.

"I'm sorry for cloistering you like this but I wanted to tell you how happy I am about you and Alison. I've always been fond of you, and I'm so pleased. I won't say any more because I don't want to embarrass you."

"I'm happy, too," I said, although it didn't sound like my voice. "Thank you."

Mrs. Arbinger looked toward the window. "Will you do me a favor?" she asked.

"Of course," I said.

"Will you look out the window? I'm not allowed out of bed and I miss seeing outside."

I got off the bed and went over to the window. There was a pond at the back of the house, and behind that a field with a horse in it, and behind that some woods.

"Can you see the pond?" Mrs. Arbinger asked.

"Yes," I said.

"Are there any geese in it?"

"No," I said.

"Oh," she said. "There will be. Are the leaves pretty?"

"Yes."

"Do you mind doing this?"

"No," I said.

"It's just that I like to picture it in my head and want to get it right. What color are the leaves?"

"Mostly yellow," I said. "Some red. It's raining."

She waited a moment before she asked the next question. "Do you and Alison really want to get married?" she asked, quietly.

I looked over at her. I had the feeling she had been watching me at the window and had turned away; she gazed up at the white tented canopy. "What?" I said.

"Forgive me if I'm being rude," she said, still not looking at me. "I just want to make sure, and I can't ask Alison."

"Sure of what?" I said.

"I don't want you to do this just for me," she said. "I know you're in love, but I also know people wait longer to get married nowadays. I just don't want you to rush into this to make me happy. You needn't do that."

I think that if she had continued to look at the canopy I would have answered differently. But she didn't. She turned her small, wrecked face toward me and smiled.

"Oh, no," I said. "We want very much to get married."

We sat there for a moment. I thought there were tears in Mrs. Arbinger's eyes, but I wasn't sure, because there seemed to be tears in my own.

The nurse came in, carrying a small silver tray. On it was a glass of beet juice.

When I went downstairs it had stopped raining. Alison and I went for a walk. We fed carrots to the fat white horse in the field, and then followed a gravel path into the woods. The sun was setting as we walked into the far side of the field an hour later, and the sight of the white horse completely disoriented me. I had thought we were walking deeper and deeper into the woods, but it was an illusion. The straight path had curved, imperceptibly, all along. As we walked around the pond, we heard a noise behind us, and when we looked back we saw a shaking V of geese appear. They descended and skidded into the pond, then collected themselves and swam over to the grassy bank. They lowered themselves into the shadows. We stood and watched until they had disappeared, until even the water in the pond had regained its composure.

Alison didn't ask me what her mother and I had talked about. I didn't tell her.

Alison and I left the Abbey the next morning before anyone else was awake. She dropped me at my apartment and drove away, and I didn't see her for a couple of months, until we met at a New Year's Eve party in Cambridge. We were sitting together on the edge of a platform bed, but it was hard to talk. The room was way too crowded, and people were dancing behind us on the bed.

"Come on," Alison shouted. "Let's go someplace quieter."

I followed her into the bathroom. Alison sat on the rim

of the bathtub, which was filled with ice and champagne bottles. No two bottles looked alike, and the idea of their being purchased separately all over town and then dumped together in the bathtub appealed to me.

"I have something to tell you," Alison said. "I should have told you before."

"What?" I said.

"My mother died."

"Oh," I said, shocked. I had thought Mrs. Arbinger would be around for a long time. "When?"

"Before Christmas. December fifteenth."

"I'm sorry," I said. Someone knocked on the door. "Go away!" I shouted.

Alison had her fingers in the icy water, pushing the bottles down and then watching them pop back up.

"Why didn't you tell me sooner?" I asked.

"I don't know," Alison said. "I hate this whole episode in my life. I wanted to forget all about it. I'm seeing a therapist, if you can believe it. She thinks I was manipulated by my mother's illness into promising things I feel guilty about not doing now."

"You mean like the wedding?"

"Yes," said Alison.

"Maybe we should get engaged, and get married, just the way we planned."

"And then what?"

"Live happily ever after," I said. "Or get divorced."

Alison smiled.

"Why did you pick me?" I asked.

"What?" She bobbed another bottle.

"Why did you ask me to do that?"

"Because you're sweet," Alison said.

"Oh," I said. "So you didn't really want to get married?"

Alison looked at me. "Oh, Patrick," she said. "Did you really think I did?"

"No," I said. I shook my head. "Of course not."

"Good," said Alison. "I don't want to have to feel guilty about that, too." She stood up, then bent over and took a bottle of champagne from its bath. "Let's drink this now," she said. "I have to leave at eleven-thirty. I'm projecting the special midnight show."

"What movie is it?" I asked.

"*Bringing Up Baby*," Alison said.

She leaned over and kissed my cheek and touched my neck. Her hand was cold and wet. She began to uncork the champagne bottle. I closed my eyes. I hate waiting for things to explode.

Slowly

Later, this is how we heard it: It was the sixth day of their honeymoon and their last day in Ireland. They decided to drive to the coast, to a beach they had passed the day before, and picnic. At the breakfast table, Jane made a list of what they needed for their meal, and after breakfast Ethan drove the rental car to the closest town and shopped. Jane went for a walk on the bridle path, saw no horses, saw deer, came back to their room, packed their bags, and went down to the terrace and waited. When Ethan had not returned in an hour and a half she mentioned this to the hotel owner, Mr. Fitzgibbon. He told her the stores didn't open till ten; her husband would return by eleven. At noon Mr. Fitzgibbon called the police in Dingle; they told him yes, an American had been in an accident. Driving on the wrong side of the road. Hit by a truck. Deader than—well, dead.

I had been the best man at their wedding. I am—was—Ethan's brother. I had introduced him to Jane Hobard, who had been my friend in college. I stood beside Ethan and watched Jane walk down the aisle. I gave him the ring; I gave it to him, and he gave it to Jane. I watched him slip it down her finger. I woke them at four o'clock the following morning and drove them down the deserted highways to the airport.

I helped them unload their bags and then I left them. I kissed Jane good-bye, but I didn't kiss Ethan. Did I shake his hand? Did I touch his shoulder? I don't remember. Probably not.

Jane did not come to the memorial service. She quit her job and moved to her parents' house on an island in a lake in Canada. I sent her a letter and waited, but got no answer. The summer passed. The week before Labor Day, her brother, Teddy, called me at work in Washington.

"Tom?" he said. "I have a mission that involves you."

"What?" I asked.

"I have been instructed to bring you to Château Hobard this weekend. I am driving up Friday evening and I am not supposed to arrive without you. What are you doing this weekend?"

"Nothing," I said.

"It's Labor Day, you know," said Teddy.

"I know."

"And you don't have plans?"

"No. Well, I was going to Maryland, to my parents'. But . . . Is this Jane's idea?"

"Yes," said Teddy.

"How is she?" I asked.

"I haven't been up in a while. She doesn't talk on the phone. Can you come? If you can get to New York Friday afternoon, I'll drive you the rest of the way."

That night I told Charles about Teddy's mission. "I take it," Charles said, "that I wasn't invited."

"Teddy didn't mention you."

"Château Hobard," Charles said. "Do they really call it that?"

"Yes," I said. "As a joke."

"Well, you should go," said Charles. "You've been summoned." Charles didn't like Jane. I had made the mistake of telling him that if I weren't gay I might have liked to marry Jane myself.

"What will you do?" I asked.

"Nothing," he said. "But don't feel that you're abandoning me."

"You could go out to my parents'," I said.

"You mean spend the weekend with Chester and Ileen? At Château Kildare?"

"Yes," I said.

"You are so wonderfully and pathetically naïve," Charles said.

Château Hobard was reached via a ferry from a small town called Big Bay. Teddy and I arrived there about three o'clock Saturday morning. We had breakfast in a diner and sat in the car, waiting for the first ferry. "Last summer I did this with Ethan," Teddy said. "It was Labor Day, too."

"I remember," I said. "It was when they got engaged."

"It's a shame," said Teddy.

I didn't say anything.

"I taught him how to wind-surf that weekend. He was terrible."

"He wasn't an athlete," I said. "I got all the athletic genes."

"That's funny," said Teddy. After a while he fell asleep; at least he slumped forward and drooled. I liked Teddy. I reclined his seat and pushed him back into it; he woke for a second and smiled at me, wiped the spittle from his face, and fell back asleep. I got out of the car and walked through the deserted town, looking in the shop windows at the mannequins and lawn mowers and books. In the half-darkness they all looked vaguely alike. Everything seemed just on the verge of being alive, poised on the edge of gesticulation. I thought about running away, finding the bus or train or taxi station and disappearing north into the wilderness. But I went nowhere. As it got light I could see the island across the lake, and as the sun rose it struck the fronts of houses there. Windows gleamed as if they had lanterns hung in them. As if the houses were on fire.

"Jane has gone to pick berries," Mrs. Hobard said. "She claims she will bake a pie."

"Oh," I said. And then, "What kind of berries?" I couldn't think of what else to say. Mrs. Hobard was showing me my room. The house was old and made of stone; my room was in a kind of tower.

"Gooseberries," said Mrs. Hobard. "There is a thicket of them up past the barn. Did you notice the barn?"

"No," I said.

"It's straight down the driveway and across the field. If you follow the path behind it—the dirt path, not the gravel one—you'll find the berries. And, I hope, Jane. Why don't you go help her?"

"O.K.," I said.

"There's an extra blanket in here," said Mrs. Hobard, opening an armoire. "It gets cold at night." She laid the blanket across the foot of the bed.

"How is Jane?" I asked.

Mrs. Hobard smoothed the blanket. "I don't know," she said. "She doesn't talk about it. I think it's good she wants to see you." She looked up at me. "Go find her," she said. "Tell her to come home for lunch."

I followed the dirt path up through the woods to a small meadow. It was the highest point on the island. I could see the lake on all sides, filled now with boats and event, although it was quiet up on the bluff. The gooseberry bushes ringed the field. They were low and scrubby and full of tent caterpillars, not berries. I walked across the meadow and found Jane lying asleep in the hot tall grass. I stood and watched her. She was lying on her back, her arms crossed over her breasts, her face turned to one side. I knelt down and looked in her pail. There were some berries in it, but mostly it was full of other things: twigs and stones and flowers. A toad leapt up against the curved cool metal, falling back into the debris. I set him free.

"Jane," I said, and my voice sounded awful, the way I've heard it when it has been recorded and played back. I moved my hand above her face so it blocked the sun, shadowed her eyes.

They opened. She smiled at me for a moment and then sat up. "Hello," she said.

"Hi," I said.

"I was sleeping," she said. "What time is it?"

"About noon." I looked up at the sun, as if I could tell time by it. It did seem to be at the top of the sky. "Your mother says to come home for lunch."

"You came," she said.

"Yes. With Teddy."

"You've never been here," she said. "What do you think?"

"It's beautiful," I said.

"You saw the house?"

"Yes."

"I got your letter," she said. "Thanks."

I shrugged. I sat down. She picked up her bucket.

"I let the frog go," I said.

"It was a toad."

"I let him go," I repeated. "He went thataway."

"I think I'm still a little asleep," said Jane. She looked up at the sky. "I sleep all the time now," she said. "I was taking these tranquilizers, but I'm not anymore. But I still sleep."

"Sleeping's cool," I said.

"I was hysterical for a while," said Jane. "You missed it. Now I'm not hysterical anymore. I just sleep."

"Should we pick more berries?" I asked.

She looked in the bucket. "The toad probably peed on all of these," she said. She emptied the bucket onto the place where she had been sleeping: the warm, matted grass. "Let's go have some lunch," she said.

"O.K.," I said. I started walking toward the path.

"Wait," said Jane. "Come here. We have to hug. I want to hug you."

I stepped through the grass and hugged her. I knew she was crying by the way she shook, and then I heard it. I held her and looked out at the water. Then I looked down at the berries and petals strewn in the grass. I closed my eyes.

"Sometimes I can't stop," Jane said, as we walked down the path through the trees. "The first time I went to Big Bay— the only time, actually—I got completely hysterical. It was rather wonderful. I went over to see *Born Free*—you know, about the lions. They show a movie at the high school every Saturday night. Very rinky-dink. Anyway, it was a big deal: my first trip to the mainland. Back to life, I guess. I went with my parents. We had dinner at the hotel, and I was fine. I was quite ordinary. I had dessert and everything. And then we went to the movie, which was in the gym—all these folding chairs and a movie screen under the basketball hoop. You would have loved it. About two minutes into it, the man-eating lion kills the native woman washing her clothes. You don't even know the woman, you've developed no sympathy for her. I mean, she's not a character. She's just this woman. Well, I completely lost it. I started crying, and I couldn't stop. All the way back home on the ferry, I cried, and when we got home they wanted to take me back over to the doctor, and somehow that stopped me. The idea of distance. Of traveling. I realized I just wanted to go to bed. You get to a point where you don't want to cry anymore, at least not cry and travel, and then it's easy to stop. That's when I started taking the tranquilizers."

"But you've stopped?"

"Yes. I don't need them anymore. I'm fine."

I looked at her. We had emerged from the woods into the pasture behind the barn. "You're fine?" I asked.

"I mean I'm better," she said. "How are you?"

There was a tree in the field and some cows lying underneath it. They seemed to be watching us. "I'm better, too," I said.

We stood for a moment, watching the cows. Jane mooed. It sounded authentic to me, but the cows took no notice.

That night, after dinner, we sat on the terrace and watched the sun set. Barrels of salmon-colored geraniums separated the flagstones from the lawn, which sloped down the hill to the lake, where it ended abruptly, as if it were a scene in a child's coloring book: lawn, water; green, blue. At the same moment in the evening's descent, when the light from the sun was falling most beautifully through the clouds, groundhogs appeared from the earth and sat, Buddha-like, on the lawn. They seemed to be waiting to sing: something ancient, in unison.

We were all there: the parents Hobard, Teddy, Jane's younger sister Eleanor, her boyfriend Scott, Jane, and I. No one said anything. We watched the sun and the groundhogs as if they were fascinating and specially rehearsed.

"There's an albino one," Eleanor finally said. "Scott and I saw it the other night. He looks like a baby polar bear."

"I've never heard of an albino groundhog," said Mrs. Hobard.

"There are albino everything," said Eleanor.

"I bet it was a rabbit," said Mrs. Hobard.

"It wasn't a rabbit," said Eleanor. "What would a rabbit be doing in a groundhog burrow?"

"Vacationing?" suggested Mrs. Hobard.

The sun and the groundhogs departed simultaneously. Mr. Hobard lit kerosene torches, and we watched bats swoop from one side of the lawn to the other. Crickets chirped. We played a game called adverbs, which was a little like charades. People had to act out a scene in the manner of an adverb while someone tried to guess what the adverb was. Mr. Hobard was dismissed to be the guesser. We decided on "surreptitiously." Mr. Hobard returned, and directed Mrs. Hobard to sell Eleanor a hat in the manner of the word. Mr. Hobard guessed "incompetently" and "lackadaisically." New participants and a new scenario were needed. While Scott tried to surreptitiously teach Teddy German, I looked across the fire-lit terrace at Jane, who was sitting on a wrought iron bench, looking down at the lake. Her cheeks and eyes were wet. I knew why she was crying, or at least I thought I did: It should have been Ethan sitting here, across the patio, or, better yet, beside her on the bench; it should have been Ethan she had canoed with that afternoon; it should have been Ethan—my brother Ethan—who woke her in the field surrounded by gooseberry bushes. That is why I thought she was crying; that is why I cried.

I got up and moved down the lawn, out of the hot flickering light, into the shadowed, bumpy groundhog turf. Behind me, the adverb was declared too difficult and the game abandoned. "You must be exhausted, Thomas," Mrs. Hobard called out to me, "and you, too, Teddy, driving all last night. I think we're all tired."

"I'm not," said Eleanor. "I'm going to swim. Do you want to swim, Scott?"

"No," said Scott. "Swimming in the dark water gives me the creeps."

"It's beautiful at night," said Eleanor. "Will you come, Jane?"

Jane stood up. "I'll come watch you," she said. "You shouldn't swim alone."

"Let's take the canoe out," said Eleanor. "We'll look in the swamp for fox fire." The two of them set off down the lawn.

"Be careful," called Mrs. Hobard.

We watched their shapes disappear toward the lake, into the trees, and then heard the canoe being launched, the slow splash of paddles, their voices. Then it was quiet.

I said good night and went up to my room in the tower. I couldn't find the light switch so I undressed in the dark. I opened the windows and leaned out into the night. The torches had been extinguished. I could hear the click of billiard balls from downstairs and, in the far distance, Eleanor's laugh. A splash.

In bed I thought about Ethan, just missing him. I realized I did not want to be there anymore, in that tower room of Château Hobard. It was not that I thought it was haunted. It was that I wished it were.

"My turn to wake you up," Jane said. She was standing beside my bed, grinning down at me. It was still dark. "I've been watching you sleep," she said. "You sleep the untroubled sleep of angels."

"How long have you been watching?" I asked.

"Not long. What were you dreaming about?"

"I don't know. I don't think I was dreaming."

"Of course you were. I could tell. Were you dreaming of Charles?"

"No," I said.

Jane sat down on the window seat beside the bed and kicked off her shoes. "How is Charles? I forgot to tell you how pleased I was to meet him. It was nice of you to bring him to the wedding."

"He said to say hello," I lied.

"He's awfully good-looking," said Jane, "and he can dance. Did you know that? Do you ever dance together?"

"No," I said.

"That's sad," said Jane. "You should." She opened the window.

"Eleanor's still out in the canoe. She got Scott to go with her. They went over to the hotel for a drink."

"What have you been doing?" I asked.

"Waiting. I won't be able to sleep until they get back." She looked out at the lake. "I think I saw the northern lights before. I was walking around the lake. I mean around the island. Come here. Come watch the sky."

"I can see from here," I said.

"But not properly," she said.

"It's too cold. I haven't got anything on."

"You're such a prude." She stood up and sat down beside me on the bed. "Move over," she said. "I'm coming in."

"There isn't much room," I said.

She got in bed beside me. For a while we said nothing. "Don't fall asleep," she said.

"I'm not," I said.

"So are you in love with this Charles?"

"I don't know," I said.

"Of course you do," she said.

"He's going to Africa," I said.

"To be an ambassador?"

"Economic attaché, at an embassy."

"Are you going with him?"

"I don't know. I doubt it."

"Why?"

"I don't think he wants me to come. I don't think the State Department does, either."

"Have you asked him?"

"Not really," I said.

"Maybe we should go to Africa, the two of us. We'll move to Africa and start a coffee plantation. At the foot of the Ngong Hills."

"Perfect," I said.

"Good," she said. "So it's all settled."

"Perfect," I repeated, sleepily.

"Don't fall asleep," Jane said.

"I won't."

We heard Eleanor's laugh out on the lake. Jane sat up. "They're coming home," she said. "In the wake of the moon. It looks lovely." She watched Eleanor and Scott paddle toward the shore. "I think they want to get married," she said.

"So why don't they?" I asked.

"Because of me. They're waiting on my account. For me to get over this."

"That's very sweet," I said.

"I know," said Jane. "Everyone's sweet. I hate it."

"Do you think I'm being sweet?"

"You're being sweetish," said Jane.

"I'm sorry."

"That was sweet," said Jane.

I didn't say anything. We lay in bed, listening to Eleanor and Scott come into the house. We listened to them climb the stairs, use the bathroom, get into bed. We listened to them make love. Then everything was quiet for a long time.

"Are you asleep?" I finally asked.

"No," said Jane. "Do you want me to leave?"

"No," I said.

"It's all right if I sleep here?"

"If you want," I said.

She turned and put her face against my neck. "You smell like him," she said. I didn't say anything. She must have felt me tense up because she laid a hand on my chest, over my heart, and said "Relax."

I tried to relax. I looked up at the ceiling. Jane continued to speak into my throat. "Did you get a postcard from Ethan?" she asked.

"Yes," I said.

"He mailed them that morning. We had written them the night before, on the terrace. We were staying at a castle. It wasn't really a castle, but they called it one. A cheat." She paused. She lifted her face away from my throat, and I could tell she was looking down at me. I continued to look at the ceiling.

"I think he knew what was going to happen," she said. "I mean, in some way he knew. Some instinctual way. He sent me a postcard. He bought it in town that morning. It was of the church in Dingle." She stopped talking. I thought she might cry.

"And what did it say?" I asked. I looked at her.

She wasn't crying. Her face was bright, her eyes and skin shone. "It said, 'Having a wonderful time. You are here.'"

Teddy was staying the week at the lake, so I went home alone. I took a bus to Toronto and flew to Washington. I got home about nine o'clock at night. Charles was out at some embassy reception. I got in bed and waited for him. I fell asleep and awoke an hour later to see Charles standing in the semi-darkness, removing his tuxedo. I felt a little as if I were dreaming. I lay there and watched him. He watched me. He unknotted his tie and it slithered out from his collar. He unwrapped his cummerbund. He unstudded his studs.

"I want to come to Africa," I said, once he was in bed.

"So come to Africa," he said.

"Do you want me to come to Africa?" I asked.

"Of course," he said. "What would Africa be without you?"

I thought for a moment. "Hot," I said. "And beautiful. Full of baobab trees, and lions."

"Exactly," said Charles.

for Stephanie Gunn

The Meeting
and Greeting Area

The new "Education" Government, in its quest for literacy, has labeled everything. The buses proclaim BUS, the benches BENCH. I was awaiting the arrival of my ex-boyfriend, Tom, in THE MEETING AND GREETING AREA of the AIR-PORT.

I hadn't seen Tom in six months, since I was posted here. Before that we had lived together in Washington, D.C. We broke up shortly before I moved. We fell slowly out of love, paratroopers, floating back down to earth, landing with a quiet thud: friends. So when Tom called and asked me if I would like a visitor, if I would travel with him as we had once planned, I said yes.

"Are you sure?" he asked, his familiar voice echoing itself.

"Of course," I said. "It will be fun. You're my favorite person to travel with. We can go up north to the mountains, where it will be cool."

"Wherever," said Tom. "It's up to you. I just want to get out of D.C. And I'd like to see you. How are you doing?"

I debated telling him about Albert, but I didn't, because Albert was something I hadn't yet figured out. "I'm fine," I said, and I heard my echo say *I'm fine*, as if I had repeated myself for emphasis.

THE MEETING AND GREETING AREA was empty. Dust blew in from the runway and was roiled by the overhead fans, each of which revolved at its own particular speed. Tom's plane was intimated rather than announced. A murmuring excitement spread through the building: Vendors woke from their drowse and dusted their ancient merchandise; the baggage wheel shuddered and began to rotate; the lights above the ticket counter flickered on. And then the plane itself appeared in a huge sky pulsing with heat.

For such a big thing it disgorged few passengers. They appeared at the top of the metal steps hastily appended to its side, one by one, like bewildered contestants, blinking at the bright sun, stunned by the heat. Tom, as polite as he is patient, was the last to emerge. I watched him glance out and around, looking for me, and I enjoyed that moment of seeing him before he saw me. It made me feel in control. I didn't move or call out—I stood still and let Tom find me.

"It's great," Tom said. "And wow, you even have a terrace."

"Everyone has a terrace here," I said. "Most people live on them. Only foreigners have air conditioning."

"Is it always this hot?"

"You get used to it," I said.

He was standing by the French doors, looking down into the garden. A woman was washing clothes in the fountain. He looked at me. "I'm excited," he said. "I'm happy to be here." He came over and touched me. We had embraced once, briefly, outside the airport. Tom had smelled of toothpaste and cologne; I could picture him performing a hurried ablution in the tiny bathroom of the plane as it bumped in over the mountains.

"Are you exhausted?" I asked. "Or hungry? I thought we could go get some lunch. There's a café at the bazaar."

"It might be nice to lie down," he said. "Just for a little while. I'm not really that hungry. I still can't believe I'm here."

"You are," I said.

We looked at each other, and then Tom looked away. "I've missed you," he said. "Seeing you makes me realize. It's weird."

This admission seemed to embarrass both of us. "I brought all the things you asked for," Tom continued. "Here, I'll show you." He opened his suitcase and removed a plastic bag of groceries: peanut butter, salad dressing, jam, a squat ball of Gouda. An elegant bottle of vodka.

"Thank you," I said. "Should we have a drink to celebrate your arrival?" A drink suddenly seemed a good idea.

"Sure," Tom said. "Whatever."

The telephone rang. "Hello," I said.

"Mission accomplished?" asked Albert.

"We just got back."

"Is it awful?"

"No," I said.

"Charles, darling, tell me."

"It's fine," I said.

"He's listening, isn't he?"

"Of course," I said.

"So it is awful," said Albert.

"It's not," I said. "We're going out to lunch. I'll talk to you later."

"I hope you'll do more than talk," said Albert.

"Good-bye," I said. "Thanks for calling."

"Wait," said Albert.

"What?"

"Don't forget tomorrow night, will you?"

"No. What time do you want us?"

"Probably eight. I'll have Irene give you a call, how would that be? Wouldn't that be proper? To have the hostess call you? You know how I like to do things properly."

"I know," I said.

"I miss you already," said Albert. "Do you miss me?"

"It goes without saying," I said, and hung up.

We brought the elegant bottle of vodka to the café. As the place emptied, we loitered at our table. The combination of my drunkenness and Tom's jet lag suited us to each other, and we spent a few hot hours in an easy camaraderie I was afraid we might have lost. A beautiful somnambulistic boy mated pairs of chairs on top of tables, overturning one onto the lap of the other. Then he swabbed the floor with a mop and a pail of dirty water. We watched him as if he were the main attraction of a floor show.

"We could go walk around the old town," I finally suggested.

"O.K.," Tom said. "In a while. It's nice just to sit here."

"Is it how you pictured?"

"I don't think so." He looked around. "But I always forget how I pictured something once I actually see it. I mean, I know I had this picture in my mind, but now it's gone."

"I know that feeling," I said.

The boy with the mop paused and leaned against it, resting. It looked as if he had fallen asleep, standing up, holding the mop.

"What goes without saying?" asked Tom.

"What?"

"Before, on the phone. You said something went without saying. What?"

"I forget," I said. "Something about work."

"That was someone from work?"

"In a way. He's with the French Embassy. We're going to his house for dinner tomorrow night."

"How did you meet him?"

"At a party."

"I thought you hated parties."

The boy tottered, awoke, and continued his job. "I do," I said. "But there isn't much else to do over here. Besides, it's important to meet people, starting out."

"Of course," said Tom. He paused. "Is he gay?"

For a moment I thought he meant the boy. Then I realized he meant Albert. "Oh, no," I said. "He's married. You'll meet his wife tomorrow."

For a brief moment, when I first met Albert at a reception in the turquoise-walled garden of the French Consulate, I thought he was ugly, his beauty is so distinct. He has a strangely elongated onslaught of a face, rather like that of a Bedlington terrier. It is the sort of preternatural face that implies there are idiots in the family, that the genes that had found amazement here must surely have collided less fortunately elsewhere.

Albert was married to a large, beautiful woman named Irene. She was not very bright, but she dressed well and could muster herself to the dim verge of charm. She drank, and handwrote all the invitations to embassy events in her beautiful conventual script. Her bedroom was separate from Albert's. They had what he called an "English" marriage.

The sun had gone down somewhere but from where we sat in the garden of the French Consulate it looked as if the sun had gone down behind everything. The air was just beginning to cool or, more aptly, become less hot. A large pitcher of martinis sweated on a carved teak table.

"So you come to us from New York?" Irene asked Thomas.

"Washington," said Tom.

"Ah, yes, Washington. I loathe Washington. Albert and

I spent a dreadful year there. When was it, darling? Eighty-three?"

"Eighty-two," said Albert.

"That's right," said Irene. "I found them surprisingly backward in Washington. Of course everything is relative. The situation here is hopeless."

"It seems very beautiful here," said Tom.

Irene looked around the garden. "Oh," she said, "but beauty is only half the game, and the easy half at that. A city needs more than beauty. It needs charm, and it needs energy. Of course I am partial, but I believe Paris to be a perfect city. Would you agree?"

"I have never been to Paris," says Tom.

"Have you really not? Imagine coming all this way, to this godforsaken spot, and never seeing Paris. It is criminal. But then I envy you, because you have that to look forward to: entering Paris for the first time."

"How does one enter Paris?" Tom asked.

Irene looked up into the sky. It was the same purple color as her dress, but it was inexorably darkening and her dress was not. "Oh," she said. "I was wrong to mention Paris. It only makes me sad."

"Irene grew up in Paris," said Albert. "She has never forgiven me for taking her away."

Irene smiled and reached out to pat Albert's cheek. "That is the least of what I haven't forgiven you for," she said.

After dinner, while Irene showed Tom her collection of gold snuffboxes, Albert and I smoked on the veranda. Tall gecko-filled trees rose up from the dense, imported foliage below. The lizards inhabited the trees as disinterestedly as lichen.

"He's so . . . enthusiastic," said Albert. "And simple."

I smiled. I had drunk more than I ought. The veranda seemed to be pitching in some silent nonexistent breeze. I held onto its marble balustrade and closed my eyes. "Actually, he's very smart," I said.

"Oh, I'm sure he is. In a simple, enthusiastic sort of way."

"You shouldn't say mean things about him," I said.

Albert inhaled. His cigar lit up, and for a second I could see all the furiously focused sparks of it. Then they went out. "May I tell you something?" he asked.

"What?" I said.

"Thomas still loves you," Albert said.

"What makes you say that?"

"Because I can tell he is in love. And I doubt seriously it is with either me or Irene. That leaves you, Charles."

"How can you tell he's in love?" I asked.

"You forget I've had some experience with these things." Albert traced the route of a blue vein up my forearm with a manicured finger.

I pulled my arm away. "Tom's my friend," I said. "I'm very fond of him, but he's just my friend."

"Famous last words," said Albert.

"I don't want to talk about this," I said.

"Of course you don't," Albert said. "This is precisely the sort of thing you avoid talking about."

"It's not my fault if Tom loves me," I said.

"I didn't say it was."

"I don't love Tom," I said. "I love you." I said this partially to disarm Albert and partially to see if it might be true. I couldn't tell. I was about to repeat it when the shutters opened. Irene and Tom appeared, silhouetted against the brilliantly lit drawing room. For a moment everyone stood still.

"When do you boys head north?" Albert asked.

"Tomorrow," I said.

"You're going up to Kunda?" Irene asked.

"Yes," I said. "And Lake Moore. And then we're going down south."

"You'd better be careful. There's been some trouble up north," Albert said. "I hear the border is hot."

"What did you think of them?" I asked. Tom and I were walking home along the muddy unmotivated river that curled through the city. I had yet to figure out in which direction it was supposed to flow, never having seen it do so.

"Irene seemed a little crazy."

"She was drunk."

"I know, but she seemed crazy, too. She tried to give me one of those snuffboxes."

"You should have taken it," I said. "What did you talk about up there?"

Tom smiled. He was kicking a piece of glass along the cobblestoned street, paying it concentrated, irksome attention. I intervened and kicked it into the river, which swallowed it without a ripple.

"I forget," Tom said.

"What did you think of Albert?"

Tom looked at me. "He's charming," he said. "In a neo-fascist kind of way."

"What do you mean?"

Tom was scuffing the pavement, looking for something else to kick. He seemed nervous. A posse of nuns on bicycles passed us, and then disappeared. The city was full of nuns. I decided to change the subject.

"So," I said. "Tomorrow we head north. Let's hope it will be cooler."

Tom stopped walking, and leaned against the river wall. A dugout canoe with a goat tethered in it was moored in the middle of the river. The goat bleated at us.

"I don't think I'm going," said Tom.

"What?" I said.

"I think maybe I should go home."

"What do you mean? You just got here."

"I know that," said Tom.

"So why do you want to go back?"

"I have a feeling maybe this won't work out."

"Why wouldn't it work out?"

Tom looked at me. He shrugged. "It's just a feeling," he said.

"It will be fine," I said. "We'll spend some time in Kunda, it will be cool and beautiful. Kunda's supposed to be really great. We like to travel together. We're good at it. Why would there be a problem?"

Tom stared at the river, at the goat in the boat, and on the far shore at the abandoned skeletons of the office buildings the Commerce Government had begun to build before its recent demise. I put my hand on his shoulder. "Everything's cool, Tommy," I said. "Relax."

I was sitting up in the king-size bed in our hotel room, safe within a flurry of mosquito netting. Tom stood beside the bed, wearing a pair of gym shorts, drying his hair with a towel monogrammed "The Royal Kunda."

"There's a lizard in the bathroom," said Tom.

"Better lizards than bugs," I said.

"There are bugs, too," said Tom. "Are you going to take a shower?"

"I'll take one in the morning."

"I've never slept under a mosquito net," Tom said. Tom is the sort of person who takes delight in doing things for the first time. He is constantly losing some sort of virginity. I once found this quality endearing. He touched the gauze shroud. "How do you get in? Do you climb under?"

"You lift it up," I said.

"Oh." He returned the towel to the bathroom, bolted the door, switched off the light, and resumed his post beside the bed. The combination of the gauze and dark masked his features, but I could feel him looking at me.

"Get in," I said. "Let's go to sleep."

He lifted the net and stooped beneath it, and then he was inside, better focused, large and luminous. I thought of him entering Paris for the first time. I moved to one side of the bed as he got in. We lay side by side for a long, silent while. I could smell his clean skin. And then, like a perfectly scheduled train, I saw his hand set out across the blank expanse of sheet between us. For a moment I thought my anticipation and dread had set it in motion—that I had somehow willed him to touch me by dreading he might. And then he did touch me; his fingers slid up and gently clasped my arm right below my elbow. It was an odd, unerotic place to hold someone. It was where you'd hold someone to pull him back from traffic, or other sudden dangers.

Kunda was full of Germans, cafés, elephants, and posters of blond women fellating bottles of Coca-Cola. Most of the buildings were made of mud; it was hard to believe that come the rains, they wouldn't all wash away.

We had wandered down through town all morning, from one terraced level to another, and noon found us on its grassy outskirts.

"We could visit the fish caves," said Tom, who was in possession of our tourist map.

"What are the fish caves?"

"I don't know. It's just on the map with a blue star. That means it's a natural phenomenon."

"Where are they?"

"Just a little bit out of town, going east." He pointed down the road.

"How far?"

"You look. I say about a mile."

We started walking east out of town. Along the roadside, people were sitting beneath jerry-built tents, trying to sell the odd objects spread out before them: gourds, widowed shoes, and strange cuts of meat swaddled in leaves. One woman had dozens of cheeping sparrows in tiny cages woven from sticks. The cages were only barely bigger than the birds. Her sign read: PLEASE SET FREE THESE BIRDS YOU WILL BE HAPPY AND PROSPEROUS. We passed the woman and turned off the road at a sign that said FAMOUS FISH CAVES. Inside a spectacular wrought iron gate a beautiful woman was selling little bunches of what appeared to be salad. Each bunch was wrapped in colored wax paper. She held them in a tray projecting from her chest, like a New Age cigarette girl.

"You buy some," she told us.

We declined her offer and walked down the path into the dry, scrubby woods. She followed us at a distance. We approached an enclave of massive boulders which surrounded a small pool of dark still water.

The woman had caught up with us. "Fish cave," she announced.

We all stood and stared at the water. The air around us was surprisingly cool. "Where are the fish?" I finally asked.

The woman indicated her colorful packages. "For food, they'll come," she said.

"That's fish food?" asked Tom.

"Yes," she said.

"It's so pretty," said Tom.

"They are special fish," she said. "You'll see if you feed them."

"How much?"

She told him, and he bought a package of greens. The care with which it had been assembled necessitated his unfolding it with reverence. Tom held a little bouquet of strange-shaped leaves and yellow clover-like flowers.

"Feed them." The beautiful woman was losing patience. She glanced back toward the gate, but we were still alone.

"All at once?" Tom asked.

She shrugged.

Tom tossed the bouquet into the black water. It spun idly for a moment, and then the pool erupted with huge blue carp. They churned the water into froth, leaping at the weeds. When they had devoured Tom's bouquet they loitered near the surface, swishing their tails, watching us.

"More?" the beautiful woman asked.

The ritual was repeated: the tossing, the feeding frenzy, followed by the blue-tinted, tail-flashing shallow lurk.

"More?"

I had the feeling we could be there forever, that those horrible fat fish would never be sated. "Let's go," I said.

"O.K.," said Tom. "No, thank you," he said to the woman. She turned and walked back toward the gate.

Tom and I remained at the fish cave. The fish sank lower as time passed, like something being erased, until the water returned to its primordial blankness. "That was something," Tom finally said. "I've never seen fish like that."

"They were more like pigs," I said.

Tom squatted and dipped his hand into the water. "It's freezing," he announced. We both watched his hand float, palm up, just below the water's dark skin. It made me nervous: The fishes' appetite had seemed carnivorous. I had a feeling Tom not only sensed but enjoyed my unease, so I squatted beside him and dangled my fingers in the water. His hand swam toward mine. Our fingers touched, but the water was so cold I couldn't feel it. I let my hand drift away.

"It's much cooler here than back in town," Tom said. "It would be a nice place for a picnic."

"We don't have anything to eat," I said.

"Let's just sit down for a while," said Tom. "Over there, by those trees."

I followed him to a grassy clearing in the flowering trees where the sun was haphazardly strewn across the ground. Bees buzzed around us.

"This is beautiful," said Tom. He was lying on his back, his head pillowed by his knapsack, his eyes closed. I stood against the tree and watched him. His hands were clasped behind his head, his face angled toward the sun. Tom loved the sun. I first saw him three years ago, on the beach at Edisto. It was very early in the morning, and the beach was empty. Tom had been lying alone in much the same position as he lay now. For a moment I thought he was dead but then I realized he was sleeping. I stood and watched him. Normally I would never stop and watch someone sleep on the beach but I was not acting normally when I met Tom, and that is how you fall in love: by not being yourself or being too much yourself or by letting go of yourself, and I did one, or perhaps all, of those things; I stood and waited for Tom to wake up and he woke up and I sat down beside him on the cool sand. And now, as I watched Tom lie in the sun here on the other side of the earth years later, I wondered if perhaps I did still love him. But what I felt was an awful staining fondness, not love.

The beautiful woman was escorting two German couples toward the fish cave. Tom opened his eyes. We watched them disappear behind the rocks. "So," said Tom. "Here we are."

"Yes," I said.

"Sit down," said Tom.

I sat down, a little wary: Tom always initiated a troubling conversation by saying "So." Whenever he said *so*, I heard *beware*.

"It's nice to lie here in the sun," he said, "and think of everyone shivering back home. It gives me great pleasure."

"Good," I said, and I meant it, as I was glad Tom was experiencing great pleasure. This was not something he often admitted.

"Actually," said Tom, "I'm not feeling great pleasure."

"Oh," I said.

"Actually, I'm feeling kind of desperate."

"About what?" I asked.

"About this," said Tom. "About us."

I said Oh again. Tom looked at me. "What are you feeling?" he asked.

There is only one question I hate more than "What are you feeling?" and that is "What are you thinking?" I believe one should be at liberty to express one's thoughts and feelings at one's own pace; to be prompted in this way is, I think, rude. I know for a fact Tom thinks otherwise. He thinks he is doing me a favor by asking these questions, but it is dangerous and stupid of him, for the responses he elicits are seldom the responses he desires. In answer to his question, I said, "What am I feeling about what?"

"Us," he said.

I shrugged. I heard the Germans exclaim over the appearance of the blue fish. I pretended to be distracted by their exclamations. "I don't know," I finally said. "I'm not feeling anything. I'm just glad, you know, that we're together, that we're friends, that we're traveling together. I think it's nice."

"Nice?" said Tom.

"I think it is," I said. "Don't you?"

Tom didn't answer. He closed his eyes. His face was no longer in the sunlight; it was laced with shade. "It's not obvious?" he asked.

"What?" I said, although of course I knew. I had known from the very beginning, from the moment Tom had crossed the tarmac and entered THE MEETING AND GREETING AREA. I had not needed Albert to tell me.

"I still love you," he said. He opened his eyes.

I didn't know what to say so I said nothing. How pathetic the unloved are, I thought. How assiduously they suffer, how they cultivate their rejection, picking again and again at their scabs.

"I just thought I should tell you," said Tom. "Although I guess I shouldn't have."

"No," I said. "I mean, I just thought, you know, that that was all over."

"I know," said Tom. "So did I."

"It's over for me," I said.

"I know," said Tom. "I know that." He stood up, and hoisted his knapsack to his shoulder. "Forget I said anything," he said. "Let's go." He began to walk back toward the road. I followed him. On the way into town we stopped and liberated a bird. Tom tore the twig cage apart. The bird jumped out and sat by the side of the dusty road. I tried to make it fly by prodding it with a stick but it wouldn't. It just sat there, stunned, it seemed, by its freedom.

Albert was right: The border was hot. That morning insurgents had invaded a mountain village. We returned to find Kunda tense with outrage and excitement and plans for a nationalist rally in the public garden that evening.

Tom and I observed from the refreshment tent, which was packed with curious, intoxicated tourists, including the two German couples from the fish cave. A marching band ringed the arid fountain, and on the grassy verges between the tree-lined paths different groups assembled. Schoolchildren, scrubbed and dressed in their blue uniforms, convened at one end of the park. They held placards—OUR BORDERS ARE SACRED—above their heads, while at the other end of the park the women milled, dressed in traditional costume, a little embarrassed by the hoopla, watching the more fervent, fist-waving men try to organize themselves into some sort of parade.

And as we watched, a parade evolved: The band led the children out of the park, followed by the women, and finally the men. It circled the large square, but since it appeared that everyone in town was marching, the parade's effect was curiously hollow. We tourists, by the very fact of our foreignness, could not even succeed as spectators. We observed in polite silence. After one revolution the marchers halted; the men hushed the band and murmured among themselves. The women and children stood about, abject and quiet. And then the men emerged from their huddle and announced their solution, which, as they reconvened, became obvious: This time the men would march and the women and children would line the streets.

"Let's go watch," Tom said.

"O.K.," I said. I tried to find our waiter, but he had joined the protesters. I dropped some money on the table, and Tom and I followed the mass exodus of women and children from the park. We stood behind the throng and watched over their heads as the all-male parade approached. Everyone seemed liberated by this new configuration; even the band sounded less rinky-dink.

The second parade was followed by a series of patriotic speeches, but as the evening waned the mood of the crowd mellowed: The schoolchildren were sent home to bed and the band began to play pop music. Couples danced on the plaza.

Tom and I were sitting on a bench near the fountain, watching the dancing, drinking beer from cold gold bottles. It had gotten late and we were exhausted, but there was something pleasurably transporting about being in the park. One felt successfully and completely in a foreign country, that one could return home and say, "One night there was a political rally in the public gardens . . ."

"I want to dance," said Tom.

"We can't dance," I said. "It's not a good idea."

"Of course it's not a good idea," said Tom. "Forget the idea. Come dance. Over there, where it's dark."

"No," I said. "It's dangerous."

"Everyone's drunk," said Tom. "They won't notice." He stood up and pulled me from the bench. We pressed through the swoon of dancing couples; everyone did seem drunk and self-intent. We made it to the other side of the park, away from the lights and the band, but even there it was obviously too public. Tom crossed the street and walked down a dirt alley. I followed him behind the buildings into a small enclosed parking lot crowded with pickup trucks. We sidled between them until we came to a place in the center where we were surrounded on all sides by trucks. None of the trucks had wheels, I noticed. The music from the park was faint yet audible. We stood for a moment, facing each other.

"Do you want to dance?" I asked.

"No," said Tom.

"Then what are we doing here?"

"I don't know," said Tom.

"Let's go back," I said.

"Wait," said Tom. He was picking rusted paint off the door of a truck. I stilled his hand with my own. I remembered them touching underwater at the fish cave. This time our hands were both hot, and I could feel his hand. I held it against the truck, but he pulled it away.

"Do you love Albert?" he asked.

"What makes you think that?"

"Just answer," he said.

"I don't know," I said. "I don't think so."

"But you've slept with him," said Tom.

"Yes," I said. "How did you know?"

"Irene told me," said Tom.

For a moment I had to think of who Irene was. And then I remembered the moment Tom and Irene reappeared on the veranda, how we had all stopped talking for a moment. I felt a little woozy so I sat down on the truck's running board. It had been Albert's idea to have Tom to dinner: He had told me not having dinner would have been childish, uncivilized.

"She told me when we went upstairs," Tom was saying. "While we were looking at her gold snuffboxes. At first I thought she was crazy. She thought I knew all about it."

"I'm sorry," I said.

"About what?"

"That I didn't tell you myself. It's just that, well, I didn't tell you because it's not a big deal."

"It's not?" asked Tom.

"No," I said.

"Is anything a big deal to you?"

"Yes," I said. "Of course."

"What?" asked Tom.

I tried to think of what was a big deal, but nothing came to mind, so I didn't answer. We were both quiet for a moment. The band seemed suddenly loud, but then I realized it wasn't the band but a sort of rickety explosion. Fireworks, I thought. I actually looked up at the sky, watching for their bright and sudden unblossoming, but the noise continued and the sky remained dark. And then the noise stopped, and I could hear the people on the plaza screaming.

As I entered my apartment the next afternoon the phone was ringing. I knew it would be Albert, and I let it ring, for I wanted to know how long Albert would wait. I stood and listened to it ring, not counting, just listening. It rang a very long time before I picked it up.

"Hello," I said.

"You're back," said Albert. "Thank God. I was worried. I heard about the violence. Are you all right?"

"Yes," I said.

"Were you at the rally? I heard there were a lot of foreigners there."

"We had just left. We were across the street, in a parking lot."

"What were you doing there?"

"Nothing. Tom wanted to dance."

"He wanted to what?"

"Dance," I said. "Everyone was dancing."

"Not for long, poor things," said Albert. "Well, thank God you're safe. Are you heading south?"

"No," I said. "Tom's gone back."

"Has he?"

"Yes," I said. "It was difficult."

"It often is," said Albert. "Well, I can't say I'm sorry. So you're alone?"

"Yes," I said.

"Are you going in to work?"

"No."

"I could come over."

"No," I said.

"What about dinner?" asked Albert. "We could have a nice dinner."

"No," I said.

"My, what a lot of no's," said Albert. He paused. "Nothing's changed, has it?"

I didn't answer.

"You must be exhausted," said Albert. "Have a stiff drink and go to bed. I'll call you later."

He hung up. So did I. I looked around the room. Tom's dress shoes stood by the terrace doors. By departing so hurriedly, he had left some of his things behind. That morning we had flown from Kunda to the capital; Tom changed planes and flew directly home. We had said good-bye in THE MEETING AND GREETING AREA. In the country to which I had been posted, leaving, saying good-bye, hadn't yet been officially sanctioned.

Nuptials & Heathens

Joan is trying to decide if Tom's habit of switching the car radio from station to station is endearing or annoying. As they drive north of Boston, into the late night and away from the good stations, he punches the buttons more and more frequently. He is never satisfied with one station for long. They are driving to his parents' house in Maine for the weekend.

She rolls up her window because it is getting cold, and puts her empty Tab can on the floor at her feet, then picks it up because she's not sure it is something she should do in his car. When they stopped for gas she took fifty-five cents from the "toll money" (they were off the highway and through with tolls) and bought a Tab from the machine. When she tilted the can under Tom's chin for him to sip from, he said, "Ugh, Tab. Couldn't you have got a soda we both liked?"

Tom's mother, Mrs. Thorenson, hears them arrive, but she doesn't get out of bed. She doesn't look so great in the middle of the night, and first impressions are first impressions. She listens to them come inside, hears them trying to be quiet, hears Tom pointing things out—"There's the ocean down there. See it?" She listens to them use the bathroom. It sounds like they're using it together—at least they're talking while Tom urinates (it sounds like a man urinating)—although Joan could be standing in the hall. Then she hears them go upstairs, together, into his room. She's glad she's not up to see that part. She hears them get into bed. She falls asleep listening for them to make love.

The sun doesn't wake Joan up. Tom does. "You better get up," he says. "We get up early here." He is standing by the bed in the pale blue tennis shorts she helped him pick out Thursday night in Herman's. Tom isn't tan, although it's August. From this angle, lying in bed with Tom standing beside her, the hair on his legs looks very unattractive. She gets out of bed and stands beside Tom in her Nike T-shirt.

"What should I wear?" she asks. "Do you get dressed up for breakfast?" When can I take a shower? she thinks to herself. Now, or after breakfast? Do they have a shower? She didn't see one in the bathroom last night.

"Not dressed up," says Tom. He pulls his matching blue-and-white-striped shirt over his head and speaks from inside it. "But dressed."

Joan looks out the window. A woman is dragging a black cat on a leash across the lawn. The cat looks dead.

"That's Deborah," says Tom. They both stand by the window and watch Deborah. "I don't know what that is she's got."

"It's a cat," says Joan.

"It looks like a skunk."

"Is your father here, too?" Joan asks. She puts on her jean skirt, then pulls off her T-shirt.

"I'm not sure," Tom says. "Let's hope not."

In the kitchen, Mrs. Thorenson is cutting up fruit for a fruit salad. She bought kiwifruit at The Fruit Basket just for this weekend, but she is unsure how to slice them. Should she peel them? The fuzzy skin looks unappetizing and vaguely dangerous. Yet, when she tries to peel them, the soft green flesh mushes up. She has, at Fanny Farmer's suggestion, quartered the strawberries, sliced (diagonally) the bananas, sectioned the grapefruit, and balled the cantaloupe with a teaspoon, but Fanny Farmer doesn't mention kiwifruit. The kiwis are hopeless. She throws them away. Good riddance to them, although at ninety-nine cents each it is a shame.

She watches Deborah tie her cat—what was its name, Gilda?—to the rail of the deck and come inside.

"Do you think it's safe to leave him out there?" Deborah asks.

"Of course," Mrs. Thorenson says. Gilbert climbs onto the canvas director's chair and lies in the sun. "Just make sure he doesn't fall off the deck and hang himself."

"He can't," says Deborah. She opens the refrigerator and looks in it. "He has on a harness, not a collar. Have they come down yet?"

"No," says Mrs. Thorenson. "But they're awake."

"She left her soap in the bathroom," Deborah says. "Clinique."

"So?" says Mrs. Thorenson.

"So, nothing. Just FYI."

The morning goes O.K. Mrs. Thorenson's fruit salad is a big hit, the coffee Deborah laced with cinnamon makes the kitchen smell nice, and Joan begins to relax. There is a shower, a nice one with a Water Pik showerhead and plenty of hot water, and after breakfast Joan takes a long shower and changes into her bathing suit.

They all sit on the deck for a while. Deborah lets Gilbert off the leash, and he sits in some bayberry bushes purring and looking dazed. At ten o'clock Mrs. Thorenson and Deborah drive to the airport to pick up Mr. Thorenson, who missed his flight the night before.

Joan and Tom go down to the beach. It's rocky except for one small area that's surrounded by railroad ties and filled with sand—bought sand, Tom explains, sand replaced every summer and after extremely high tides. They keep sacks of it in the boathouse.

But it's like a little oasis, and Tom and Joan lie on it, on an old bedspread that has a Wizard of Oz motif, only Dorothy doesn't look like Judy Garland, she looks like Heidi. She's blonde and dressed in lederhosen.

The blonde, skipping Dorothys unnerve Joan, but when she closes her eyes and traces the indentation down Tom's warm back again and again—a gesture she usually reserves for after they have made love—she begins to feel better, and by the time Deborah appears on the little beach, with Gilbert back on his leash, she's almost happy. It's not so bad here. It's nice.

"Daddy missed that plane, too," Deborah announces. "Mommy's beginning to get worried."

"Can't she call?" asks Tom. He doesn't open his eyes.

"She did. There's no answer." Deborah drops the leash and wades into the waves. Gilbert crouches on the beach looking terrified.

Joan sits up and watches Deborah in the water. When she was in college, Deborah was married to a Pakistani exchange student. Tom told Joan this, but also told her it is no longer mentioned. His exact words were "dead and buried."

"Have you been in the water yet?" Deborah calls.

"No," Joan shouts, "but I'm hot."

"Come in," Deborah shouts back. "It's great."

Joan gets up and steps over Gilbert, who flinches. She stands with her feet in the moist sand at the edge of the water, allowing the waves to come to her. She feels dizzy standing up.

Deborah splashes in toward shore, peels off her tank top

and throws it on the beach. It lands near Gilbert, who bolts up the path toward the house. Deborah runs back out and dives under a wave. She has nothing on under the tank top.

"I forgot to take my contacts out," Joan says to no one: Deborah is underwater, and Tom doesn't hear her.

Deborah's head, brown shoulders, and white breasts slip out of the water and she flings her hair back from her face. "Come on," she calls to Joan. "It's great!"

"I have to take my contacts out," Joan yells. "I'll be right back."

Deborah makes some facial expression that Joan can't interpret: it could be irritation or sympathy or disgust.

Joan touches Tom's back with one of her wet toes, and says, for the third time in as many minutes, "I forgot to take my contacts out. Can I go up?"

"Sure," says Tom. "Would you bring down the suntan lotion? I think my shoulders are getting burned."

"They are," says Joan. "You better be careful. Turn over."

Mrs. Thorenson is sitting on the deck under a huge lavender-and-white-striped umbrella, drinking orange juice.

"I'm sorry my husband is ruining your weekend," she says, as Joan comes up the path. Her sunglasses have a pink plastic triangle over the nose, which she has flipped up, so it looks like a tiny horn coming out from between her eyes.

Joan was not aware that Mr. Thorenson was ruining her weekend. "Oh, hardly," she says, while she thinks about what she should say. "I'm having a good time."

"I'm not," says Mrs. Thorenson. "Maybe it would be better if he didn't come. Did Tom tell you he's found religion?"

Tom had mentioned something about Mr. Thorenson's newfound religious zeal, saying it was all because the doctors made him give up bridge, because he was getting "obsessive."

But Joan isn't sure what this has to do with him missing all these planes: Is he one of those weirdos who try to sell flowers in airports? Surely he's not that bad.

Joan decides to play it safe and resorts to her now standard line. "I've come up to take my contact lenses out," she says. "I'm going in for a swim."

Mrs. Thorenson takes a sip of her drink. An ice cube falls out of the glass and onto the wooden deck, where it quickly begins melting in the sun. The melting ice cube reminds Joan of the speedup movies she used to see of crocuses blooming, only in reverse.

"I didn't know you wore contacts," Mrs. Thorenson says.

"Yes," Joan says. "For years."

"Come here," says Mrs. Thorenson. "Let me see." She reaches out her tanned hand and motions Joan over. "Are they hard or soft?"

"Hard," says Joan. She bends down and lets Mrs. Thorenson hold her chin and turn her face sideways. She opens her eyes wide. She's looking at a wooden sign nailed to the side of the house that says WELCOME SHIPMATES.

"So you do," says Mrs. Thorenson. Her hot breath lands on Joan's cheek. There is more than juice in that glass, Joan thinks.

Before Joan returns, Deborah gets out of the water and puts her tank top back on. "Where's Gilbert?"

Tom sits up. "He ran up to the house. I don't think he liked it down here."

"Do you like Gilbert?" asks Deborah. She sits down on the bedspread where Joan had been lying, forming a big wet spot.

"He's all right," says Tom. "I don't know."

"You could at least cheer up a little," says Deborah. She puts on her punk sunglasses. "What's the matter?"

"Nothing," says Tom. "Let me try them on."

Deborah gives him the sunglasses. He tries them on. They do things for him. "They look great," says Deborah. She reaches over and takes them off. "But they look greater on me."

"Do you like Joan?" asks Tom.

"Why?" asks Deborah. "Are you going to marry her?"

"I'm going to ask her," Tom says.

"Seriously?" says Deborah. "You're kidding."

"No," says Tom. "I'm serious. At least about asking her."

"I can't believe it," says Deborah. "I thought you just met her."

"At Christmas," Tom says. "Last Christmas." He lies back down. "It's summer now," he says as if it just dawned on him.

"When are you going to ask her?" says Deborah. "I want to watch."

"I'm not sure," says Tom. "Sometime this weekend. When the moment is right."

"Jesus Christ," says Deborah. "I can't believe you're going to get married."

"But do you like her?"

Before Deborah can answer, Joan stumbles onto the beach. "I can't see anything," she says. "Where's the water?"

After lunch Mrs. Thorenson has Tom hold the ladder while she ties TV dinner trays to the cherry tree. Their clatter and reflection scare the birds away. Mrs. Thorenson went out and bought ten macaroni-and-cheese TV dinners (the cheapest) before she realized she could have used aluminum pie plates. The women's magazine had recommended the TV dinner trays, instead of just throwing them away. Mrs. Thorenson doesn't really like cherries—they have pits—but it bothers her that the birds get them. The sea gulls are always sitting fatly under the tree, their breasts stained red.

Joan is sitting on the ground shucking corn for dinner. Some of the silk is picked up and carried off by the breeze, and it hangs like lighted hair in the air. Joan watches it disappear into the pine trees.

Mrs. Thorenson's head is hidden by leaves and TV dinner trays, but Joan is listening to her talk. "I wish this were a peach tree. Wouldn't it be nice if this were a peach tree? This tree was a gift from a woman I never liked. She stayed here one weekend when we first built the house and she gave us this cherry tree as a house gift. I don't remember how it got planted. I remember it sat in a burlap bag for a long time after she left.

"That was back when Daddy came up on the seaplane with Mr. Thomas Friday nights and landed on Great Snake Pond. Do you remember? We'd go over there after dinner and wait on the dock and you and Deborah would have flashlights—it would just be getting dark. And the plane would appear and get closer and closer and land with a splash and Daddy would get out on the dock in his business suit, holding his briefcase, dropped from the sky. Do you remember?"

"No," says Tom. "I must have repressed it."

"Why would you have repressed it?" Mrs. Thorenson asks. A TV dinner tray falls out of the tree.

"I don't know," says Tom. "Maybe it was painful."

"You were probably just too young," Mrs. Thorenson says. "Maybe Deborah remembers. Deborah must."

Tom looks over to see if Joan is watching, and when he sees she is, he mimes kicking the ladder out from under Mrs. Thorenson. Tom is sulking because his shoulders are sunburned. Tom is a sulker, Joan is realizing. When they changed out of their bathing suits, Tom noticed the red streaks beginning to bloom across his white shoulders. He blamed Joan, accusing her of not applying the sunblock properly. As he stands under the tree, he keeps craning his neck to get a better view of his back.

Joan watches, amused, but there's something about the leafy pattern of shadows moving across Tom's mottled skin that makes him look a little leprous from behind. This thought nauseates her, so she concentrates on the corn. When she first met Tom at her old boyfriend's Christmas party, she thought he was wonderful. He was very good-looking, and a great, tireless dancer, and after the party he insisted they go out for breakfast. On their way home in the cab, Tom shot the stoplights from red to green, and he hit every one, and as the cab flew down the deserted avenue, Joan began to think she might be falling in love. It was very magical. But the next morning she worried it might have been the wicked punch. And ever since it's followed that pattern: Tom will do something nice—buy her flowers, make love to her especially well, invite her to Maine—something that will intoxicate her, but then a few minutes or hours or days later she'll lose interest in him again. One of the reasons she came to Maine was to get a grip on all this and decide one way or another. She pulls the silk off the last ear of corn. She feels lightheaded, but it's not the wine she is drinking that makes her feel giddy. It's something else. What is it? Joan thinks. Then she realizes. It's because she knows she doesn't love Tom. All these months she has been trying to convince herself otherwise. But now—right now—she knows. As she stuffs the last strands of corn silk into the brown paper bag she feels truly out of love with Tom. Everything will change now, she has a feeling, everything will be all right. She laughs. She can't help it.

"What are you laughing at?" asks Tom.

"Nothing," says Joan. "I'm just happy."

"Are you?" says Tom. He smiles. "So am I."

At dinner, at a restaurant called Oysters & Oxes, Tom asks Joan to marry him. The waiter arrives with a bottle of champagne Tom secretly ordered on a trip to the men's room, and the whole uncorking procedure gives Joan some time to think about how she should say no.

Then the waiter is gone, and she's left with Tom sitting across from her, a glass of champagne raised in front of him, repeating his embarrassing proposal. Joan's champagne glass is still on the table and she can feel the bubbly mist cooling her throat.

Tom's serious face glowing sincerely in the candlelight makes her feel sad and guilty. How could she have let things go this far? This is a predicament she associates with movies—old movies—or with her mother's time.

"Marry?" she says, as if it's a word with many shades of meaning.

"Yes," says Tom. "Don't you think we should?"

"No," says Joan.

Tom puts down his champagne glass. "Oh," he says. He picks it up again and drinks from it.

Joan thinks, This is so wrong. She's sure that all the people she knows who are married decided mutually while watching TV or baking bread or wallpapering their apartments. She and Tom do none of these things. They go to the movies and out to dinner once or twice a week and sleep together on the weekends, but they've never been through anything together or gone on a trip or even had a big fight. It's just not a serious relationship. Why doesn't Tom know this? It's scary to think that he can be in love with her on the basis of so little.

She excuses herself and goes down to the women's room. There is a hand-lettered sign that looks like an invitation taped to the mirror, explaining that, since the women's room is below sea level, please don't flush tampons down the toilet.

When she comes back the mussels have disappeared. She drinks some champagne. "I'm sorry," she says. "You surprised me."

"It's O.K.," says Tom. "We can talk about it later."

She should tell him no, never, but she doesn't. She just smiles. "It was very nice of you," she says. "Thank you."

Tom shrugs. He is playing with the champagne cork, making it roll on the table in little lopsided circles. Joan thinks, If I said yes, he'd keep the cork as a souvenir, and every year on the anniversary of this date, he'd bring it out and show it to me.

When they get back to the house Deborah is standing in the sandy driveway. It is windy and the wind seems to blow even the stars around in the sky. Joan is a little drunk.

"Gilbert got away," Deborah announces, as they get out of the car. "I can't find him."

This domestic tragedy immediately cheers Joan; it's a welcome relief from the silent tension between her and Tom. The wind is waking her up, too.

"Gil-bert!" Joan shouts into the blowing bushes.

"I thought I could hear him meowing," Deborah says, "but I can't tell where it's coming from."

They all listen for a minute, but they don't hear Gilbert. Deborah shines her flashlight into the scrubby pine trees. Joan sits on the hood of the car and takes her shoes off. The tops of her feet are sunburnt. "Maybe he's down by the water," she says.

"Maybe he's dead," Tom says.

"I'm going to go look on the beach," Joan says, partly because she wants to see the water at night, partly because she wants to get away by herself. She gives Tom a look she hopes discourages him from joining her.

"Do you want a flashlight?" asks Deborah. "There's another one in the drawer beneath the breadbox."

"No," says Joan. She hops off the car. "It's bright out." She's right: the moon and the stars seem to be unusually—

and unnervingly—near, as if they've dropped out of their niches and are falling.

"I'm going to go look over by Cooke's," says Deborah. "There was a dead rabbit over there last weekend Gilbert might have smelled. Come with me," she says to Tom. "I'm scared."

She and Tom walk down the driveway, across the dirt road, and into the woods. Deborah shines the flashlight at the ground; toadstools poke through the matted pine needles, forming little tents.

"So?" says Deborah.

"So, what?"

"So did you ask her?"

"Yes," says Tom. He kicks a toadstool and watches the white floweret fly through the air out of their circle of light. "She said no."

"Oh," says Deborah.

Tom stops walking and leans against a pine tree. He picks some lichen off the bark.

Deborah shines the flashlight at his face. "Are you sad?" she asks.

Tom looks at her, but can't see, because of the bright light in his eyes. "A little," he says. "I don't know."

"I wouldn't be too sad," says Deborah. "She seems like kind of a pill to me."

"Oh," says Tom.

"I mean, I'm sure she's nice. Are you really O.K.?"

"I'm O.K.," says Tom. "I just feel like a fool."

Deborah turns her flashlight off. "Gilbert's not really lost," she says. "I just made that up so I could get you away."

"Did Daddy come?"

"No," says Deborah. "But he called. From Dallas. He said there are a lot of heathens in Dallas."

"There are heathens everywhere," says Tom. "I'm a heathen."

"Don't tell Daddy that," Deborah says. She laughs.

"Where is Gilbert?"

"In my room."

"Maybe Joan will get lost looking for him," says Tom. "Maybe she'll never come back."

"Maybe," says Deborah.

Joan walks around the house and onto the croquet lawn. The wickets grow out of the ground like strange curving reeds. Everything looks different, Joan thinks, when you're drunk and it's dark and windy and your life is changing. All she wants to do is get back to the city and start over again. She's already forgotten about Gilbert.

As she walks down the sloping field of wickets, something catches her eye on the other side of the house—the cherry tree. It's blowing in the wind and looks as if it's trying to shake the TV dinner trays off its limbs, and as Joan watches, one does come off, and sails, gleaming, into the night.

Aria

Someone recognized me as I waited for the elevator. "Are you Melanie Minor?" the man asked. He was a handsome young man, home from work, wheeling a bicycle, his trousers clipped at his ankles.

"Yes," I said. The elevator arrived. My friend Rudy lives in an old apartment building; the elevator comes to you, but you have to open the door yourself. And close it behind you.

The bicycle man did this. "I saw you in *Dorian Gray* at Glimmerglass. I thought you were the best thing in it. You made a wonderful Sibyl."

"Thank you," I said.

"Are you singing in New York?" he asked.

"Not this year," I said.

"I'd love to hear you again," he said. "You have a fabulous voice. And you were very funny, I thought."

"Thank you," I said.

"Is anything happening with that production?" he asked.

"No," I said. "Kaput."

The elevator stopped at his floor. I held the door for him, so he could extract his bicycle. "It was nice to meet you," he said. "Good night."

"Good night," I said. I pulled the door shut and ascended. I felt happy, which I did not want to feel, for it was not a happy occasion: this was the last time I would be visiting Rudy at his home. What had been his home. In the morning he was leaving, moving to Iowa, back to his parents, from whence he came. He had AIDS and had decided to leave New York. To go home and lead a very simple, quiet life. His lover, Michael, had died a year ago. Rudy had decided then to leave, but it had taken him a year, a whole year, to unloose himself from his life in New York, and during that year I could feel him withdrawing himself as he cast off his possessions. It was as if he wanted to disappear, not die. Tonight I was coming to say goodbye, and collect his cat, Gray. Michael's cat, actually. Originally. Then Rudy's. About to be mine.

I walked down the hushed industrially carpeted hallway and stood outside the black lacquered door, and paused for a moment, pushing my happiness—it was excitement more than happiness, a bubbling thrill—down. Then I knocked, even though Rudy had a doorbell. I like the contact of knocking. It is more personal.

"Come in," Rudy shouted. He sounded a little annoyed, and the first thing he said after I had entered was, "Why did you knock?"

"For the sound of it," I said. I handed him the flowers I had brought. I knew it was foolish to bring flowers to someone who was moving out of his apartment, but I often brought Rudy flowers, and I wanted to bring him flowers one last time.

"Thank you," he said. They were very large, quite ugly, marigolds. Orange marigolds, the orange of imitation cheese. But I liked them, and hoped Rudy might, because they were so unabashedly the color they were. They did not pretend.

"I think I still have a jar of cranapple juice," he said. "If we drink it, I can put them in the jar."

He opened the refrigerator, which was almost empty. A

bottle of champagne, a folded foil crescent of cream cheese, and the juice.

"But wait," he said, "I don't have any glasses."

"Oh, spill it down the drain," I said, reaching for the jar. "And we'll drink the champagne. What's it from, anyway?"

"The champagne? I don't know. Or I've forgotten. It's been there for about a year."

I emptied the cranapple juice down the sink and then rinsed the jar. The cabinets were all open, exposing their shelf paper like underwear, as if to prove they were empty. "Here," I said, reaching for the flowers, "give them to me."

Rudy did, and then leaned against the counter. Only about half of the flowers fit in the jar. "We'll throw the rest of these away," I said.

"It seems a shame to throw away flowers."

"I wasn't thinking when I bought them," I said. "I should have thought you wouldn't have anything to put them in. Can we drink the champagne? At least have a taste? Or are you saving it?"

"I was going to leave it for the new people," said Rudy. He opened the refrigerator and took out the bottle. "But fuck the new people. Let's drink it. Here," he said, "you open it. It makes me nervous."

I opened the bottle and covered it quickly with my mouth to prevent it from foaming over. This also allowed me not to make a toast, for which I was grateful, because what was there to toast?

I held the bottle out to Rudy.

"Let's go in the living room," he said. "If we're going to stand, we may as well stand in the nicest room."

"Where are you going to sleep tonight?" I asked him, as I followed him down the long hall.

"On the floor," he said. "I've kept the mattress. The new people can throw it away."

There was nothing in the living room except the evening sun falling through the windows and graphing the hardwood floor. We leaned against the window ledge, and looked down into the garden, through the thin-limbed, tenacious trees. I think they are called Trees of Heaven, although I do not know why.

"When did the movers come?" I asked.

"Today," said Rudy.

"I know," I said, "but when? This morning?"

"Yes," he said. "Very early. They woke me up. Are they movers when they're moving it all to storage? Or are they called something else? Storers?"

"They're still movers," I said. "They moved it all, didn't they?"

Rudy looked around at the emptiness, as if to make sure they hadn't missed anything. "Yes," he said.

"I remember when you moved in here," I said. "And it was empty just like this. And we had a picnic dinner on the floor."

"Yes," said Rudy, "with Michael."

"Yes," I said. "With Michael." I always leave the dead out, yet Rudy includes them. Mentioning the dead to me seems impolite. I know this is not how it should be, but it is how it is with me. "And Michael tapdanced and the people from downstairs came up and complained," I added, for once the dead have been mentioned I feel the need to elaborate to prove that I am not scared of them. But the truth is they are dead, no matter how desperately you include them. Michael is dead.

"Where's Gray?" I asked.

"In the closet," said Rudy. "The movers scared her, and now that there's nothing in here she's disoriented."

"I've got the litterbox all set up," I said. "And I bought that special food, so I'm sure she'll be fine."

"I forgot to set aside her carrying case," said Rudy. "So the movers took it. Maybe we can find a box or something in the trash."

"No," I said. "I'll take her in my arms. I'll carry her."

We drank the bottle of champagne, passing it back and forth like teenagers, and then we went for a walk, in the bold late-summer twilight.

"Where do you want to go?" I asked, as we stood on the street, which was gloriously lit at one end by the sunset. "Should we go to the park? Or would you like to walk over to the pier?"

"The park," Rudy said. "I don't want to cross the highway."

We walked slowly. I held his arm with both of mine, for support and in farewell. I've known Rudy for eighteen years. We were, I think, the first real friends either of us ever had. At least that was true for me. We met at college when we were both finally turning into ourselves, and we were the first people to encourage each other in who we would be. And for many years we had been those people. I had been an opera singer and Rudy had played the cello. The thing was that I was going to continue being that person, and maybe even become another person, and Rudy would not. Or maybe very quickly he would, far away from me, in Iowa. I held his arm, like a pipe beneath his shirt, thin and hard and cold, with both of my hands.

It was a small park with a fountain. If you squinted so you couldn't read the shop signs across the street, you could feel you were in Europe. Yet it wasn't really a park: it was a gated traffic island with wounded trees and benches. And the fountain.

"How's your opera?" Rudy asked, after we had sat down. He was panting a little.

He meant my life, which has been a bit operatic lately.

For six years I have been in love with a man named Thomas. He is wealthy and powerful. And married. At least he *was* married. He was married to a woman named Felicia, but she committed suicide six months ago. She flung herself over the terrace of their apartment. *Flung herself* is wrong, I'm sure. I don't know the proper verb for that action. Ever since that happened Thomas has stopped seeing me. Death has made him faithful. He could betray a woman but not her memory. Or at least that is what I imagine. I suppose he could be seeing someone else but I don't think he is. I really don't.

"Nothing's happened," I said.

"He hasn't even called you?" Rudy asked.

"No."

"Do you call him?"

"I call him all the time," I said. "Whenever I think of it. More than before. I never talk for long. I just tell him where I am, where I'm going, what I'm doing. I have this need for him to know what I'm doing. Or for me to think he knows what I'm doing. For him to have knowledge of my life. I refuse to relinquish him."

"Do you think he listens to his messages?"

"Yes," I said. "Who doesn't listen to their messages?"

"Then eventually he'll call you," said Rudy. "Or answer the phone, perhaps. He hasn't changed the number?"

"No," I said.

"Then he will answer the phone, eventually."

Saying yes might jinx it, so I said nothing. I looked at the fountain. It was the type in which water flowed from one basin into another, filling that one, and falling again, and again, finally into a large pool, from which one supposed it was mysteriously siphoned and recirculated. "Tell me what it's like," I said.

"What?" asked Rudy.

"Where you're going. Your parents' house. So I can picture you."

"I thought you said you would visit me."

"I will. But until then, tell me."

We were both looking at the fountain. I realized I did not plan to visit Rudy.

"It's a ranch," he said. "It's painted red. The shutters are white. There are pine trees, tall pine trees, in the yard. They were not always tall, though. One year I remember we put Christmas lights on one. Wound them around it, and it wasn't so very tall."

"Is it on a country road?" I asked. "Or in the town?"

"In the town. It backs up to the high school. To the football field."

"Then you can watch them practicing," I said, "the beautiful young boys, grunting and banging against one another."

"Yes," said Rudy.

Suddenly the light altered. The sun had set. A bare-chested man pushed a shopping cart of bottles up to the fountain and began rinsing them in its basin. We watched him for a while. I didn't know what to say to Rudy. I knew that he was going away and that I might not ever see him again, but I didn't know how to act about this. This was not a situation that had arisen before in our friendship, or in my life. I wished I were the kind of person who could live without learning how to live first. Finally, I said—and this was forced, I had to make myself say it, even though it was the truth—finally I said, "I love you."

I looked at Rudy. He was looking at the man washing his bottles. He moved his mouth into what stood for, but wasn't, a smile.

When we got back to Rudy's apartment something terrible happened. Gray was still in the closet, hiding, crouched in the corner, facing the wall, admitting that everything was gone. When I leaned down to pick her up, she yowled—she screamed—and tried to grab the floor, the walls, anything, everything, with her claws. She scratched my arms, forming long, thin furrows of blood.

Rudy started to cry. He went down the hall and into the bedroom. He closed the door. I stood there near the closet, holding Gray, trying to comfort her. It was like a goal: to comfort the cat, as if the cat stood for something. I held her and stroked her and talked to her. Finally she grew less rigid in my arms. But I knew if I released my grasp even a little she would bolt. Then it was quiet and I stood there for a long time, hoping that Rudy would come out from the bedroom. It was dark by now, and I irrationally thought that since the apartment was empty the lights wouldn't work. So I walked down the hall in the dark and stood outside his bedroom door.

I didn't knock. "Rudy?" I said.

After a moment he said yes.

"I'm going to leave now," I said. "Are you all right?"

He didn't answer. It was a stupid question.

"May I come in?" I asked.

"No," he said. "I'm sorry. I can't—I'm sorry. Please just go."

I stood there for another moment. I knew I had failed him. I was crying. I wanted to put my hand against the door, touch it, but I was afraid of losing the cat. "I'll call you in the morning," I said, and then I left.

In the taxi the cat clung to me, scared but tenderly, as if she knew she was mine. In my apartment I showed her the litterbox, set her down in it, but she jumped from it, spraying gravel, and ran beneath the bed. I sat quietly for a while on the couch. I had a dull, thumping headache from the champagne. I lay down and fell asleep, and when I woke up I couldn't tell if minutes or hours had passed. I went into the kitchen and drank a tall glass of water. And then I drank another. And then I sat down at the table and dialed Thomas's number.

"It's me," I told his machine. "I'm at home. It's Wednesday night. I'm not sure what time. Late, I think. For some reason I don't want to know what time it is. I fell asleep, and just woke up. I said goodbye to Rudy tonight. He's leaving tomorrow. Actually I didn't say goodbye. We couldn't seem to say goodbye. I suppose that's natural. A man recognized me today. That's the first time that's ever happened. I mean a complete stranger, on the street. He had seen me in *Dorian*. He said I was wonderful. I suppose if they stop you on the street they have to say you're wonderful. Actually it wasn't on the street. It was at Rudy's apartment. I have a cat now. Rudy's cat. It's under the bed. I'm not wonderful though, am I? Thomas, are you there? I don't think so, although you might be since it's so late. If it is late. I may have woken you. I hope I did. I wish you were there. I wish you were here. I wish you were someplace where I could talk to you." I paused for a moment. "No, not talk to you," I said. "See you. Touch you."

Freddie's Haircut

"What is it about your life you don't like? What is it you want to change?" Drew, Freddie's roommate, was in the bathroom, talking to Joan, the cat. Freddie went in and sat on the sink. Drew was sitting on the closed toilet, and Joan was crouching in the litterbox. Recently, she had taken to spending most of her time in the litterbox, leaving it only to eat or occasionally watch the traffic on Avenue A.

"We love you, Joan," Drew continued. Joan looked up at them suspiciously and raked the litter with her tail. "Be careful," Drew said to Freddie. "The sink might break." Freddie sat on the rim of the bathtub. "She's been in there all night," Drew said. "I don't understand it. I'm trying to talk her through it."

"Come on, Joan," Freddie offered. "Lighten up."

"You better get out of there soon," Drew said. "If you think I'm going to tolerate this behavior you're crazy."

"Maybe she is crazy," said Freddie. "Maybe she's been inside too long. Cabin fever."

Drew prodded Joan with his bare foot. She leapt out of the box, and ran into the hall closet. Freddie began to brush his teeth.

"What are you doing tonight?" Drew said. Drew worked

from ten at night to six in the morning in a record store that was open twenty-four hours a day. He had been held up twice. Once the cash register deflected a bullet he claims would have killed him. During the day he went to the New York Restaurant School. The only time Freddie saw him was first thing in the morning.

Freddie looked in the mirror. He appeared rabid. "I'm thinking about getting my ear pierced."

"Why?"

"Why not?" said Freddie. "To look cool. I think it looks cool."

"Mine got infected," Drew said. "Get it done right."

"There's nothing else to do," said Freddie. He spread some Ultra Brite on his front teeth with his middle finger. He hoped this would make them gleam.

Freddie worked for a textile company that specialized in reproducing discontinued fabrics. That afternoon he was standing by the elevators watching the envelopes fall down the mail chute. They dropped as quickly as birds shot from the sky. In a few minutes he could push the down button and go home.

Mrs. Grimes, the office manager, opened the glass lobby doors and said, "Freddie, can I see you in my office before you leave?" Mrs. Grimes's first name was Bernice but she pronounced it Berenice. Freddie had heard her answer the phone.

"Now?" said Freddie.

"In a minute," she said. "What are you doing out here?"

"Someone said a letter was stuck. I was checking it out."

Mrs. Grimes looked disapprovingly at the mail chute. Then she looked disapprovingly at Freddie's new cowboy boots. Then she went back into the lobby.

———

Mrs. Grimes's office was on the twenty-fourth floor, and by the time Freddie arrived—via the spiral staircase reserved for executives—she was sitting behind her desk, energetically pushing the buttons on a calculator. Her long fingernails prevented her from expending her total fury. "Sit down," she said, without looking up.

The only chair was occupied by Mrs. Grimes's dachshund-shaped handbag. Freddie was afraid to move it.

"Sit down," Mrs. Grimes repeated, this time looking up.

Freddie picked up the handbag and sat with it on his lap. Then he put it on the floor.

"I see nothing to be except frank," Mrs. Grimes began, confusing Freddie immediately. "Are you stealing blue Uni-ball pens?"

Freddie was the supply distributor for the twenty-fifth floor. He had stolen a stapler and a Rolodex for the apartment, but he had stolen no pens. "No," he said.

"I ask because, according to my information, several gross are missing."

Since Freddie wasn't sure how many were involved in a gross, he couldn't tell how grave the situation was. "I haven't taken any," he said. "I don't need pens."

"You could sell them," Mrs. Grimes suggested.

Freddie shrugged.

"Do you lock your closet whenever you vacate it?"

"Yes," Freddie lied.

"Then I am afraid the blame must be yours. I will let it pass this time, but I will keep a close watch on the comings and goings of pens on the twenty-fifth floor. And I will not hesitate to charge any further losses against your paycheck."

"O.K.," Freddie said. He stood up and put the handbag on the chair. It rolled to its side and a pack of cigarettes fell on the floor. Freddie leaned down and picked them up.

"Leave them," Mrs. Grimes said. "Don't touch them."

———

A girl who looked about thirteen sat behind a glass case filled with earrings and roach clips, reading *Interview* magazine. Freddie looked in the case. Some of the earrings looked like they were made out of tabs from beer cans.

"Can I help you?" the girl asked.

"I think so," said Freddie. He sat down on a stool.

"We close at eleven," the girl said, although it was only a little after ten.

"I want an ear pierced," Freddie said. "Just one."

"You'll have to pay for two. It's a flat rate."

"O.K.," Freddie said.

"Pain or no pain?" the girl asked.

"Are you serious?"

"Yes," the girl said. She picked up an apparatus that looked like the embosser Freddie's mother used to personalize her stationery. "Some people like the pain. It makes the experience more real. It's not that bad."

"I want no pain," Freddie said.

"O.K.," the girl said. She went in the back of the store and returned with an ice cube. It was already beginning to melt in her palm. "Which ear?" she asked.

"Oh," said Freddie. "I'm not sure."

"Are you gay?"

"No," said Freddie.

"Then the right one. Left means you're gay."

"Are you sure?"

"Of course," said the girl. "Here. Hold this against your lobe till it melts."

Freddie held the ice cube against his right ear lobe. "Do I get to pick out the earring?"

"No," said the girl. "You have to have a fourteen-karat gold stud."

"Is that included?"

"No. It's fifteen dollars. I can give you just one for ten."

"So it's fourteen dollars altogether?" Freddie asked. His cheek was getting wet from the melting ice.

The girl nodded. "Is that melted yet?"

Freddie held up the thin disk of ice.

"A few more minutes," she said. She opened a bottle of rubbing alcohol and took a cotton ball out of a plastic bag. "I could put two holes in one ear," she said. "That looks good."

"Can I take it out?" Freddie asked.

"Not for six weeks. Otherwise your hole closes."

The ice slivered out of Freddie's hand and fell to the floor. He wiped his wet fingers on his pants.

"O.K.," the girl said. "One or two?"

"One," said Freddie.

She motioned for him to lean forward and wiped his ear with the cotton ball. Then she fingered his lobe and said, "Can you feel this?"

"No," Freddie said. The girl lifted the piercer and rested her hand against Freddie's cheek, steadying his head with her other hand. Freddie felt like he was being comforted. He closed his eyes, and felt his lashes scrape against the girl's throat.

No one noticed—or commented on—Freddie's earring until he went home for his sister's graduation-from-midwifery-school party. It was Freddie's idea to cut a sheet cake in the form of a baby and cover it with flesh-colored frosting. He was surrounded by chunks of cake and puddles of food coloring. The baby kept getting smaller and smaller. His mother was spraying rosettes of cheese food from an aerosol can onto crackers. "I've tried not to notice that thing in your ear," she said. "Is it really an earring?"

"It is," said Freddie.

"What does it mean? Or would I rather not know?"

"It doesn't mean anything," Freddie said. He touched the tiny stud, coating it with pink frosting.

"First gypsies wore earrings," said his mother. "Then Catholics. Then normal girls. And now my son. Where will it end?"

"With pets," Freddie said.

There was a girl who worked in Deferred Sales whom Freddie liked. He sent her anonymous gifts of unrequisitioned supplies through the mail. On Friday afternoon she opened the supply-closet door and said, "Rumor has it you're the man with the stuff."

Freddie was arranging bottles of liquid paper on a shelf. "Stuff?" he said. "You mean supplies?"

"In a way," she said. "Supplies for living." She closed the door and sat on a stool.

Freddie didn't understand. "Huh?" he said.

The girl opened a bottle of pink liquid paper and began painting her thumbnail. "It's a madhouse out there," she said. "Do you mind if I hang out for a minute?"

"No," said Freddie.

"I'm Diane," the girl said.

"I know," said Freddie.

"What I meant before was, do you have any pot?"

"Who said I had pot?"

"I thought it was common knowledge. I thought people were always escaping to the supply closet to get high."

"Not this one," Freddie said.

Diane observed her pink nail and switched to ledger-green liquid paper.

"I'd check the mailroom," said Freddie. "If you're that desperate."

"I'm not desperate. I'm just a little tense." Diane capped the bottle and fanned her polished nails at arm's length. "I like your cowboy boots," she said. "They're so pointy. Do they hurt?"

"No," Freddie lied.

"You must have weird feet then."

"Do you like my earring?" Freddie asked.

"You have an earring?"

Freddie bared his ear. "No one notices."

"Are you gay?"

"No," said Freddie. "It's the right ear."

"That means you're gay."

"No. It means you're straight."

"If you want people to notice it, you should get your hair cut."

"You think so?" asked Freddie. "How short?"

"I don't know." Diane stood up. "I could cut it for you. Do you have scissors?"

"Of course," said Freddie. "But do you know how?"

"I've done it before. I love to cut people's hair. I cut my boyfriend's." She opened the cabinet. "Where are the scissors?"

Before Freddie could dissuade her, Diane found a pair of scissors and began to snip them ferociously in the air. "Sit on the stool," she commanded. "I'll just cut a little around the ears."

"Are you sure about this?"

"Don't worry."

Freddie sat on the stool. Diane ran her fingers through his hair. "You have funny hair," she said. "It sticks out funny."

"I didn't wash it this morning," Freddie explained. "We didn't have any hot water."

Diane started snipping. She handed the cut hair to Freddie. Someone knocked on the door.

"Shit," Diane said. She tried to throw the scissors back into the cabinet but they landed on the floor, and separated.

Mrs. Grimes opened the door. Freddie jumped up from the stool, and his cut hair flurried to the floor. All three of them watched it for a second.

"Excuse me," Diane said. "I was just leaving."

Mrs. Grimes watched Diane leave. "I see you've been getting a haircut, Freddie," she said.

"I guess so," said Freddie.

"I think I should like to see you in my office before you leave today."

"O.K.," said Freddie.

Mrs. Grimes went out and closed the door. Freddie picked up his cut hair and put it in an inter-office envelope. He sent it to Diane.

Drew was whipping egg whites with a rat-tail comb when Freddie got home. He looked at Freddie's head and said, "What happened?"

"Everything," said Freddie.

"No. Really. What happened to your hair?"

"It got cut. At least some of it. And I got fired."

"You got fired? Why?"

"For getting my hair cut," said Freddie.

"They can't fire you for being ugly, can they?"

"Thanks," said Freddie. "That's just what I needed to hear. No, this girl was cutting my hair in the closet and the office manager found us."

"And she fired you?"

"Yeah," said Freddie.

"She fired you because you were getting your hair cut?"

"She also thought I was stealing pens."

"Were you?"

"No," said Freddie.

"You need a drink," said Drew. He inserted the comb into the meringue and watched to see if it would stand. It did. "Let me fix you a drink."

Drew mixed some vodka with some orange juice and gave it to Freddie. Freddie drank it. "What am I going to do?" he said.

"It'll all work out," Drew said. "But I'd get my hair fixed before I look for another job."

After Drew left for work Freddie took a shower and washed his hair. It didn't look much better clean. He was trying to decide if he could fix it himself when the phone rang. It always seemed to ring when Freddie was naked.

"Hello," he said.

"Hi," said his mother. "This is me."

"Hi," said Freddie.

"What's the matter?"

"Nothing."

"Oh," said his mother. "I was calling to see if you got the check."

"What check?" asked Freddie.

"The check I sent you. You didn't get it?"

"No," said Freddie. "Not yet."

"Well, I thought you could use a little extra money. It's just for fifteen dollars."

"Thanks," said Freddie.

"What are you doing?"

"Nothing. I might go out and get my hair cut later."

"Isn't it too late for that?"

"Some places around here are open late. Till midnight."

"How's work?"

"O.K.," said Freddie.

"Monica delivered her first official baby today."

"Oh," said Freddie. "How did it go?"

"Fine, I guess. She said it was a little difficult because the woman insisted on having it in the dark. I think it's absurd: having your baby at home in bed with all the lights out."

"It's the new thing," said Freddie. "It's supposed to be better for the baby."

"You were born in an operating room. I don't remember anything. The last thing I remember is lying on the couch timing the pains and watching a war movie. All these planes flying back and forth, back and forth. I forget the rest."

Freddie couldn't think of what to say. He wanted to say, "I got fired," but it was all too complicated and horrible to admit. "I've got to go," he said.

"I'll talk to you soon," said his mother. "I hope you get a nice haircut. Freddie?"

"What?"

"I'm sorry about what I said about your earring. I mean, I shouldn't have said it. I think it's fine for you to have an earring. Really, I do. I hope I didn't upset you."

"No," said Freddie.

"O.K., honey. Bye-bye."

"Bye," said Freddie.

There were two people in the haircutting place when Freddie arrived. A woman was sitting in one of the chairs watching herself drink coffee from a paper cup in the mirror. It was as if she were watching TV and starring on it at the same time. A man with a zebra-striped mohawk was sweeping the cut hair on the floor into a pile. Freddie stood inside the door.

Finally the woman turned away from the mirror and said, "Do you want your hair cut or something?"

"Yes," said Freddie.

She got out of the chair and motioned for Freddie to take her place. He did.

The woman took a comb out of a jar of blue liquid and poked Freddie's head. "It looks like it's just been cut," she said.

"It was a mistake," said Freddie. "Can you fix it?"

"Sure," the woman said.

"I want it cut the way it is now, only a little shorter."

"No you don't," the woman said. "We'll fix it up."

"How?" asked Freddie.

"Trust me," the woman said. She opened a drawer and removed a set of hedge clippers.

"What are they?" asked Freddie.

"They're shears," said the woman. "They give your hair a lot more texture. And height."

"Oh," said Freddie.

The woman tousled Freddie's hair and attacked it with the shears, snipping randomly at the tufted locks. "I'm cutting on the angle," she said. "To add fullness."

Freddie watched in the mirror, fascinated. Even the skunk-like man laid down his broom and watched. The woman tousled with one hand and snipped with the other, establishing a rhythm that was oddly soothing for all its fury. Freddie felt like he was outside, hatless, in a terrible storm.

He did not cry until he got home. He managed to pay the woman—even tip her—and walk home, all the time hoping that his hair would look better in his own, familiar mirror.

He went into the dark bathroom and could sense Joan crouching in the litterbox. Freddie knew why she was there. One day she was sitting on the window sill, watching the traffic while he was washing dishes. He dropped a plate, and as it shattered, he heard Joan screech, and when he looked up, the window sill was empty. He ran downstairs—two flights—and found her, stunned but alive, flattened against the sidewalk. He carried her upstairs, and ever since then she crouched near to the floor in small, contained places. Freddie doesn't know why he feels responsible for this. Technically, it was an accident.

When he turned on the bathroom light and saw himself in the mirror his worst fears were confirmed. His spiky hair looked menacing and hideous, and as he leaned toward his reflection it occurred to him that even he, even now, did not deserve to look this ugly.

Not the Point

The halls of the high school are teeming with manic, barely dressed students, and I press myself against the tile wall and let them pass. There is something frighteningly erotic about this sea of bodies: Girls' stomachs and boys' shoulders are bared in a combination of what seems to be narcissism and lust, as if they have emerged, not from History, but from some orgy, and are roaming the corridors in an effort to re-group, return to their lairs, and continue doing whatever it is they do behind these steamy glass doors.

After a few minutes, a bell shrills, the halls clear, and the school regains its composure. I find my way to the guidance office, and Mrs. King, Ellery's counselor. She asks me to sit down.

"Mr. Groener couldn't come?"

"No," I say. "He's in the Philippines."

"Philadelphia?"

"No, the Philippines."

"The Philippines?"

"On business."

"Of course," says Mrs. King, as if I were lying. "Well, I've taken the liberty of asking the school nurse to join us. I hope that's all right with you?"

I nod.

"Ellery's problems—or troubles—are not only academic. That's why Mr. Katikonas wanted to speak with us."

"Who's Mr. Katikonas?"

"Oh, he's the nurse. Miss Holloran retired, and, in an effort to update our health offerings, we've hired Mr. Katikonas. He has a background in drug and alcohol abuse, as well as adolescent psychology. Educational nursing has changed since our day." Mrs. King pauses, and then adds, "Not that Ellery's problems are stimulus-effected."

I smile.

Mr. Katikonas enters the small cubicle. He is wearing jeans and a T-shirt that says "Say No" on its chest. If I had met him in the hall I would have thought he was a student. He shakes hands with me, and then with Mrs. King, as if he knows each of us equally poorly. Perhaps he does. He looks around for a chair, but there isn't one.

"Oh," says Mrs. King. "You can get a chair from Willy's office."

"That's O.K.," says the nurse. "I'd rather stand." He leans against the wall.

"Well," says Mrs. King, "Mr. Katikonas and I wanted to talk to you about Ellery. Mainly about the sunglasses."

"I guessed," I say.

"You're aware of the problem?" Mrs. King asks.

"Yes."

"So he wears them at home?" the nurse asks.

I pause, think about lying. But I don't. "Yes," I say.

"All the time?"

"Yes."

"Do you have any idea why?"

"No."

"Have you talked to him about them?" Mrs. King is obviously our group leader.

"A little," I say.

"And what did he say?"

"Nothing, really," I say. "I mean, I just kind of kidded him . . . I didn't want to make a big deal out of it."

"He could be doing serious retinal damage," the nurse interjects.

"Oh . . ." I say.

"I'm sure that's true, John, but that's not the point," says Mrs. King. "I think the glasses are a psychological shield he's building up around himself . . . they're a symbol for a deeper problem. The problem isn't really the sunglasses."

"Nevertheless," says the nurse, "he could be damaging his eyes. I feel it's important to make that point. From a health point of view."

"Thank you," I say.

"Mrs. Groener?" Mrs. King asks.

"Yes," I say.

"Could this be linked with . . . I mean, Ellery's record mentions his brother's recent death. Since he's a new student, I'm afraid I don't know him as well as some of my other students. But do you think this is linked with that?"

Ellery's twin brother, Patrick, committed suicide last year. We're still trying to adjust, I think. We moved to this new town, and now we're getting ready to move to the Philippines, where my husband's been transferred (at his own request). I don't answer. I don't yet know how to answer questions like these.

"Excuse me," Mrs. King says.

"No," I say. "It's O.K. I just really don't know."

"Of course," she says. "To return to the matter at hand. This school has no specific policy regarding the wearing of sunglasses. However, we do forbid the wearing of clothes and accessories that are either dangerous or that divert attention from the purpose of education. I think the sunglasses could fall into either of those categories."

"Yes," I say. "I suppose they could."

"So we're thinking of forbidding Ellery to wear them in the building."

"But I thought the problem wasn't the sunglasses," I say.

"But it's the . . . the manifestation of the problem," Mrs. King says. "It's all we have to go on."

"I'd just like to see Ellery out of those shades," the nurse says. "Then we can take it from there."

"Would you agree to that?" Mrs. King asks.

"What would happen if he refused to take them off?" I ask.

"He wouldn't be allowed to attend classes. We'd put him in ICE."

"In what?"

"ICE. Isolated Continuing Education. Instead of suspending or expelling our students, we try to keep them in the building, but don't allow them to attend classes or mix with other students."

"It sounds like prison," I say.

"It's a very successful program," Mrs. King says. "It might sound drastic, but it does get us results. Of course it's supplemented with psychological counseling. It's just what some kids need."

"Maybe I should talk to Ellery again," I say.

"By all means, do," says Mrs. King.

"Hey, listen," the nurse says. "We don't want to do anything without your knowledge and cooperation. And it's much better if the problem is approached by you rather than us."

"But there is a problem," says Mrs. King. "And it does have to be approached."

I nod.

"One more question," the nurse says. "I'm just curious. Why did you name him Ellery?"

When I get home from the high school there's a strange car parked in front of the house. I pull into the driveway, and as

I walk up the front steps, a woman gets out of the car and crosses the lawn.

"Do you live here?" she asks.

"Yes," I say.

"I came about the garage sale? Vinnie Olloppia—she bought your Osterizer—told me."

"Oh," I say. "Well, come in."

"Where's the stuff?"

"It's inside," I say. "I'm selling the contents of the house."

"Everything?" she asks.

I unlock the front door. "Yes," I say. "We're moving overseas."

"Where to?"

"The Philippines," I say. "My husband is there now. I'm just trying to get the house sold."

"You shouldn't tell people that," the woman says. "I mean, that you're living alone."

"My son is here," I say. And, because Carly is lying in the front hall, I add, "And my dog."

"Does he bite?" the woman asks.

"No," I say.

Carly sighs. We step over him and go into the living room.

"Wow. This is all for sale? Everything?"

"Yes," I say. "My husband's bought a furnished house."

"You could put this in storage," the woman suggests. "I can't imagine selling all my things. Aren't you sad?"

"No," I say. "You can look around. Excuse me a minute."

I go into my bedroom and lie down on the bed. Carly noses open the door and walks over and looks at me. He doesn't like it when you close doors. "Hi, Carly," I say. I stroke his nose, and his ears. Carly has glaucoma and is almost blind. The vet told me that moving him into another new, unfamiliar house would be "torture" for him. Not that we would take him all the way to Manila. We'll have to put him to sleep soon. I'll have to put him to sleep soon.

I can hear the lady walking around the living room. She could be stealing everything, for all I know. That would be nice. That would be the easiest way to get rid of it.

I get up, wash my face, and go back to the living room. The woman isn't there. I go into the kitchen. She's holding open a cupboard door, looking inside. She closes it when she sees me. Real quick.

"I'm sorry," she says.

"No," I say. "It's fine. Look."

"I'm trying to find some things for my daughter. She just got married, and moved into a beautiful condo—in the Riverwarren?—but she won't buy anything for it. She got some things as wedding presents, of course. A bed and a TV and a kitchen table. But she won't get anything else. She doesn't take any interest in fixing the place up. Don't you think that's strange?"

"Yes," I say.

"I'm thinking that if I get a few things, start her off, you know, she'll make an effort. Her husband's just as bad. They lie on the bed, watch TV, and eat frozen food. Oh, she has a microwave, too."

"Would you like something to drink?"

"No, thanks," she says. "Are you selling these pots and pans?"

"Everything," I say.

"How much do you want for these? Are they genuine Revere Ware?"

"Yes," I say. They were my wedding presents. "Twenty dollars?"

"That sounds reasonable." She takes the pots out of the cupboard and arranges them on the kitchen table, stacking them inside of one another. "Listen," she says. "Do you think I could come back with my daughter? Maybe seeing all this stuff, might, you know, excite her."

"Sure," I say.

"But I'll take these pots now. Are you sure just twenty? For the whole set?"

"Yes," I say.

The woman opens her bag and rummages in it. It's shaped like a little wooden picnic basket. She hands me a twenty. "Here you go," she says. "Maybe I'll come back this evening? With Debbie? Would that be O.K.?"

"Sure," I say.

I walk her to the front door. Carly's back in the front hall. We both step over him. He sighs.

I stand inside the door and watch the woman drive away. Then I take the twenty and put it, along with all the other money I've made, in the empty dog biscuit box I keep on top of the refrigerator.

I haven't been sleeping much nights, so I take a nap. Carly joins me. We are awakened by Ellery, home from school, playing his stereo: the soundtrack from *Carousel*. Ellery has strange taste in music.

I knock on his door, and when he doesn't answer I open it. He's lying on his bed, on his back, his sunglasses on. He wears different ones. I forgot to mention that to the guidance counselor. Surely it's not as obsessive if he changes them? The worst are the mirrored ones. The wraparound ones he has on now are thin and curved, so you can't see his eyes, even if you sit beside him and make an effort.

"Hello, Ellery," I say. I turn the music down: "June Is Bustin' Out All Over."

"Hi," Ellery says.

Carly, ignored, noses his chest. "Hello, Carly," Ellery says.

"How was school?" I ask.

"Wonderful," says Ellery. "I learned a lot of new things today."

"I was there," I say.

"I know," says Ellery. "Fiona Fitzhugh told me. She said you had your skirt on backward."

"I didn't have my skirt on backward. It buttons up the back."

"Are you sure?" asks Ellery.

Suddenly, I'm not sure. Have I been wearing it wrong all this time? "You can wear it either way," I rationalize.

"What were you doing in school?" Ellery asks. "Signing up for the bake sale?"

"Is there going to be a bake sale?" I stupidly ask, before I realize he is being sarcastic.

Ellery moans.

"I was seeing Mrs. King. And the nurse. The male nurse."

"I didn't know I was diseased," says Ellery.

"About your sunglasses," I say.

"Ah," says Ellery.

"If you don't stop wearing them, they'll put you on ICE," I say, proud of myself for remembering this vernacular. Maybe it makes up for my bake sale faux pas.

"People say it's actually cooler in ICE. You can put your head down on the desk and sleep if you want."

"Then it would suit you," I say. Ellery smiles, but not being able to see his eyes, it's hard to interpret this smile. I guess it's a mean little smile, though.

"And you're doing irreparable damage to your retinas," I say.

"They can transplant retinas, now, can't they?" Ellery asks.

I think this is a smug remark, especially with poor Carly sitting here with her egg-white eyes. "If you were Carly, you wouldn't say things like that," I say.

Ellery turns away from me, onto his side, so he's facing the wall. He doesn't say anything. From this angle he reminds me of Patrick. Patrick always slept on his side, his bony hip tenting the sheet, forming a little alpine mountainscape. Ellery usually sleeps on his back, the blankets rising smoothly over him, like water.

The record finishes. The needle rises, and clicks itself off. The only sound is Carly's labored breathing. "I'm still here," I say.

Ellery doesn't answer.

"Do you want me to turn the record over?"

He still doesn't answer. And then I notice his back moving: shaking, ever so slightly, the way it shakes when he's crying, but trying to hold himself still.

I should call Carly and go for a walk, but instead I go into my bedroom and look through Patrick's things. If I had known he was going to die like that, I would have saved everything: his splayed toothbrushes, his outgrown sneakers, every hair that was ever cut from his head. All I have are report cards, pictures, and some Mother's Day cards he made me in Sunday school. When he died, my sister, in a well-intentioned but misguided effort to comfort me, said maybe it was good that Ellery and he were twins, so much alike— that having Ellery was a little like still having Patrick. You have to be their mother to know how absurd that is. There was nothing alike about them. Their elbows were different. Their walks. They had their own auras. For instance, the afternoon I found the bathroom door locked, that awful quiet, I knew it would be Patrick I found inside, once the door was knocked down. I was right. Or: If one of them touched me lightly, with one finger, on my back, I could tell, without turning, without looking, whose finger it was.

———

I start to make (canned) chili for dinner before I remember I sold all my pots. I keep missing things this way. The other night I went to vacuum and the vacuum was gone. I spoon the opened can of chili into Carly's bowl and call her. She lumbers into the kitchen, smells the food, then sits down, confused, looking at, but not really seeing, me.

"You don't like it?" I say. "It's chili."

Carly just stares. She looks sad. But then dogs always look sad, don't they? That's not true. Carly used to look happy. Sometimes she still grins.

Ellery comes into the kitchen. The hair on one side of his head is bouffanted from sleep. "Is Daddy coming home for dinner?" he asks, although he knows his father is on the other side of our planet.

"He should be home any minute," I say.

"Oh, good," says Ellery. "It will be nice to see him. Are you cooking us a great dinner?"

"You bet," I say, grabbing his shoulders and kissing his neck, before he stops playing whatever game it is we're playing.

Ellery drives us down to Pronto! Pizza!. I'm a little worried about letting him drive with his sunglasses at night, but he appears to see fine, although he's neurotic about signalling: He even puts his blinker on when he turns into the parking space.

Ellery says he doesn't care what kind of pizza we get, and to punish him for his apathy, I order pizza with green peppers, which I know he dislikes. He good-naturedly picks the peppers off his slices, making me feel terrible. I had expected he would complain. Children are always magnanimous when you'd rather they weren't.

"Daddy should call tonight," I say.

"Oh," says Ellery.

If I hadn't ordered the green peppers I would remove

them from my slices, too. They taste rubbery and inorganic.

"Will you stay up and talk to him?"

"Maybe," says Ellery. "I'm kind of tired."

"You slept all afternoon."

Ellery shrugs. We eat for a while in silence. Ellery, the fastest eater I've ever known, finishes first and watches me. Or at least I think he's watching (the sunglasses).

"Do you want one of my slices?" I ask. "I can't eat all of this."

"I've made up my mind," Ellery says, ignoring my offer.

"About what?"

"The Philippines," Ellery says.

"What do you mean?" I'm not following him.

"I'm not going."

I put my slice of pizza down, and seeing it, half-eaten on the paper plate, nauseates me. I wipe my greasy hands on a napkin, and cover the remaining pizza with it. "What are you talking about?"

Ellery doesn't say anything. How I wish he would take those sunglasses off.

"What are you talking about?" I repeat, and for the first time, I realize I've been waiting for this: I know.

"I'm not going to move to the Philippines. It just doesn't make sense."

"But I thought you wanted to. We've discussed all this. You're the one who thought it would be so great . . ."

"I've changed my mind," says Ellery. "I still think you should go. I still think it makes sense for you and Daddy."

"And it doesn't make sense for you?"

"No. I have one more year of high school. I'll finish it here, and then get a job. Or go to college, or something."

"And where will you live?"

"Well, at the rate you're selling the house, I can live there. And if you finally sell it, I can live with someone, or something. Or get an apartment."

"And I'm supposed to move to the Philippines and just leave you here?"

"I'm almost eighteen," Ellery says. He begins to stack our refuse on the tray.

"Wait," I say. I take my paper cup of soda and drink from it. Ellery takes the tray and dumps it in the garbage can. He studies the jukebox. I don't know what to do. I feel as if I might start crying, but something about flexing my cheek muscles to sip through the straw comforts me, helps hold my face together. I drain the soda and keep on sucking, inhaling nothing but cold, sweet air.

We drive for a while in silence. Punky-looking kids stand under the streetlights drinking beer.

"Can I drop you off and take the car?" Ellery asks.

"Where are you going?"

"To Fiona Fitzhugh's. We have a physiology lab practical tomorrow and Fiona has the cat."

"What cat?"

"The cat we're dissecting."

"You're dissecting a cat? That's disgusting. Why can't you dissect frogs?"

"One does," Ellery says patiently, "in biology, in ninth grade. In physiology, one dissects cats. Fiona and I are going to quiz each other."

"It sounds romantic," I say.

"It's not a date," Ellery says.

"You're allowed to take the cats home?"

"Not really. But Mr. Gey says that as long as he doesn't see you take it and as long as it's back in the refrigerator by 8:30 he doesn't mind. Fiona has this huge pocketbook. It was easy. Want to hear something?"

"Is it about dissecting cats?"

"No," says Ellery. "People."

"Sure," I say, brightly.

"Mr. Gey was telling us, in the lab where he studies—he's getting his Ph.D. or something—they're dissecting cadavers, and they keep them in this big walk-in freezer and inside the freezer, on the door is a sign that says YOU ARE NOT LOCKED IN! Who do you think it's for?"

"What do you mean?"

"Do you think it's for the cadavers, you know, if they come back to life, or something, or the people dissecting them, like if they freak out in there?"

"I have no idea," I say. "Who?"

Ellery chuckles. A strange, forgotten sound. "No one knows. Mr. Gey had us vote. With our heads down and everything."

"Does Mr. Gey have a problem?" I ask.

"Mr. Gey is cool," Ellery says.

"Oh," I say. "Well, who did you vote for?"

For a second Ellery doesn't answer. Then he turns to look at me, the streetlights reflecting across his sunglasses. "I voted twice," he says. "I think the sign was there for everyone involved."

Ellery drops me off, and I walk across tufted, crab-grassy lawn, the only imperfect one on our block. There's a note stuck in the front door. It says: "Brought my daughter to see your furniture. Sorry to miss you. We'll come back tomorrow eve. (Wed) If you won't be here will you kindly call?" It's signed Doris Something and underneath that is a phone number. On the other side is a P.S.: "You should leave lights on to discourage burglars."

I'm counting the money in the dog biscuit box when the phone rings. I've counted three hundred dollars, and there's still more. Ellery came home about an hour ago, smelling faintly of formaldehyde, took a shower, and went to bed.

It's tomorrow morning in the Philippines. When I talk to

Leonard in these circumstances—he a day ahead of me—I feel as if I've lost him somehow, as if he's lived longer than I; that in the hours he's gained he's learned something I don't know. It's the time, not the distance, that separates us. In the Philippines, Leonard goes home for lunch. He has a chauffeur and a housekeeper. I'm going to love it when I get there. That's what he tells me, when we talk, once a week.

The operator asks for me, and I say I'm me, and then Leonard gets on, and says hello. Sometimes he sounds far away, and sometimes he sounds like he's calling from next door. Tonight he sounds far away. He says he misses me; that he loves me.

Then he asks about Ellery and Carly—I lie and say they're both doing fine—and then he asks about the house. I lie again and tell him someone's about to make an offer.

We talk for a while and then Leonard tells me again how much I will love the house; he bangs the telephone on the floor so I can hear the green slate tiles in the kitchen, and then he starts to hang up.

"Leonard?" I say.

"What?" he says.

"Wait," I say. I'm not sure how I'm going to say what I know I want to say next. We both listen to the static for a moment.

"I don't think I'm going to come," I finally say, listening to my voice unravel across all those miles of cold, dark cable.

"What?" Leonard says.

"Maybe it would be better if Ellery and I stayed here."

"What are you talking about?" Leonard asks. "What's happened?"

"Nothing. Nothing's happened. But Ellery doesn't want to move. I think that's good, don't you? I mean, I think he's a little happier here, now. He went on a date tonight."

"Really?" Leonard says. "That's wonderful, great, but

that doesn't mean you can't come to the Philippines, Arlene. That's crazy."

"I know," I say. "But . . . maybe you can get transferred back, or something . . ."

"Arlene, I've taken this job. I've got to stay here at least a year, now. At least. I owe them that. And this house . . ."

"I know," I say. "I know that. But it will be O.K. A year . . . I mean, it will only be for a year. That's not too long."

"What are you saying? I don't believe this," Leonard says. "What's happening, Arlene? What about us? I miss you."

"Stop calling me Arlene," I say. Whenever Leonard talks to me on the phone, he keeps inserting my name into the conversation, as if, since he can't see me, he might forget who he's talking to.

"What?" he asks.

"Nothing. I miss you, too," I say. "I do. But . . ."

"But what?"

"I don't think I can move again," I say.

"But Arlene—honey—you're the one who wanted to get the hell away . . . this was your idea."

This is true, but it's not the point. I think for a moment, and then, carefully, say, "No. Not without Ellery."

Leonard doesn't say anything. I listen to our chorus of static.

"Well, this is a real shock," he finally says. "I'm going to have to think about this. Have you thought about this?"

"Yes," I say. "I mean, not really. Ellery just told me."

"Well, why don't we both think about this then? Maybe there's another way to work this. I'll call again tomorrow."

"That sounds good," I say. "I'm sorry."

"Don't be sorry," Leonard says. He pauses. "Is Ellery there? Can I talk to him?"

"He's sleeping," I say. "Do you want me to wake him?"

"Oh, no," says Leonard. "Don't wake him up. Tell him I said . . ."

"What?"

"Tell him I said hi," Leonard says. "Tell him I love him."

After I hang up the phone I let Carly out and stand in the dark backyard with her, watching her squat. I walk down the slope to the clothesline and take down the sheets that have been hanging for a couple of days. They still smell clean, and they feel cool, slightly damp. I think about putting them on my bed: It would be a little like sleeping outdoors. Carly, disoriented, starts to whimper. Her eyesight is especially bad at night. I call her. She walks over to me and inserts her muzzle between my legs: Safe.

We go through the house and I turn all the lights off, burglars or not. I make my bed with the clean, cool sheets, but instead of attempting to sleep, I go into Ellery's room. He doesn't wear his sunglasses in bed. I was very relieved, the first night I came in here, to discover that. It makes it not so bad, somehow. That may sound sick, but you have to measure these things. It's how you bear it. Ellery is lying on his back, his arms akimbo, with one loosely curled fist resting in each eye socket, as if even in sleep there is some bright light he cannot bear.

But it's O.K. I take his hands by their unscathed wrists and gently move them to his side. Ellery doesn't wake up; he assimilates this gesture into the narrative of his dream. His exposed eyelids flicker with secret vision.

The Half
You Don't Know

Miss Alice Paul was in a quandary. Ever since Rose had died, everything had gone wrong. And it wasn't getting better—it had been a month already, but it was no better. It was worse, she thought: much worse. Right this minute, Rose's grandson, a man named Knight, was up in the attic going through Rose's things, and there was nothing she could do about it. She stood in the upstairs hall, clutching the folding stairs that had collapsed from the ceiling. She had tried to climb them, but she couldn't. She had trouble enough getting up the regular stairs.

The problem was, nobody was telling her anything. It looked like they were moving Rose's stuff out of the house, or maybe Knight was moving in? Miss Alice Paul had lived in this house for about twenty years, ever since she met Rose at the Del Ray Luncheonette counter. They were both eating BLTs on white toast. It had made perfect sense for them to move in together—Rose was widowed and Miss Alice Paul was the tragic victim of a brief, annulled and (she hoped) forgotten marriage, but now that Rose was dead it turned out the house was really her daughter's, and nobody was talking about what would become of her. It was just too awful for words.

"Knight?" Alice Paul called up the stairs. He had a radio going up there. "Knight!" She shouted louder.

He turned the radio down. Good. "Yes?" he said.

"Are you sure I can't help with that? What are you doing?"

"Just going through this stuff. It's mostly junk, Miss Paul. I don't know the last time anyone's been up here."

"Yes, but what are you going to do with it?"

"Well, throw it out, most likely."

"Oh, dear. You don't suppose I could see it first? I mean, there might be something that was special to me, something you'd overlook."

"Well, sure you can see it. I have to bring it all down anyway. You can look through it then."

Well, that was a relief. God only knew what was up there, and what that boy might throw away. "Would you like a cold drink or something? Is it hot up there?"

But there was no answer. He had turned the radio back up. Miss Alice Paul went downstairs to the kitchen. She made a cup of tea and then put on her coat and went outside. It was a sunny day, mild for November, and she had read that sunlight can cure depression, so she was trying to sit outside whenever possible.

Deirdre Kassbaum was hanging out her wash next door. Or no, she was taking it down, folding it. Miss Alice Paul walked over to the fence.

"Do you need some help?" she asked.

Deirdre took a clothespin out of her mouth. "Oh, hi, Miss Paul."

Miss Paul repeated her offer.

"No thanks. I'm just going to finish these off in the dryer. They're still kind of damp."

"It's a nice day for air drying," Alice Paul said. Maybe I could go live with the Kassbaums, she thought. They've got that whole upstairs they never use. I could rent a room. Mr. Kassbaum drinks, but he's not a mean drunk.

"I see Knight's here," Mrs. Kassbaum said. "Is that his truck?"

"No. He rented it."

"Is he moving you out?"

"No," said Miss Alice Paul. She was trying to think how much people rented rooms for nowadays. The last time she rented a room, it was twelve dollars a week. Double that: twenty-five dollars—would that be enough? "I mean I don't know. I don't know what's going to happen."

"Well, are they selling the house?" Mrs. Kassbaum left the laundry basket on the lawn and walked over to the fence.

"I don't know," said Miss Alice Paul. "They won't tell me anything. It's driving me crazy."

"Well, that's a shame. But you shouldn't get all worried. I'm sure it'll work out just fine. Plus, you've got your rights. They can't just kick you out after twenty-two years. It's a thing called squatting, squatter's rights. They had an article about it in the *Digest*. Not that they'd kick you out. But you got to find out what's going on. She left the house to Knight?"

"Well, not really. Her daughter up in Norwell owns it. She was renting it to Rose."

"Well, can't she rent it to you?"

"I doubt I can afford it. I'll probably have to rent a room someplace."

"Oh, you don't want to do that. Rent a room? Living with strangers, sharing a bathroom. That would be so depressing, don't you think?" Mrs. Kassbaum patted Miss Paul's arm. "What you have to do, honey, is talk to him, find out what they're planning. Knight's a nice man. You know that. Go in and talk to him, and put your mind at rest."

Miss Paul turned around and looked back at the house. She could hear the radio coming out of the open attic window. The sun had gone around to the front, leaving the backyard in shadow. I missed the sun, she thought. It would be shining in the living room window now, creating a familiar pattern on the rug and the couch. If Rose were alive she would put down the blinds, so the sun wouldn't fade the upholstery.

Miss Alice Paul was trying to check her pocketbook under the table without Knight seeing her. They were sitting at a booth in the Casa Adobe, a Mexican restaurant, and Miss Alice Paul wasn't sure who was paying. Knight was the one who had suggested going out to dinner, and before she could think of an excuse not to he had her in the car. She was pretty sure she had a five-dollar bill, so she had ordered a taco plate, which was the cheapest thing on the menu, even though she had no idea what a taco was, but Knight had said that wasn't enough for dinner and had changed her order to a deluxe burrito platter—something she just knew she couldn't afford, let alone eat.

"You lose something?" Knight said. He was drinking a beer. He had peeled its foil collar back and was drinking it straight from the bottle. At a restaurant. Just imagine.

"I just want to be sure I have enough money," Miss Alice Paul said. "I don't want to have to do the dishes." She tried to laugh, but it didn't sound too good.

"Oh, forget that," Knight said. "This is my treat."

"Well, many thanks, but I couldn't allow that. Though it is sweet of you."

"Oh, come on." Knight reached across the table and grabbed her pocketbook from her hands, putting it on the seat beside him. "Now just relax," he said. "Are you sure you don't want a glass of wine? They have sangria, I think."

"No, thank you." Miss Alice Paul leaned back and tried to think straight. He's taken my bag, she thought. Good God. "Could I have my bag back?" she asked.

"Of course," said Knight. "On one condition."

"What's that?"

"On the condition that you don't open it until we get home. O.K.?"

"If you insist," Miss Alice Paul said.

"I do," said Knight. "I insist."

Their deluxe platters arrived. "Good Lord," said Miss Paul. She couldn't help it. It just looked such a mess.

"Dig in," said Knight.

"I thought we'd have Thanksgiving at the house," Knight said. They were driving home from the restaurant, through a part of town Miss Alice Paul didn't seem to recognize. I don't get out much anymore, she thought. Everything's changing.

"What house?" she said.

"Your house," Knight said. "At Aunt Gran's." Aunt Gran was what they called Rose. She had never figured out why. Everyone in their family had pointless, misleading, disrespectful names: Rose's sixty-year-old daughter was called Topsy, and her daughter—Knight's sister—was sometimes called Ellen and sometimes called Nina, and Ellen's two children were called Kittery and Dominick. Hardly American names. She made sure they all called her Miss Alice Paul.

"There's more room there, and it's stupid to go back and forth from the lake. Is that O.K.?"

Miss Alice Paul was confused. What did he mean? He said *your house*. And who all was coming? "Who's coming?" she said.

"Topsy, and Ellen and Kittery and Dominick. They're coming down for the weekend. I figure the women can stay with you, and Dominick can stay with me. Or sleep on the couch. I don't know."

"I didn't buy a turkey." Was she supposed to do all the cooking? She hadn't cooked a turkey in years. Decades.

"No. Topsy said she was bringing one. And I'm making pies. You don't have to worry about anything." He pulled into a gas station. It was self-serve. "Excuse me," he said, before getting out.

Excuse me. He's a nice man, Miss Alice Paul told herself. He has manners, and he's quiet and he was listening to classical music on the radio. He was a professor at the university. He taught history or something. For a while he had lived with another professor, a man named John, who had sometimes come to Sunday dinner, but John had been killed about two years ago. His car cracked up, driving out to the lake in the winter. All that ice. Had he been drunk? Most men drink. Hector Kassbaum. Knight drinking that beer from the bottle. Disgusting. She watched him pump the gas. He was trying to get the numbers even, pumping little spurts. He paid the girl, and got back into the car.

In the driveway she realized she had forgotten to leave any lights on. Rose always left the porch light on, and one in the living room. It was strange to see the house so dark. Like nobody lived in it. She sat there for a moment.

"Want me to come in with you?" Knight said.

"Would you?" Miss Alice Paul asked. "Just for a minute."

"Sure," he said. He opened his door and came around and opened hers.

He held her elbow going up the front walk. "I should have left a light on," she said. "Rose always did. I forgot."

He grunted. He was looking up at the sky. She looked up, too. It was filled with stars. She felt dizzy looking up, and leaned closer to him.

"It's dark," he said. "Careful."

I'll ask him when we get inside, she thought. I'll offer him some coffee—do I have any coffee?—and ask him what he meant when he said *your house*. He let go of her arm on the front step and opened the screen door. He reached in to open the front door, but it was locked. "Do you have keys?" he asked.

Did she? She forgot the door locked when she closed it.

She didn't think she had keys. It was all his fault, making her go out to dinner, getting her agitated; she had forgotten all about the keys when she left. But maybe they were in her bag. "Let me see," she said. She opened her bag and tried to look, but it was too dark. She backed up into the moonlight and almost fell off the stoop. He grabbed her. "Woops," he said, taking her bag. "Let me look."

This was awful, she thought. He's going through my bag now. He took out her change purse and her plastic rain hat and her tissues. He felt around with his big hand. "Nope," he said. He reassembled her purse and handed it to her. "You wait here," he said. "I'll go around back. I can get in through the cellar, I think."

He disappeared behind the house. She looked back up at the sky. Birds were flying around the edges of the trees. Were they bats? They sure flew funny—jerky and silent. Don't look at them, she thought. Just stand here. Don't think of anything.

She waited what seemed like a long time. Then a light came on in the living room, and the front door opened. "Come in," he said. But something had changed. It was him inside first. It made it different.

"Come in," he repeated. He opened the screen door wider. He snapped on the porch light. "Oh, no," he said, when he saw her face. "What's the matter? Miss Paul?"

Am I crying? she wondered. I must be. That must be it.

Rose's daughter Topsy was washing the dishes, and Miss Alice Paul was drying and putting away, supposedly because she knew where things went. But she didn't. Half this stuff she had never seen before, so she just put things where she could find space. She'd sort it out later. After they all left tomorrow.

"It's nice to have a little peace and quiet for a change,"

said Topsy. "I hope this weekend wasn't too hectic for you."

"Oh, no," Miss Paul said, thinking, It will be peace and quiet when you're gone. Actually it hadn't been that bad. They were nice people even if there were too many of them. And they all shouted a lot. Tonight everyone had gone to the movies. They tried to make her go, but she just hated the movies. All that filthy language.

"Well, I'm glad we have this chance to talk, Miss Paul. There's something we have to discuss." Topsy had finished washing the dishes. She chased the suds down the drain and turned the faucet off.

Miss Alice Paul was drying the pronged bulbous foot of the electric mixer. She drew the towel back and forth between its curves. For some reason she couldn't stop. Finally the towel got all tangled up and Topsy took it away from her.

"Let's sit down," she said. "The rest of this can dry overnight." They sat at the table. "I was wondering if you had thought about where you might like to live, now that Rose is gone. As you probably know, we're planning to rent this house starting the first of the year."

"I didn't know," said Miss Alice Paul.

"Well, this old house is too big for you, anyway. It's too big for any one person."

"How much are you renting it for?"

"We're going to ask six hundred dollars a month."

That was highway robbery, thought Miss Paul. She's lying to me. "I doubt you'll find anyone willing to pay that," she said.

"In fact, we already have. That's why we have to talk. Do you have any relatives, Miss Paul, or friends, who could . . ."

"Everybody's dead. You might as well take me out into the street and drive the car right over me. That's what you should do."

"Don't talk crazy, now, Miss Paul. There are plenty of solutions. Knight tells me there's a real nice . . . place out by the lake. Have you ever heard of St. Luke's?"

St. Luke's was the rest home out by the lake. The very idea. "Course I have. But that's for—I'm not going to St. Luke's. I used to be a volunteer at St. Luke's. It's not a place for decent people. It's trash out there."

"Knight tells me it's real nice. I was thinking maybe we could drive out there tomorrow and have a look. I think they've fixed it up real nice since you—"

"You don't understand," said Miss Alice Paul. "I don't care if they got the Taj Mahal out there."

"Well, I don't think I can promise you the Taj Mahal, but what say we go take a look? It can't hurt to look, can it?"

People are just awful, Miss Alice Paul thought.

"So what do you say, Miss Paul? Let's go take a look."

"No," said Miss Alice Paul.

"Oh, come on, Miss Paul. It won't hurt you to look. Can't you do that much? We're just trying to help you, remember."

"No. I'm sorry, but no. Just no."

"Well," said Topsy. "I think that's a shame. I think you could be real happy out there."

"No," said Miss Alice Paul.

Kittery, the girl, Rose's great-granddaughter, was giving Miss Alice Paul a facial. Miss Alice Paul was sitting on a chair pushed away from the kitchen table, a plastic produce bag stuck on her head to hold her hair back. She was smiling—things had worked out as well as they could. At Christmas they had moved her up north to Norwell. They had a big old house—the biggest house she had ever seen. There was one whole floor they didn't even use.

Kittery was rubbing a peach-colored cream into her

cheeks. It felt good. "This is apricot," she said. "It's really for younger skin, I think, like teenagers, but we'll just keep it on for a minute. It's got ground-up apricot. Wait till you see your glow!" Kittery had a job selling this stuff door-to-door. She also had a boyfriend who was a black man.

Dominick came in from the front hall.

"Hi," said Kittery.

Dominick said hi and opened the refrigerator. He was her favorite. They played gin rummy sometimes.

"How are you, Dominick?" she asked.

"I'm cold."

"Then shut the refrigerator," said Kittery.

Dominick shut it but continued to regard it.

"I'm thirsty," he announced. "What are we having for dinner?"

"You're on your own," Kittery said. "Topsy's spending the night at Knox Farm, and Ellen's at dance class." Ellen was their mother. She was plain nuts.

"Why's Topsy staying over there?"

"She said she had a lot to do and didn't want to drive home in the snow. I'm fasting. I heard on the radio that today is a national fast day. I'm starting now. Actually about an hour ago."

"What about Miss Alice Paul?" Dominick reopened the refrigerator. He took out a carton of orange juice.

"Well, you might fix her something when you make your own dinner. Are you hungry, Miss Alice Paul?"

"Vaguely," said Miss Alice Paul.

"I could make an omelet," said Dominick. "We learned how today in home ec. Do we have an omelet pan?"

"It's stinging," said Miss Alice Paul. "Is it supposed to sting?"

"Yes," said Kittery. "That means it's penetrating the epidermis."

"Do you want an omelet?"

"What kind?" asked Kittery.

"I was asking Miss Paul. I thought you were fasting."

"I think you're supposed to start in the morning. I'll do it tomorrow. Do you want an omelet, Miss Alice Paul? When we're done with your facial?"

"This is stinging like the dickens."

"We'll rinse it off. You got to put your head down between your legs, though, so the blood will rush to your face. That's a Lottie Dale secret. That's how you get the glow."

Everyone at the senior citizen nutrition lunch was pretending that noon was really midnight, and they were going to count down and then blow their horns and celebrate the New Year. They had to have their lunch—beef stew—an hour earlier today, at eleven o'clock. Miss Alice Paul hated coming to nutrition lunches. Topsy made her. She said it was good for her to get out of the house.

Miss Alice Paul had taken off her party hat twice, and both times Pauline Carlson had come round and told her to put it back on.

"Miss Alice Paul, don't be a party pooper," she said. "Let's cooperate. If one person takes their hat off, everyone will want to."

"So let them," Miss Alice Paul said.

"What kind of party would that be?" Pauline said. She put the hat—which looked like toilet paper rolls covered in tin foil—back on Miss Alice Paul's head and adjusted the elastic under her chin. Miss Alice Paul felt self-conscious because she knew she hadn't plucked all her whiskers that morning. She couldn't find her tweezers. The girl had stolen them, she was pretty sure.

A woman dressed up as the Statue of Liberty was coming around with Dixie cups filled with ginger ale. "Save this for the toast," she said, every time she put a cup on someone's tray. "Don't drink it yet."

The woman on Miss Alice Paul's left had fallen asleep, and the woman on her right didn't speak English. God only knew what she spoke—gobbledygook, it sounded like.

Miss Alice Paul got up to go to the bathroom.

"Where are you going?" Mrs. Carlson asked.

"To the ladies' room."

"Do you want someone to go with you?"

"No," said Miss Alice Paul.

"Well, hurry back. We don't want you to miss the countdown."

In the bathroom Miss Alice Paul unhitched her garter belt; she thought that pantyhose were somehow morally inferior to stockings. It was nice and quiet. She could hear them counting down outside. The fools. She covered the seat with toilet paper and sat on it, hearing the roar of noon in the cafeteria. Then she urinated as hard as she could, trying to block out their noise with her own.

When the senior citizens had successfully toasted the New Year, Mrs. Carlson closed the shades and dimmed the lights. She clapped her hands for silence and, being the type of woman she was, got it. "Happy New Year!" she shouted, and raised both her arms above her head as if she were a successful political candidate. "Well, we have a special New Year's treat for you. Something nice and romantic and beautiful to watch. I'm happy to introduce Dillon and Deanne, from the Tuxedo Dance Academy, who are going to entertain us with some ballroom dancing."

Dillon and Deanne squeezed through the jungle of tables and wheelchairs and stood in a clearing in the middle of the cafeteria. They smiled and waved to the senior citizens. "Music, maestro," Dillon said, none too enthusiastically.

Mrs. Carlson lowered the needle to a record on the phonograph, which began playing at the wrong speed. Dillon and Deanne laughed and boogied frenetically for a moment, and then began to waltz as the speed was adjusted and the tune of "Auld Lang Syne" became recognizable.

Miss Alice Paul returned from the bathroom to find the cafeteria dark and rearranged. She couldn't find her seat so she stood against the wall. It was snowing out. Two people were dancing in the middle of the room. Miss Alice Paul recognized the woman from the bathroom. She had come in and changed—from a nylon snow suit into a ball gown. She had asked Miss Alice Paul to zip her up. Miss Alice Paul thought she had seen a tattoo on her back, but she could have been mistaken.

They finished dancing; some people applauded. Several in the group had fallen asleep. People always fell asleep when they turned the lights out. That was why they didn't show movies anymore.

"Well," Mrs. Carlson announced, breathlessly, as if she had been dancing herself, "wasn't that beautiful? Poetry in motion, is what I call it! Guess what? Dillon and Deanne have offered to dance with some of us! Let's show them how agile we are. Who'd like to dance?"

Miss Alice Paul was looking out at the snow falling in the parking lot. A bus drew up to the curb and collected a line of people. She was wondering where the bus was going when Dillon appeared at her side and asked her to dance. For a moment she was confused—the snow had been falling with a disorienting richness, like fabric disintegrating in the sky— but then the lights dimmed again and Dillon led her through the tables, and she thought, Do I remember how to dance? She found she did: The motions were all still there some- where, and she moved closer to Dillon and closed her eyes, which helped. She heard Dillon say "You're good," and she felt herself squeezing his arm, a strange, involuntary gesture, and her hand felt the shape of his biceps beneath his coat and held it and Dillon said "Let's try something," and he began to dance more intricately and Miss Alice Paul followed him, her feet articulating a language she thought she had forgotten, and for the first time in ages, she realized she knew what she was doing and she couldn't help laughing a little and Dillon said "Let's dip," and they did; they dipped, and when Miss Alice Paul opened her eyes she found that she and Dillon were the only ones dancing and that everyone was watching them.

No one realized Miss Alice Paul had bolted till Knight called on New Year's Eve, saying she had been picked up at the Bloomington bus station for loitering. Apparently she had gotten on a bus after the nutrition lunch and took it all the way to Bloomington, but once she got there she didn't know what to do. The police found her crying in the station.

No one ever did figure out what exactly had happened, because Miss Alice Paul stopped talking. She also kept her eyes closed most of the time after she came back to Norwell, squeezed tight, as if every moment were a scary scene in a movie.

At first everyone thought she was just mad at them and not talking out of spite, but after a few weeks, when she still hadn't said anything, Topsy called Carleen Dempster, the therapist at the Norwell Mental Health Center. Carleen told Topsy to bring Miss Alice Paul in for a visit, but Miss Alice Paul wouldn't go. She just shook her head when Topsy suggested they go see a friend.

So Carleen made a house call, one night after dinner. While Dominick loaded the dishwasher, Topsy filled her in.

"Now, is she a relation of yours?" Carleen asked. She took out a little spiral notebook and wrote "Miss Alice Paul" on the top of a page.

"No," said Topsy. "She was a friend of my mother's."

"And now she's living with you?"

"Well, when my mother died, there was no place else for her to go. They lived together for about thirty years."

"Doesn't she have family?"

"No."

"Well, now, does she pay rent?"

"No," said Topsy. "She doesn't have any money."

"She has no income? What about Social Security?"

"She doesn't get any."

"What about welfare?"

"No," said Topsy. "She's just an old gentlewoman. She never worked. She was a pink lady for a while, I think, but that's volunteer."

"And she didn't pay rent when she lived with your mother?"

"I don't think so."

"But you're not sure?"

"She just helped out," said Topsy.

"Doing what?"

"I don't know. With the cooking and cleaning, I suppose."

"And she wasn't paid?"

"She wasn't an employee. She was a friend."

"And what about your mother's estate?"

"What about it?"

"Was this Miss Paul recognized by the estate?"

"No, this Miss Paul wasn't."

"So now she's just living off the goodness of your heart?"

"Yes, although she doesn't quite see it that way. She wanted to stay down in Bloomington, in my mother's house. Actually, it belongs to me. I was renting it to my mother."

"And you couldn't rent it to Miss Paul?"

"Like I said, she hasn't got any money."

"Well, who buys her clothes and all?"

"I don't know. She has things. They're all about a hundred years old. I bought her a new winter coat, but she doesn't wear it."

"Well, this sounds real complicated. She should have

been on welfare all along. She must have some money coming to her."

"Well, I told you, she stopped talking. Ever since she came back from Bloomington."

"When did she go to Bloomington?"

"Over New Year's."

"And she hasn't talked since then?"

"No. At least not to me."

"She talked to me," said Dominick. He closed the dishwasher.

"Did she?" asked Topsy. "When?"

"The other night."

"What'd she say?" asked Carleen.

"Well, it was . . . I don't know if I should tell you."

"Course you should," said Topsy. "Why not?"

"She's real sad," said Dominick. "She said she wanted to die. She asked me to run her over with the car."

"Oh, she asked me that, too," said Topsy. "I think that's just a ploy for sympathy."

"Well, you can't be too sure," said Carleen. "How old is she?"

"Well, I'm not sure. My mother was eighty-three, and Miss Alice Paul was about the same age. About that, I'd say."

"And do you want her to continue living here?"

"What do you mean? What can we do?"

"Well, maybe she should be at Heritage Hills."

"I don't think she'd like that," Topsy said.

"Well, let's ask her," said Carleen. "Where is she?"

"She's upstairs. She goes right up after dinner, sits in the dark. It's like she doesn't want to be here at all. Like she just wants to ignore everything."

"Dear oh dear," said Carleen. She followed Topsy up the back stairs. The door to Miss Alice Paul's room was closed. Topsy knocked.

"She won't say 'Come in,' or anything," Topsy said. She opened the door.

Miss Alice Paul was sitting on the bed, one hand braced on either side of her. The room was dark except for some stripes from the porch light. Topsy turned on the overhead light.

"Miss Alice Paul, this is the woman I was telling you about who wants to help you," Topsy said. "Her name is Mrs. Dempster."

Miss Alice Paul sat perfectly still, her eyes closed. Carleen walked over and put one of her hands on top of one of Miss Alice Paul's. Miss Alice Paul drew hers away.

"Hi, Miss Paul," Carleen said. "I'm real glad to meet you."

"Maybe I'll just leave you two alone," Topsy said.

"That'd be just great," said Carleen. "I'll be down in a while."

When Topsy had retreated Carleen turned the light off. "We'll just sit here in the dark," she said. "We don't need that old light, do we? I always did like to sit in the dark. It's real comforting." She sat down on the bed next to Miss Alice Paul and for a while she didn't say anything.

"What a real nice quilt this is," she finally said. "Did you make it?"

Miss Alice Paul didn't respond.

"I took a quilting class at Adult School a couple years ago, but all we ever made were pillows. Mine came out all lumpy. You need such patience to be a good quilter. It's a dying art, you know. It is for sure. 'Cause you see, it was women who did it, and now they're just all doing something else." She paused. "I mean, they all have jobs or something. I like my job, but sometimes I think it would be nice to have the time to do more things with my hands, things like quilting. Or just plain sewing."

Miss Alice Paul seemed to have relaxed a little. It was hard to tell.

"Miss Paul, I don't want to tell you what to do. I mean, I respect you, and if you don't want to talk to me, well, I think that's fine. I mean that. It's fine. But I think you should. I think you should talk to me because I can help you. And things aren't going to get better unless someone helps you. They're going to get worse."

She paused and put her hand back on top of Miss Alice Paul's. Miss Paul folded her hands in her lap. "You don't know the half of it," she said.

"What?" said Carleen. "Excuse me?"

Miss Alice Paul cleared her throat. "I was married once," she said. "And I'm not a widow and I'm not a wife and I'm not a divorcée."

Carleen thought it would be impolite to ask what indeed she was, even though Miss Alice Paul seemed to be waiting for that exact question.

"My marriage was annulled," Miss Alice Paul said. "It was annulled by the court and the Church after twenty-eight days."

"Well, huh," said Carleen, with great interest. And then, when Miss Alice Paul failed to continue she asked, "Why was it annulled?"

"I got married to Thomas Oliver Lippincott, which was not, of course, his real name. He had another wife. She was in a sanatorium up in Saranac, New York. He thought she was going to die of tuberculosis, but she did not die of tuberculosis."

"She got better?" Carleen asked.

Miss Alice Paul nodded her head, once, with vehemence.

"Miss Paul?" Carleen asked.

Miss Alice Paul stood and walked over to her dresser. She took a pin from her pin cushion, which was shaped like a gigantic mutant strawberry. She held it out in the dark, something shiny in her palm, for Carleen to see. "Sara Teasdale gave me this pin," she said. "Do you know of Sara Teasdale?"

"I don't think I do," said Carleen.

"Sara Teasdale was a poet. I met her in New York City, and I admired her brooch, and she gave it to me. She took it off her coat and gave it to me. It's made of agate and amber. She took it off her coat and said, 'If you like it, please do have it.' "

"Wow," said Carleen. "How interesting."

"Do you like it?" Miss Alice Paul asked. She walked back over to the bed, her arm outstretched, and stopped when her hand was in a patch of stray porchlight. A fat bumblebee rested in her palm.

"It's very pretty," said Carleen. "But I don't really wear—"

"Here," said Miss Alice Paul. "If you like it, please do have it."

The girl didn't take the pin. She left it on Miss Alice Paul's dresser. It looked as if it had been flying around the room and landed there. For a moment Miss Alice Paul tried to believe it was a real bee, that she was afraid of it. Then she picked it up and clutched it in her palm. The metal wings bit into her skin, but it wasn't like holding an object. It was like holding a feeling. This is pain, Miss Alice Paul thought. The harder she clutched it, the better it felt.

After a minute she opened her hand to see if her palm was bleeding, but it wasn't. There were just lines, red and calligraphic, like a Chinese character.

"There's a magician in the solarium," the girl said. "How does that sound?"

"What?" asked Miss Alice Paul.

"This afternoon's event is MAGIC. Do you want to go down to the solarium for a magic show?"

"I don't believe in magic," said Miss Alice Paul. "It's all just tricks."

"But they're fun to watch," the girl said. "Don't you think?"

"Why don't you go," suggested Miss Alice Paul, "and tell me all about it?"

"I think you're supposed to go," said the girl. "Your chart says you can go to all events."

"Does it say I must go? Is this Russia?"

"I guess you don't have to. I'll put down you were asleep."

"Don't lie on my account," said Miss Alice Paul. "I can't have that on my conscience."

"Why don't you just come down for a little while? If you don't like it, I'll bring you back up. I promise."

"What's your name?" asked Miss Alice Paul.

"Jane," said the girl.

"All right, Jane," said Miss Alice Paul. "I surrender."

"Good. I should think you'd like to get out of this room."

Miss Alice Paul looked around her hospital room. Since she had broken her ankle, she had been moved from The Lodge, the nicest building in Heritage Hills, into the intermediate care pavilion. She should never have tried to escape out the window at night. Not that she believed her ankle was really broken—she had walked to have it x-rayed. She was sure they had put a cast on her leg and her in a wheelchair and moved her to intermediate care only to keep her immobilized.

The solarium was not accurately named. It was illuminated not by the sun but by long tubes of fluorescent lights. The couches and chairs had, like their inhabitants, found their way to the solarium after what appeared to be long and taxing lives.

The magician, a lady in a green velvet tuxedo, was pouring water into a handkerchief folded to resemble a vase. When the pitcher was empty, she snapped the handkerchief open, revealing nothing but air. She paused for applause, but received none.

Her next trick required a volunteer, and she was vainly seeking one when Jane appeared beside Miss Alice Paul's wheelchair. "You've got a visitor," she said.

"A visitor?" asked Miss Alice Paul. "Who?"

"A friend," said Jane. "A boy. He's waiting in your room. I'll bring you up."

It was a boy: the boy. He was standing by the window, looking out, when Miss Alice Paul was wheeled in.

"I'll leave you two alone," Jane said. "Have a nice visit."

"Hi, Miss Alice Paul," the boy said. "Remember me?"

"Of course," she said. But she couldn't think of his name. He was just the boy. There had been the boy, and the girl, and the two ladies. The crazy one and the mean one. She had always liked the boy the best.

"I'm Dominick," he said, as if he knew she didn't know his name.

"Of course, Dominick," Miss Alice Paul said. "It's nice of you to come. Sit down."

He went to sit on her bed but then he noticed the bars were up, so he sat on the windowsill. He nodded out the window. "I was outside cutting the grass and I thought I'd come in and see you. See how you are. I haven't seen you in a while."

"No," said Miss Alice Paul.

"What happened to your foot?"

"They tell me it's broken."

"How did it happen?"

"An accident," said Miss Alice Paul.

"Does it hurt?"

"I don't feel it," said Miss Alice Paul. She looked at her foot, which was extended straight out in front of her, like a sword. She had forgotten about her feet. They were so far away from the rest of her. She had lost interest in them. Every other Thursday, she was lined up with the other residents, barefoot, in the corridor, and a podiatrist, who sat on a little rolling platform, scooted down the row, his head bowed over their gnarled, naked feet, trimming their toenails. Like Jesus washing the apostles' feet.

"It took me a while to find you," Dominick said. "This is a big place."

"Well, I used to be over there." Miss Alice Paul started to wave toward The Lodge, but then she realized she had no idea where it was. "But they moved me because of my foot. It was nicer over there."

"Maybe you'll get moved back," Dominick said.

"Maybe," said Miss Alice Paul. "I doubt it."

"Oh," said Dominick. He sounded disappointed.

"How are you?" asked Miss Alice Paul. "You said you were cutting grass?"

"Yes," said Dominick. "I have a job cutting grass. All over the county."

"That sounds . . . interesting," Miss Alice Paul said.

"Not really," said Dominick. "But it's nice to be outdoors."

"How's school?" asked Miss Alice Paul.

"It's over. I graduated. I start college in the fall."

"Where are you going?"

"Indiana University. Bloomington."

"I used to live in Bloomington," said Miss Alice Paul.

"I know," said Dominick. "With Aunt Gran."

Rose. If only Rose hadn't died.

"What will you study?"

"I'm not sure."

"What do you want to do?" She almost added, when you grow up, but she stopped herself.

Dominick shrugged. "I don't know."

"How's your sister?"

"Good. At least I think. She moved to California."

"To be a movie star?"

"No," said Dominick.

"What does she want to do?"

"She's not sure," said Dominick.

What unmotivated children, Miss Alice Paul thought. They'll get nowhere.

"And your mother?" she asked, thinking, I'll ask about the mother, but I won't ask about the grandmother. I'll be damned if I ask after her.

"She's O.K." He stood up. "I should get back to work," he said. "I just wanted to stop by."

"It was very kind of you," said Miss Alice Paul. "I'm sorry I can't offer you anything to eat."

"That's O.K.," said Dominick. "I just had lunch."

"Well, it was so nice of you to come."

Dominick smiled. "It was nice to see you," he said. "I've been thinking about you." He paused in the door. "Maybe I'll come again, before I leave for school."

"Please do," said Miss Alice Paul. "If you find the time."

"Is there anything you need? I could maybe bring you something."

"Oh, no," said Miss Alice Paul. She gestured around her little room. "I have everything I need right here. I'm quite . . . fine. But thank you."

"So long," said Dominick. "Take care."

"Good-bye," said Miss Alice Paul. He went out into the hall, apparently the wrong way, because he reappeared, walking in the opposite direction. He smiled at her, waved, was gone.

After a moment she tried to move her chair over to the window so she could watch him come out the front. But the girl had put the brake on, and she couldn't release it. She pulled with all her might but it wouldn't budge. Damn it, she thought. Damn it to hell.

Departing

Marian was far enough away from the two men to suggest, rather than guarantee, their privacy. Robert lay in the sun on the lawn; Lyle sat nearby in an Adirondack chair in the shade. Marian—their hostess—sat nearer the river, painting with a child's watercolor set. She dunked the tiny brush into a goblet of water that stood on the grass beside her.

It was a lovely yard to sit in, and to paint, although Marian's painting was not a success: the colors in the tiny compact were all wrong. They were intense and synthetic, and her attempts to mix them on the paper to suggest the sun-stunned colors around her had only muddied them. But the scene itself was lovely: the old stone house and the long lawn, studded with trees, that sloped down between high unkempt hedges toward the river.

"Take you, for instance," Marian heard Robert say to Lyle. "You look better now than you did at thirty."

"Am better looking," corrected—and conceded—Lyle. "But how do you know? You didn't know me when I was thirty."

"Marian showed me a picture," said Robert. "Of you and Tony in Egypt."

"Oh," said Lyle, "did she?"

Marian glanced up from her painting and found that Lyle was looking over at her. He made a face. "How's the painting?" he called. Robert turned his head.

"It's a mess," she said. And then, as if such a judgment precluded its continuation, she ripped the thick, damp page from the pad and crumpled it up.

Lyle had brought the paints for Roland, his godson, the child of Marian and John. John was working in the garden beyond the hedge. Every so often they could hear him whistling, talking, or singing to himself. John enjoyed being alone on the other side of the hedge. He spent most of the summer there. Lyle was an old friend of John and Marian's and had spent countless weekends at their house with Tony, his lover. Last summer Tony had died. Lyle had been solitary and despondent all winter and spring, and everyone had urged him to get out and meet people, but no one had expected him to meet someone so quickly—especially someone as young and as unlike Tony as was Robert.

"I wanted to see it," said Lyle. He meant her painting.

"I'll do another," Marian said. "I'll do one of you two." She moved her chair and in doing so overturned the goblet. "That was careless," she said.

"I'll fill it up," said Robert. He stood and crossed the lawn.

She handed him the glass. "Thank you," she said. She expected him to walk up to the spigot beside the back stoop, but instead he walked toward the river. Of course, she thought, Robert's a stranger here: he doesn't know where the spigot is. She knew this did not make him inferior in any way but she had an urge to think so. Stop it, she told herself. She watched him squat on a rock at the river's edge, dip the glass, and return. The water was much clearer than she had imagined. It was clear, seen a glass at a time; only all together was it opaque.

"Now go lie down," she said, "and pretend I'm not here."

Robert resumed his position, but Lyle had stood up.

"Sit down," said Marian. "I'm going to paint you."

Lyle frowned at her, and she understood that he did not wish to be painted with Robert. She wondered if she had once painted Lyle and Tony. She must have, although she did not remember.

"I feel in desperate need of a nap," Lyle said. Marian and Robert watched him walk toward, and into, the house.

"I don't know how he can be tired," said Robert. "We've just lay about all day."

Lain about, Marian wanted to say, but then she remembered that Robert was young and not properly educated, so she said, "Sometimes indolence can be exhausting." She sat down in Lyle's vacant chair. She felt she should offer to paint Robert but she didn't really want to. His back, which had appeared smooth and brown from a distance, was actually, she now realized, mottled by acne scars.

"I thought Lyle brought those for Roland," Robert said, nodding at the paints.

"He did," said Marian, "but Roland is a baby. Lyle is a loving, but inattentive, godfather."

"I didn't know Lyle was Roland's godfather."

"Yes," said Marian. Tony as well, she thought.

"Lyle said he wanted Roland to be an artist. That's why he bought the paints."

"If only it were that easy," said Marian. "Or rather, thank God it's not."

"What do you want him to be?"

Roland was eleven months old and sickly. Marian wanted him to be alive the next morning. She avoided the question by asking, "Do you like children?"

Robert flipped a few pages of the magazine. "I like their hands," he said. "And feet."

Marian found this answer unnerving. It was as if she had asked him what part of the chicken he preferred. She looked away for a moment, trying to think of an appropriate response. None came to mind. "How old are you?" she asked.

"Twenty-four," said Robert. He looked at her. "I was twenty-four in June. How old are you?"

"Thirty-eight," said Marian.

"Ages are fascinating," said Robert.

He wants me to ask why, thought Marian, but I don't want to hear him tell me. It is something he has read in a book. "Where did you and Lyle meet?" she asked. She, at least, would be direct.

"At an ACT UP meeting," said Robert.

"I didn't know Lyle was going to ACT UP meetings."

"He just went to one," said Robert.

"And are you very involved? Do you go to those demonstrations?"

"Yes," said Robert. "Sometimes."

"I think it's all so terribly important, what ACT UP is doing," Marian said.

This comment was followed by an awkward silence, which Marian interrupted by saying, "I'd better check on Roland."

"Of course," said Robert, but in a way that let Marian know he knew she wanted to be away from him.

"We're so happy you're here," she said.

"So am I," said Robert.

"And we're happy to see you with Lyle," said Marian. "We're happy about that."

Robert did not respond to this comment.

"What are you doing this summer?" Marian asked. "Lyle told me you were an actor."

"Actually, I'm a painter. But I have a job."

"Really? Where?"

"As a waiter. In an Indian restaurant."

"Are you Indian?"

"Half," said Robert. "My father was Indian."

"Was?"

"Is. He lives in India."

"Do you see him?"

Robert thought for a moment, as if this question required contemplation. "No," he said. "I haven't in a while. I don't think he likes how I've turned out."

"Oh," said Marian, "that you're an actor?"

"I'm really a waiter," said Robert. "I meant he doesn't like that I'm gay."

"What a shame," said Marian.

"Would you be happy if Roland was gay?"

"Happy? Well, yes, I suppose. If he were happy."

"But you wouldn't be happy first. You'd wait for him to be happy and then be happy?"

"Actually, to tell you the truth," said Marian, "this isn't something I've given any thought to. Roland isn't even a year old. It seems a bit premature."

"Of course," said Robert. And then, after a moment, he added, "I'm sorry."

"There's no need to apologize," said Marian.

They were silent a moment. A bee alit on the lip of Marian's glass of river water, and they both observed it. She waved it away. "I'd better go check on him," she said. "We'll be eating about eight, so if you get hungry before then please help yourself to anything you can find. There's lots of fruit in the kitchen."

"Thank you," said Robert.

Robert fell asleep on the lawn, his face pressed against the magazine he had been reading, so that when he awoke, he found the page blurred. Some of the ink had rubbed off, forming a smudged, moist tattoo on his cheek. He walked up to the house. There was a large bowl of fruit on the kitchen table. He ate a peach, sucked the juice from his fingers, and went upstairs.

He passed a room where Marian sat in a rocking chair before an open window nursing Roland. They both seemed to be asleep. Roland had slipped off Marian's nipple but he worked his mouth nevertheless. Robert continued walking down the hall, thinking that every room he passed might reveal a similarly transporting sight, like a museum in a dream. At the end of the hall and down a few steps was the room he and Lyle were sharing. Robert pushed open the door, bowed his head beneath the low door frame, and entered.

Lyle was sleeping naked on the bed. The strong afternoon light infused itself through the peony-patterned curtains drawn across the windows. Robert sat on the bed. Lyle's back was sweating; Robert resisted the urge to bend over and lick it. Most of his urges concerning Lyle were resisted. He traced the indentation of Lyle's spine down into the tight valley of his buttocks. This motion, though intended to, did not rouse Lyle. And then Robert realized that Lyle was awake, and pretending to sleep: a telltale skein of tension appeared across his shoulders. Robert removed his hand. He stood beside the bed for a moment, looking down at Lyle, who continued to feign sleep. An insect could be heard but not seen in the room. Robert left the room. He went outside and stood in the front yard for a moment, and then walked up the long dirt driveway. It was a communal driveway, with tributaries leading to other houses, which, Robert supposed, made it technically a road. But it had the feel of a driveway. The paved road it adjoined was surprisingly heavily traveled. The cars went by quickly and noisily, blowing up hot storms of wind and dust as they passed. Robert turned around, but instead of walking back along the driveway he veered into the woods.

———

Lyle was lying on the bed, thinking of Tony, when he heard Robert come into the room. He closed his eyes. I just need a moment to compose myself, he thought. A moment. He felt Robert sit beside him, felt Robert's fingers touch and descend his back. Robert is amorous, he thought. It is both a delight and a burden. Tony would have come into the hot, still room and lay down without a word. On the other bed. But Tony is dead, Lyle told himself. It was something he told himself repeatedly and yet it never ceased to have an effect, an incessant paparazzi flash that followed him everywhere. Tony is dead and so now I am in this room with Robert. With Robert who is standing up. Who's leaving.

Lyle lay on the bed for a while, trying to think something clear and definite, but everything his mind touched seemed to lack a necessary, focusing dimension. Except for *Tony is dead*. He put on his bathing suit and a T-shirt and a pair of sandals and went downstairs. He walked out the back door and down the lawn, through a chink in the hedge, and into the garden. John was doing something fierce with a hoe: thrusting it into the ground, wriggling it, and removing it. Lyle stood outside the gate for a moment, watching John, and then he said, "You're such a hard worker. You put the rest of us to shame."

John poked the hoe into the ground and turned around. He wiped his brow with the back of his hand. "You don't really mean that," he said.

"I think you're a hard worker."

"I meant the shame part," said John. "You were never one to be intimidated by physical labor."

"I suppose not," said Lyle. "Yet one feels one should. It is so much more evident than mental labor."

John sensed a complicated conversation he had no energy for. "I'm ready for a swim," he said.

"Good," said Lyle. "So am I."

They began to walk down toward the river. "I like Robert," John said. "He seems nice."

"Yes," said Lyle. "He is nothing if not nice."

"What does that mean?" asked John, irritably, for he wanted to talk directly, and that was something Lyle sometimes had to be coaxed into doing.

Lyle sensed his impatience. "I'm doing a terrible thing."

"What?" asked John.

"I am . . . I have no business being with Robert. I'm not ready."

"How do you know?"

"I know," said Lyle. "Being here makes it awfully clear. It was very sweet of Marian to give us another room, but still. Being here with you and Marian, in summer, it's just . . . I feel as if I'm betraying Tony."

"That's to be expected," said John. They had reached the bank of the river. A slender wooden pier extended itself into the water. They walked to the end of it, carefully avoiding the planks that had lost their grips.

"I should stop seeing him," said Lyle.

"Why?"

"It isn't right. It isn't fair."

"Do you like being with him?"

"Yes," said Lyle. "I do."

"And it's obvious he enjoys being with you."

Lyle shrugged. John unlaced his sneakers and took off his shorts and underwear. He stood for a moment, naked, his toes curled around the edge of the final plank. John liked people but did not enjoy talking to them about their personal lives. It had always seemed to him an odd thing to talk about. Besides, he was no good at it. So he reached out and touched Lyle's shoulder. "Relax," he said. "That's why you're here." He dove into the river. He didn't resurface until the stain of his entrance had been absorbed. He had swum out very far.

Lyle considered for a moment shedding his bathing suit, but did not. His dive was less exact.

Robert came out of the woods onto the bank of the river. Lyle and John were swimming out in the middle. Or not swimming—treading water, being slowly carried downstream with the current. Robert stood for a moment, watching them, wondering what to do. Should he call out? Should he join them? Or should he disappear back into the woods? That would be the easiest thing, he thought, the weakest, the most characteristic of me. But once he realized that, he could not do it without shaming himself, so he took off his clothes and waded out into the river. He held his arms up in the air and felt the chill ascend his body. The mud was slimy and unpleasant beneath his feet. He dove into the water with enough noise and force so that when he surfaced both John and Lyle were looking toward him. He tried to wave at them while he swam but the movement was awkward. He was a mediocre swimmer and the distance to them was greater than he had thought. He arrived at their side breathless.

"There you are," said Lyle, as if John and he had been searching the river for him.

"I went for a walk," Robert said, between gasps, "and then saw you swimming. So I joined you."

"Good idea," said John.

"It's beautiful," said Robert.

They were all three silent for a moment. Robert had the feeling he had interrupted something. "I think I'll swim to the other side," he said.

"You'd better get your breath back first," said John.

"I'm fine," said Robert. "It's just the cold that makes me pant." He began swimming to the opposite shore. When he turned around, John and Lyle were swimming toward the house. Robert floated on his back and watched them get out of the water and stand on the dock. They waved at him to return, but he purposely misinterpreted their gesture and waved back. He waited until they were walking up the lawn before he began swimming to where he had left his clothes. The sun had sunk behind the trees, and the water, luminous moments ago, was now dark.

Lyle was waiting for him, sitting in a lawn chair carefully placed on the one small ragged patch of sun that remained. "How was your swim?" he asked.

"Good," said Robert.

"I didn't know you were such a swimmer."

Robert didn't know what to say. He was not a swimmer. It had been a miserable swim. He felt for a moment like crying. Lyle reached up and touched one of Robert's nipples, which was shriveled with cold. "How about a hot shower?" he asked. "It's time to get ready for dinner."

Upstairs, in the bedroom, Robert shut the door. Lyle sat on the bed. Robert came over and knelt on the floor, placing his face on Lyle's lap, on his damp bathing suit. It smelled of the river, and, more faintly, of Lyle. He could see Lyle's hand poised on the peony-patterned bedspread. He picked it up and placed it on top of his own head. Lyle held it still for a moment, and then began to sift his fingers through Robert's hair.

Birds had inhabited the garden John had deserted, pecking at the moist, upset earth.

Robert, showered and dressed for dinner, opened the door to the back staircase, which descended from the upstairs hall to the kitchen, and heard Marian's voice.

"What do you think of him?" she was saying.

"He seems nice," said John. "Young."

"I don't like him," said Marian.

"Why not?"

"He's . . . there's something prickly about him."

"Well, it must be awkward for him. Coming here, and us being so close to Lyle. And having been so close to Tony."

"I understand that. I mean apart from that. There's just something about—I hate young people who are judgmental. Who observe you and judge you and think they know better. He's like that, I can tell."

"But you're judging him."

"Well, of course. I mean, everyone judges everybody. You can't help but form impressions. But you can be—well, tactful. I don't think he's very tactful."

"He seems tactful enough to me."

"It's not tact, then. It's something more contrary. I don't know what it is. I just sense it."

"Well, it's nice to see Lyle with someone again."

"He's all wrong for Lyle. It won't last."

"Of course it won't last. That's why you should be nice to him. It's just something Lyle's going through, part of his healing."

"It just makes me miss Tony so dreadfully."

"We all miss Tony. Do you mean for this to boil?"

"Oh no, darling. Turn it down."

Robert closed the door. He waited there for Lyle, and they went downstairs together.

There was a guest for dinner—an older, glamorous woman named Rosa Ponti. She drove up the driveway in her little red sports car and pulled onto the lawn, parking in front of the house, as if she were in a commercial for automobiles.

They ate outside beneath a big tree. Roland slept in a basket. Terra-cotta pots held sweating bottles of white wine. Their talk was general and convivial. When the meal was finished, Marian stood up and began stacking plates. "Let me help you," said Robert, standing up as well.

"No, no," said Marian. "Sit down."

John and Lyle and Rosa Ponti were seated. Rosa was smoking a thin brown cigarette, exhaling drifts of smoke over her shoulder into the darkness. "No," said Robert. "I'll help." He wanted to hurt Marian in some way, and helping her when she did not want help was the best way he knew how. They carried the dishes up the terraced steps to the house. Lanterns glowed in the tumbled pachysandra. They paused at the kitchen door, both with their hands full. "Here," said Robert, shifting his load, reaching out for the door. He dropped a plate on the bricks. The sound of it smashing seemed very loud.

"Oh no," he said. "I'm sorry."

"Just get the door," said Marian. "It's nothing. No— don't try to pick it up. I'll get the broom."

John appeared behind them. He opened the door and took some dishes from them. Robert heard Rosa laughing at something Lyle had said down in the garden.

They piled the dishes in the sink. The light in the kitchen seemed unusually bright and artificial after the candlelit gloom of the backyard. Robert began to rinse the plates un- der the tap but Marian said, "Leave them, please. Join the others."

"Are you sure I can't help?"

"I'll give you a shout when I'm ready with the dessert," said Marian. She actually pushed him a little.

Back at the table Rosa Ponti was drawing the floor plan of the apartment she had just bought in Lucca on a blank page of her Filofax. Then she drew another of how the apart- ment would be when the renovation was complete. The floor, she announced, would be sheathed in anodized aluminum.

Marian came down the steps sideways, balancing a large platter to one side of her. Everyone stopped talking and watched her descent, as if she were a Ziegfeld girl. She waited for Rosa to remove her sketch, and then lay the platter on the middle of the table. A pyramid of lacy, nearly transparent cookies was surrounded by grapes. The grapes were red, their underbellies flushed lime green.

Robert could feel Lyle's bare foot caressing the muscle of his calf beneath the table, but Lyle was not looking at him. He was smoking one of Rosa Ponti's cigarettes, and in the way he held and inhaled the cigarette Robert could tell he had once been a smoker. Robert watched Lyle smoke, his arm extended along the back of Rosa Ponti's chair, inches from her bare neck. He was not flirting, Robert knew, but simply being charming.

Robert reached out and tugged at a bunch of grapes, plucking one from its thin stem, so that just a touch of its moist insides remained behind on the stalk.

"Oh, darling, here," said Marian. She picked up a pair of tiny scissors and held them toward Robert. They glowed in the candlelight.

Robert put a grape into his mouth, and held it there, intact. He was confused.

Lyle removed his hand from the back of Rosa Ponti's chair and took the scissors from Marian. "You use these to cut a small bunch of grapes," he said to Robert, "instead of yanking them off one by one." He demonstrated this phenomenon, and then held the scissors toward Robert.

Robert did not take the scissors.

"Oh, don't tame him!" cried Rosa Ponti. "Let him be free! Let us all be free of these stupid affectations!" She grabbed the scissors from Lyle and flung them over her shoulder.

Everyone was silent for a moment, and the drone of the insects and the chafe of the leaves in the trees, which hovered above them in great dark clouds, were suddenly evident. Rosa Ponti laughed a little, but to herself. She pushed back her chair, got up, and retrieved the scissors from where they had fallen on the lawn. She placed them on the table. Everyone looked at them. They were lovely: gold, their loops a trellis engraved with vines.

Marian picked them up. "They were my grandmother's," she said.

Soon thereafter the party dispersed. Marian and Roland disappeared upstairs, John and Rosa Ponti did the washing up, and Lyle and Robert went for a walk along the river.

When the lights of the house had disappeared behind them, Robert said, "John and Marian think I'm all wrong for you."

"No, they don't," said Lyle, who was walking a few steps behind Robert. He held his hand out a ways in front of him, for he was having trouble seeing in the darkness. Robert, judging by how fast he was walking, was not.

"Yes, they do," said Robert.

"Do you mean about the scissors? That was just Marian being Marian."

"I don't mean about the scissors. I heard them talking and saying they didn't like me and they don't think I'm right for you and that we won't last."

Lyle took this opportunity to stop walking and said, rather stupidly, "What? Were you eavesdropping?"

"Yes," said Robert.

"Where? When?"

"At the top of the stairs. Before dinner."

"You shouldn't have been."

"Why?"

"Because it's wrong. It's impolite."

"Like eating grapes without scissors?"

"No," said Lyle. "That's different."

"How is it different?"

"That's culturally impolite, while eavesdropping is— well, the impoliteness is more intrinsic."

"How can something be intrinsically impolite?"

"Some things can. Like murder."

"But I didn't murder anyone. I just opened a door and overheard a conversation."

"I wish you hadn't listened."

"I'm sure you do. But I did."

"Well, you shouldn't take to heart what you weren't meant to hear. That's a good rule."

"I think just the opposite. I think things you weren't meant to hear are often the most important. Nobody tells you things directly."

"So you're going to make a big deal out of this?"

"Mentioning it is making a big deal?"

Lyle considered for a moment. "No, I suppose not. But can't we just forget it?"

"We? You can."

"And you?"

"Why should I?"

"Because what's the point of dwelling on it? What good does that achieve?"

"I hate when you do this," said Robert.

"Do what?" said Lyle.

"Make things into a debate."

"We're just talking," said Lyle. "It isn't a debate."

"Then talk to me," said Robert. "What do you think?"

"About what?"

"About what Marian said. Do you think I'm right for you? Do you think we'll last?"

"I think it's a bit premature to think in those terms." Lyle wished there were a place to sit down. Mostly he wished to be back at the house and helping with the cleaning up. He could picture the bright kitchen, the plates stacked in the sink, and Rosa Ponti and John laughing. "I think," he said, carefully picking his way among words, like a cat walking through wet grass, "I think that at this point in my life, no one is right for me. In fact I doubt that I'll ever find anyone who is right for me again."

"Was Tony right for you?"

Lyle looked out at the river. This is what I deserve, he thought, for getting involved with a twenty-four-year-old: discussions about Mr. Right.

"Was he?" Robert insisted.

Right? thought Lyle. At moments Tony had been right, but then he had been wrong, too. But at moments it had hurt, and it hurt more now, when he was dead, how right Tony had been, for it had been a rightness that seemed to preclude all others; a rightness that had staked its territories in Lyle's heart, had followed his rivers to their sources, and left flags there, high in the uncharted parts of him. "Yes," he said. "In some ways, Tony was right."

"And I'm not."

"I didn't say that. I don't know yet. I've only known you a short time. I think this whole conversation is foolish."

"But if you had to guess."

"I would never want to guess about something as important as that."

"But if you had to. If I made you."

Lyle was still looking at the river. "I would guess no," he said.

"And what?" said Robert. "I'm supposed to just stay here and . . . bleed?"

"You are not bleeding."

"I feel like I'm bleeding. Like what's me, the inside liquid part of me, is oozing out. Like I'm losing myself."

"You're just being melodramatic," said Lyle. "You're not losing yourself. In fact, I doubt very much that you've even found yourself yet."

"I hate that worst of all," said Robert. "I hate when someone else tells you what's happening inside yourself."

"Then you should be careful what you tell people. Especially when you articulate your hurts."

They stood there for a moment.

"I'm going," said Robert.

"Wait," said Lyle. "I'll come back with you."

"No," said Robert. "I'm not going back to the house."

"Where are you going?"

"I'm going home," said Robert.

"And how are you getting there?"

"I'll walk. I'll walk to the train station and take a train."

"The train station is ten miles from here. And I doubt very much the trains run this late."

"I have no problem walking ten miles. And I have no problem waiting for a train."

"Come back to the house," said Lyle. "And we'll leave first thing in the morning."

"No," said Robert. "I'm leaving now." He began to walk into the dark woods purposefully, as if a trail were clearly marked to the railroad station.

Lyle tried to make himself call out, or follow, but did neither. It had been wrong to bring Robert here. He had done it because he thought it might have worked. There was a way, he felt, that things between them could succeed, but it was not a way that included weekends at John and Marian's. It was a strange way more difficult than that. And standing alone in the woods, Lyle felt old and tired and not inclined toward difficulty. In fact, he realized, at the very moment, he felt inclined toward nothing at all.

Sunday evening Marian drove Lyle to the station. The light had gone stark, and was attacking the trees with a clarity that suggested autumn. Yet it was midsummer.

In the parking lot Lyle went to get out of the car but Marian touched his arm and said, "No. Stay a minute."

Lyle closed the door. Marian dusted the steering wheel with her middle finger, round and round, and then looked at it: clean. "I feel so . . . awful," she said.

"Why?" asked Lyle.

"I feel it was my fault," said Marian.

"It wasn't," said Lyle. "I told you. It was something between us. It had nothing to do with you."

"But when you arrived you were both so happy."

"Yes," said Lyle. "But it wasn't you."

"I wasn't nice to him," said Marian.

Lyle said nothing. He looked down the empty curve of track, but there was no train.

"I don't know if I like him or not," said Marian. She was talking to the steering wheel. "I mean, to be honest, I don't think I do. But it wasn't about him, how I was behaving. How awful I was."

"What was it about?" asked Lyle.

Marian looked at him as if he were simple. "It was about Tony," she said. "It was about you and Tony."

"Oh," said Lyle. "Yes."

"I couldn't allow myself to be nice to him, I was awful to him, I drove him away, I did it, I know I did, and it's unforgivable. It is."

"I think the train is coming," said Lyle.

"Will you invite him back?" Marian asked. "Make him come. And we'll have a really lovely weekend, I promise, it will just be very relaxed and . . . lovely."

"He won't come," said Lyle. He opened the door, and stepped out of the car.

"But ask him," said Marian. "Promise you will. Or should I call him? Why don't you give me his number and I'll call him?"

"Let me talk to him first," said Lyle. He closed the door.

"Call me," said Marian. "As soon as you have."

"I will," said Lyle.

"Promise," said Marian.

The train was just pulling in. Lyle hurried up the stairs to the platform. There was an overpass above the tracks, and Marian watched him run across it, and descend the stairs on the other side, where she lost sight of him behind the arriving, and then departing, train.

Just Relax

It all started at the airport. My mother had promised to pick me up, but she wasn't there. Then I was informed that the airline had lost my luggage somewhere between Zaire and New York, and right after I finished filling out a three-page claim form my younger sister, Daria, and her boyfriend, Charles, appeared and told me that my mother had become a performance artist and sold her apartment, and that I could stay with them for ten days, and after that I'd have to find my own place or go to L.A. and live with my father. Then Charles and Daria had a fight about how to get home from the airport: Daria wanted to take a cab, but Charles thought we should take some special express bus. They were so angry at each other that Daria got in a cab and Charles got on the bus, and before I could get in either they were both gone. I met an Argentine businessman, and we shared a cab back to the city; halfway there he asked the cabbie to pull over, and in the parking lot of a mall in Queens he and the cabbie snorted coke the man had just smuggled into the country. It was then that I started missing the Peace Corps.

The coked-up businessman got out of the cab at the Waldorf Astoria. He invited me up to his room, but I told him

I had contracted a disease in Africa and been sent home to die. I gave the driver Daria's address and we headed downtown. He dropped me off on a very odd street. It was made of cobblestones, and it didn't have any cars parked on it, or sidewalks. None of the doors was numbered, and they weren't normal, friendly looking doors: They were steel doors with no handles or anything on them, the kind you can only open from inside. I was about to go find another taxi—I hadn't figured out where I was going to ask it to take me—when one of the doors opened and Daria and Charles walked out.

They had changed. They were obviously dressed to go out someplace fancy. Daria saw me standing in the street and said, "Oh, Lainie, great, we left a message on our machine telling you to meet us at Minnie's, but now you can just come with us. You probably never would have found it yourself, anyway."

"Who's Minnie?" I asked.

"Who's Minnie?" Charles laughed. "I know you've been in Africa, but really, Elaine. Who's Minnie?"

"Minnie's is a restaurant," Daria said. "Charles, go fetch a cab."

Charles, apparently chastened, looked down at his shoes for a moment—they were patent leather cowboy boots—and then trotted up to the corner.

Daria waited till he was out of earshot before she spoke. "I'm sorry about the airport," she said. "I know you probably think I behaved terribly, but this is a new relationship, and I think it's important to stick up for yourself right from the start, otherwise things just get so helplessly spastic. . . ."

"Do you think I could use your bathroom before we go anywhere? And shouldn't I change?"

Daria, who had been watching Charles's receding back, looked at me. "Well, you do look awful," she sighed. "We'll run up and see what we can do."

At Minnie's we found Charles sitting at a table on its own little platform, drinking a glass of champagne. Most of the tables were on their own platforms, so walking across the restaurant was a sickening experience: You kept going up a few steps, then down a few.

"Oh, champagne," squealed Daria, helping herself to a glass. "What a good idea." She kissed Charles. Charles grinned and raised his glass.

"Cheers," he said. "To a new career." He turned to me. "Welcome home, Elaine."

Even though I didn't have a glass of champagne or a new career, I thought this was awfully sweet of Charles, so I just smiled and lifted my water glass.

"Charles, you jerk, give her some champagne!" Daria said. She hit his still upraised arm, spilling some of the peach-colored liquid.

"Oh, sorry," Charles said. He reached into the bucket, extracted the dripping bottle, and poured me a glass.

"Don't you want to know what my new career is?" Daria asked.

"Oh," I said. "I thought . . ."

"No, no, guess," Daria said. "I bet she can't guess," she said to Charles.

After she was graduated from college, Daria had gotten a job as an assistant buyer at Bloomingdale's. The last I had heard, she was manager of Men's Notions: umbrellas, wallets, and sunglasses.

"Are you still at Bloomingdale's?" I asked.

"God, no," said Daria. "Really."

"Look at her face," said Charles. "It shows on her face."

I looked at Daria's face. She was flushed, and I noticed her eyebrows were unnaturally bushy and dark. Had they been dyed?

"Are you an actress?"

"Close," said Daria. "A model. I've already done two shows. One was a designer showcase."

"She wore underwear," said Charles.

"It wasn't underwear," said Daria. "It just kind of looked like underwear."

"Are you tall enough to be a model?" I asked.

"Well, not really. But it's mostly in how you carry yourself, how you move. I move very well. They're very excited about the way I move."

"Have you told Mom?"

"It was her idea. This guy who is acting as her manager also books models, and she showed him a picture of me, and we all had dinner, and he got me the shows. The first one was a little skeevy—they still haven't paid me—but the second show was completely legit. I got five hundred dollars, and they had a big buffet. Caviar. Everything."

In the ladies' room, Daria filled me in on Charles. She had met him at Bloomingdale's, when he special-ordered a sharkskin wallet. He was only nineteen, but he was very rich, and he wanted to be an actor.

Daria was applying black lipstick with a little paintbrush, peering into the mirror. I was standing next to the sink, my back against the cool tile wall. The floor and ceiling were made of mirrors, so I felt like I was floating. I was starting to feel jet-lagged, and trying to remember the last time I slept.

"Do you like Charles?" Daria asked. She looked at me in the mirror.

"I'm not sure," I said. "He seems pleasant."

"Pleasant?" Daria said. "Pleasant? Well, that's a new concept."

"Can we go home soon?" I asked. "I'm a little exhausted."

"Oh, take one of these," Daria said. She opened her bag and took out an aqua pill. "They gave us these before the show. They animate you. They aren't harmful."

"How do you know?" I asked.

"How do I know?" Daria gave me a despairing look. "Elaine, just look at me," she said. "Do I look harmed?"

We were dancing at some club. Or rather: Daria and Charles and a boy with aluminum foil gym shorts and no shirt were dancing together, and I was sitting on a chair that was shaped like a hand, sitting in the palm and leaning back against the fingers. The pill Daria had given me was having an odd effect. I kept forgetting I was myself, drifting off somewhere, only to suddenly find I was back in the hand chair. This was not completely unpleasant.

Charles and Daria trotted off the dance floor, leaving the blond boy dancing alone. He didn't seem to notice.

"Is that your beer?" Daria asked. She pointed to a Rolling Rock on the table—a little, upturned hand—next to my chair. It was half full.

"No," I said.

Daria picked it up, looked at it, then drank from it. She handed it to Charles.

"This is disgusting," he said. Nevertheless, he took a slug and offered it to me. I declined.

"Charles wants to go to Mars," Daria said. "But I want to go to Des Moines. You decide."

"Can't we just go home?" I asked.

"Home?" asked Charles, as if this were the name of some new club he hadn't yet heard of.

"But Lainie, this is your first night in New York. We wanted to make it special."

"It's been very special," I said. "I'd just like to go home."

"I suppose we could go home," said Charles, turning the idea over in his mind.

Daria took the beer bottle from him and finished it. "All right," she said. "If it's what you really want. We'll go home. But we'll stop on the way for breakfast: French Toast! Eggs Benni!"

The next morning, while Charles and Daria went to an acting class for models, I began my job search. I went out to get a newspaper, but I got stuck in the elevator. I couldn't get it to move. After about twenty minutes it started to ascend on its own accord. It stopped, and the door opened. A woman stood there with a little piggy-looking dog on a leash.

"Are you going down?" she asked.

"I'm trying to," I said. "I don't know how to work this."

The woman gave me an unfriendly look and got in the elevator. She cranked some strange handle and the elevator started to descend none too smoothly. The dog stood on the floor, snorting, and looking up at me.

"What kind of dog is that?"

"What?" the woman said.

I repeated my question.

"This dog?" the woman said, pointing to the dog, as if there were several in the elevator.

"Yes," I said.

"A bull terrier."

The elevator landed with a thud and the woman opened the gates. We were about a foot below the main floor. I stepped up and out, and so did the woman, but the dog stayed in the elevator.

"Spanky, I'm not going to pick you up," the woman said. She pulled on the leash and dragged Spanky out of the elevator. This experience didn't seem to help his breathing problem.

"Is there a paper store around here?" I asked the woman.

"A paper store?"

"To buy a newspaper? I'm looking for a job."

"Well, the last place I'd look is in a newspaper. Don't you have any connections?"

"Not really," I said. "I just got out of the Peace Corps."

"What's that?" the woman asked.

"You've never heard of the Peace Corps?"

"Is it a band?"

"No," I said. "It's this program whereby Americans are sent to help people in developing nations."

"Help them with what?"

"Different things. I helped people in Africa on a cooperative farm."

Spanky started to eat a Coke can that was lying in the gutter.

"You don't want a dog, do you?" the woman asked. "This was my ex-boyfriend's dog. The meanest thing he ever did to me was leave Spanky. Actually, it was probably the meanest thing he ever did to Spanky, too."

I felt kind of sorry for Spanky, despite his general awfulness, but I didn't feel in a position to take him. Plus, I felt as if we were digressing. "Is there a place to get a paper?" I asked.

"A paper," the woman said. "Well, I usually just grab one from outside of someone's door. But I suppose you could buy one at Igor's. For about ten million dollars, probably."

"Where's Igor's?"

"It's on the corner. The purple awning. Would you buy me some cigarettes while you're there? Igor won't let me come in anymore. Spanky messed on his floor."

"What kind?"

"Number two," the woman said.

"No, I mean what kind of cigarettes?"

"Oh, that. Gauloises."

It was when I got back in Daria's apartment with a copy of *Backstage*—the only paper Igor's carried—that I started to panic. The paper was full of ads, but they all seemed to be people advertising themselves; the only real jobs were word-processing jobs for actors "between engagements." I could type about three words a minute. On the second-to-last page was an ad that said: "NO ACTORS . . . JUST PEOPLE. No Equity, No Experience Necessary. We just want YOU. Pilgrim Acres, Massachusetts' newest theme park, needs all types for recreational acting/being. Excellent pay, benefits, more. Call now."

I called the number. "Hello," a man said.

"Is this Pilgrim Acres?" I asked.

"Yes."

"I'm calling about the ad in *Backstage*. For people?"

"Yes."

"Do you have jobs?"

"What's your dress size?"

I told him.

"Are you reasonably attractive?"

I said yes.

"Then we have a job," he said. "If you get here by five o'clock."

"Five o'clock when?"

"Tonight," he said.

When I hung up I was elated, and only a little scared. I had never been to Boston, but my mother, who grew up there, had always said it was a "small, manageable" city, and I was sure there couldn't be as many creepy people there as there seemed to be in New York. And I was proud of myself for having gotten a job in what must have been record time. I packed some of Daria's clothes—winter clothes so she couldn't accuse me of taking things she needed—and wrote her a note and went to Penn Station and took a train to Boston. I arrived at Pilgrim Acres at a quarter to five.

The next day I started work. Mr. Antonini, the man who ran the park, said Elaine wasn't a good Pilgrim name and gave me a list of suitable names to choose from. I selected Ann, but he said they already had six Anns, so I picked Clara. First I was assigned to the Apothecary's, but then two women fainted in the Bakery, and since I had been in Africa, Mr. Antonini thought maybe I'd do better in the heat and switched me.

A few nights later I was sitting on the back steps of a row house in Medford spraying a hose at a baby standing up in an inflated swimming pool. The baby's name was Dido, and I was living with his mother and father, Louisa and Curly. Curly taught American history and lifestyles at Medford High School, and Louisa was going to a school to learn how to install cable TV in people's houses. I had met Curly—he was named after the cowboy in *Oklahoma!*—at Pilgrim Acres. A lot of teachers worked there in the summer. Curly suggested I rent their attic instead of staying in the barracks-like dorms at the park. The only problem was that I didn't think Louisa liked me very much. Either that or she couldn't speak English—she spoke only Spanish to both Curly and Dido.

Dido was shrieking from pleasure (I think) as I ran the hose up and down his pink little body. Louisa was at school and Curly was in the kitchen, fixing dinner.

After a few minutes Dido's pink little body started turning blue, so I took him out of the pool, wrapped him in a towel, and took him into the kitchen. I put a fresh diaper on him, then sat him in his high chair.

The phone rang. Curly picked it up. "Hello," he said, and then, "No. We have no Lainie here. No Elaine, either. You have the wrong number."

"Wait," I said. "I think that's for me." I took the receiver out of Curly's hand. He shrugged.

"Hello," I said.

"What was that all about?" asked Daria.

"Daria," I said. I had left a message on her machine

telling her where I could be reached, but I hadn't expected to hear from her so soon.

"Who answered the phone?" she asked.

"That was Curly," I said.

"Doesn't he know your name?"

"I changed my name," I said. "I'm Clara now."

"Why did you change your name?"

"It's a long story," I said.

"Well, then, some other day," said Daria. "Listen, Elaine, are you all right? I'm worried about you, just taking off like that."

"I'm fine," I said.

"Are you sure? I mean, I'm sorry if I seemed inhospitable before. If you want to come back to the city, you can stay here. It's no big deal. Why don't you come back?"

"I don't think so," I said. "I like it here."

"Well, Edith called." Edith is our mother. "She wanted to know what was happening with you, and I told her about this Pilgrim thing and I think she's coming to see you. She's performing at some hospital or something. So be warned."

"Oh, no," I said. "I don't think I'm ready for her yet."

"Are you really O.K.?" Daria asked. "Who's this Curly person?"

"He's my landlord," I said. "He works at the Pilgrim Acres."

"Oh, speaking of jobs, make sure you buy next month's *Glamour*. I'm in it."

"Congratulations," I said. "That's great."

"Yeah, well it could have been better. I'm a DON'T picture."

It was warm in the Bakery, especially in the long Pilgrim dresses we had to wear, but I liked the job. I started to forget all about the Peace Corps and indigenous fertilizers and New York and Daria, and the simple routine of bread baking—

mixing the dough, letting it rise, punching it down, shaping it, setting the moist unbaked loaves out on the paddle, pushing them into the oven, removing them an hour later, and then selling warm slices to the tourists for a quarter—seemed like the best job in the world. Some mornings I'd take an early bus out and just walk around the deserted village, up and down the wooden sidewalks, past the herb garden and chicken yards, across the dirt road and around the Village Green, past the Butcher's and the Seamstress's and the Blacksmith's and the Apothecary's, then into the Bakery, where I'd start sifting and measuring the flour. Then I started staying later at night: The Bakery closed at 4:30, but I'd walk around in my Pilgrim costume, smiling at the tourists, sitting on the benches, letting them take pictures of me holding their fat fragrant babies, waiting for dark and the fireworks display they had every night. And I'd ride the late bus home, still dressed like a Pilgrim, and walk to Curly and Louisa's house, and inside they'd be lying on the couch, watching Spanish TV, and I'd walk upstairs past Dido's room, where he slept in his crib, softly illuminated by the Virgin Mary night-light, up another flight past Curly and Louisa's room, up, up into the dark, hot attic.

One day when I came back from my morning break, Becky, the Pilgrim who ran the Bakery, told me a woman had come in and asked for me. I knew it must be my mother. About noon she reappeared with a man. They both were wearing jumpsuits and sunglasses.

"Darling," my mother said. "This is Henry, my manager."

Henry nodded. He ate one of the twenty-five-cent slices.

"Can you come out for some lunch with us?" my mother asked. "I can't talk in this place."

"I've got to wait a few minutes. I have some bread in the oven."

"I'll take the bread out," said Becky. "You can go."

"Thanks," I said. I took my apron off and walked outside with my mother and Henry.

"Can't you take that costume off?" my mother asked.

"I change at home," I said.

"Where's home?"

"I'm staying with some people in Medford. Should we go to the pub?" I asked. "It's really the only place to eat here."

"Can't we go to a normal restaurant? Henry has a car."

"I'm not supposed to leave the Village," I said. "Plus I only have half an hour."

Henry said he wanted to take a look at the working windmill, and headed down Main Street. My mother and I went into the pub. From outside it looked like an old English pub—thatched roof, gables, and leaded glass windows—but inside it was set up like a cafeteria. We both got a chef's salad and sat at a plank table.

"I'm performing tonight at the Mansard House, a private clinic for alcoholic women," my mother said. "I'd ask you to come, but I don't think I'm ready to perform in front of family yet. I've drawn on quite a lot of my unhappy experience with your father, and it might be painful for you."

"What do you do?" I asked. I couldn't picture my mother as a performance artist. After she left my father, she decided to become an actress, and I saw her once play Mrs. Cratchit in an off-Broadway musical based on *A Christmas Carol*. She sang a song called "Another Sad Christmas, Another Sad Goose."

"I really can't talk about it," my mother said. "A performance can't be explained, it has to be experienced."

"Oh," I said.

She looked at me. "Darling, I hate to see you like this. All dressed up like a Pilgrim with no place to go." She laughed, then continued. "No, really. I'm sorry. But we've got to get you out of here."

"What do you mean?" I said. "I like this job."

"Elaine, let's be serious. You can't be a Pilgrim for the rest of your life. Now, the reason I brought Henry along was so he could see you. He's been very good about helping Daria with her new career, and I'm sure he could do the same for you. I do wish you weren't wearing that dress. And the wimple! Can you take that off, so he can at least see your hair?"

"No," I said. "It's a costume. I've got to wear it as long as I'm on the grounds."

"What if we went out to the car? Does the parking lot count?"

I suddenly realized how annoying my mother was, so I said, "What's the story with Henry?"

"What do you mean?"

"Are you sleeping with him?"

"Elaine!" my mother said. "What kind of question is that?"

"Who is he? Where did you find him? He looks like a creep."

"I beg your pardon," my mother said. "But Henry is not a creep. Henry has helped turn my life around. I'd still be sitting in that roach-infested apartment if Henry hadn't taken an interest in me."

"That's another thing," I said. "Thanks for selling the apartment. What happened to all my stuff? Did you just toss it down the incinerator?"

My mother laid down her wooden fork and looked at me for a second. "You know, Elaine," she finally said, "just because you're having a little trouble shifting your life into first gear doesn't mean you have to take your frustration out on me. I am no longer the emotional quicker-picker-upper I once was. I am an adult woman pursuing her own life. I had a perfect right to do everything I've done, and if you don't approve, that's too bad. And I didn't toss your 'stuff' in the incinerator. I am paying for it to be stored in a climate controlled, mildew-free warehouse in Long Island City. So spare me."

I didn't know what to say. I wanted to get up and walk out, but something about the Pilgrim costume prohibited a dramatic exit. So I just sat there, and picked at the American cheese slices in my salad.

My mother sighed. "I'm sorry," she said. "I guess I'm a little on edge. I still get anxious about performing."

I still didn't say anything. I felt a little like I felt after I took the aqua pill Daria gave me: I had to concentrate hard to remember that I was myself, sitting there.

"Are you O.K.?" my mother asked. "Are you sure you aren't ill? Maybe you caught something in Africa. They have some terrible diseases over there, you know. Megan Foster was telling me about her sister who got bit by some fish and started to grow scales. Perhaps you should see a doctor? Are you taking vitamins?"

"I'm fine," I said. "I have to get back to work. It was nice to see you. Good luck with your performance."

"Oh, darling," my mother said. "Don't sulk. I said I was sorry. Is this some kind of Moonie thing? Have you been brainwashed?"

This time I didn't answer. I just stood up and walked out.

When I got to the Bakery I felt sick. I sat down in the back room, but the heat from the ovens made me feel worse, so I went out and sat on the shaded back stoop. Becky looked out the Dutch door. "What happened? Are you all right?" she asked.

"I feel funny," I said.

"You look terrible."

I stood up, but I felt dizzy, so I sat down again.

"Why don't you go home?" Becky said. "Take the afternoon off. Just relax."

When I arrived at Curly's and Louisa's, my key wouldn't fit in the lock. Someone had changed it. I knocked on the door. I knew someone was home because I could hear the radio playing. I kept knocking, and after a while, I used my foot too.

Louisa opened the door, but only wide enough so she could see me. She had the chain fastened. "Go away," she said. So she did speak English.

"What's the matter?" I asked. "Why did you change the lock?"

"I know about you and Curly," Louisa said. "You must go away now, before I kill you."

"What are you talking about? Where's Curly?"

"I now understand that you try to steal Curly. That you come into our happy home and try to steal him. But no way. I always suspect you." Louisa closed the door. I knocked again, but she didn't answer it. She turned the radio up.

There was a paper bag on the porch containing Daria's winter clothes. I left them there. I walked up to the corner and went into the bar where Curly sometimes went before dinner, but it was too early. I decided to wait. I ordered a vodka gimlet and got four because it was both ladies' day and happy hour. I drank two of them, and by the time I finished the second one I knew what I wanted to do.

I got up and left some money and took the T into Boston. I went straight to the Peace Corps offices, and explained my situation to a man in a suit. He was wearing a button that said "THE NEW PEACE CORPS." This unnerved me since I wasn't sure if I had been in the old Peace Corps or the new Peace Corps, or what the difference was. When I had finished my story, he didn't say anything for a minute. We both just sat there.

Then he said, "You did resign, didn't you?"

"Yes," I said. "But it was a mistake. I want to withdraw my resignation."

"You can't," he said. "You have to reapply."

"But that's absurd," I said. "Can't I just go back?"

"No," he said. "This is all very complicated. You have to reapply, and then, if you are accepted, you'll have to be reassigned."

"I can't just go back to Slemba?"

"No," he said. "Why don't you take some time to think about this? It's probably just culture shock. It does take some time to readjust. Going back isn't always the solution."

"But I made a terrible mistake. I don't know why I didn't stay. I should have stayed."

"Why didn't you, then?"

"Well, I thought I wanted to come back and start a life here and a career and all that, but I've realized I don't."

"What?" he asked.

"Nothing," I said.

"The Peace Corps is not an escape. You can't use it to escape."

"I'm not escaping. That's why I want to go right back. If I stay here, I'll get another job or something, and that will be something to escape. But right now I don't have anything to escape from. Nothing. So it's not an escape." I thought this was a very good point, but the man just looked at me oddly.

"I'm sorry," he said. "I really think you should give this some time and thought. If you decide to reapply, I'll personally supervise your application and make sure it gets processed with the utmost expediency. But that's all I can do for you."

I took the application he handed me and went outside and sat in the plaza and started to fill it out, but halfway through, the pen I had stolen from the receptionist's desk ran out of ink, but it ran out slowly, so the application was all scratched out and awful looking, and I started to cry. I hadn't cried once, during this whole ordeal, but once I started, I couldn't stop.

When I did stop crying, I realized my application now looked even worse: It was tear-stained and crumpled, so I tore it up and threw it away. I thought about going up and getting another application, but it was after five o'clock.

I must have sat there a long time because suddenly I realized it was getting dark. I thought about going back to Medford and trying to talk to Curly, but for some reason I knew it would be a waste of time. And I was sick of wasting my time. The plaza was starting to look ornery in the fading light, so I got up and tried to find a bus out to Pilgrim Acres. I figured I'd stay there for the night.

I wasn't planning on hitchhiking, but a car stopped beside me. "Need a ride?" the guy asked.

"Where are you going?"

"Out to Stockbridge," he said.

I got in the car. It seemed like the only thing to do. The man looked back over his shoulder, and pulled into the traffic. He didn't say anything for a minute. Then he looked over at me.

"Going to a party?" he asked.

I still had my Pilgrim costume on. "No," I said. "I work at Pilgrim Acres."

"Is that open nights?"

"Not usually," I said, "but tonight we're doing a special reenactment of the Battle of Gettysburg."

"Oh," the man said. "That sounds interesting."

"It's fascinating," I said. Then I realized he might want

to come see it, so I added, "If you like that kind of thing. Most people find it really boring."

We drove a little further in silence. Then the man said, "I'm Drake. What's your name?"

"Clara," I said.

I told Drake to drop me at the exit because I knew if the guard saw the car drive up to the main gate, he would be suspicious. So I walked down the exit ramp and the mile out to Pilgrim Acres. The park was surrounded by a stockade fence topped with barbed wire, but I knew there was a gate by the cow field that was left unlocked. I had thought the cows would be put into a barn or something for the night, but they were still in the field. They were sitting under a tree, but as I walked across the field they stood up and watched me. They looked very ghostly in the moonlight: Their white patches shone like freshly spilled paint around the holes of their dark patches, and they swayed their big heads in a sleepy, curious way.

I climbed over the fence into the herb garden. Except for the cows, Pilgrim Acres was deserted. Even the swans in the swan pond had disappeared someplace. I walked up Main Street to the Bakery.

For a few minutes I just stood there; it looked so lovely, all shut up and quiet, the flowers in the window boxes curled tight for the night. But then I took out my keys and went in, locking the door behind me. I was afraid to turn on the lights in case the guard could see, so I lit a candle. There were two rocking chairs in the parlor, supposedly antiques. They had velvet ropes tied across their arms so tourists couldn't sit in them. I took the rope off one and sat down. I wondered who had sat there last—maybe a real Pilgrim.

I sat there and rocked, holding the candle. I watched it burn down, rocking the whole time.

Memorial Day

I am eating my grapefruit with a grapefruit spoon my mother bought last summer from a door-to-door salesman on a large three-wheeled bike. My mother and I were sitting on the front steps that day and we watched him glide down the street, into our driveway, and up our front walk. He opened his case on the handlebars, and it was full of fruit appliances: pineapple corers, melon ballers, watermelon seeders, orange-juice squeezers, and grapefruit spoons. My mother bought four of the spoons and the man pedaled himself out of our lives.

That was about a year ago. Since then a lot has changed, I think as I pry the grapefruit pulp away from the skin with the serrated edge of the spoon. Since then, my mother has remarried, my father has moved to California, and I have stopped talking. Actually, I talk quite a lot at school, but never at home. I have nothing to say to anyone here.

Across the table from me, drinking Postum, is my new stepfather. He wasn't here last year. I don't think he was anywhere last year. His name is Lonnie, and my mother met him at a Seth Speaks seminar. Seth is this guy without a body who speaks out of the mouth of this lady and tells you how to fix your life. Both Lonnie and my mother have fixed their lives. "One day at a time," my mother says every morning, smiling at Lonnie and then, less happily, at me.

Lonnie is only thirteen years older than I am; he is twenty-nine but looks about fourteen. When the three of us go out together, he is taken to be my brother.

"Listen to this," Lonnie says. Both Lonnie and my mother continue to talk to me, consult with me, and read things to me, in the hope that I will forget and speak. "If gypsy moths continue to destroy trees at their present rate, North America will become a desert incapable of supporting any life by the year 4000." Lonnie has a morbid sense of humor and delights in macabre newspaper fillers. Because he knows I won't answer, he doesn't glance up at me. He continues to stare at his paper and says, "Wow. Think of that."

I look out the window. My mother is sitting in an inflated rubber boat in the swimming pool, scrubbing the fiberglass walls with a stiff brush and Mr. Clean. They get stained during the winter. She does this every Memorial Day. We always open the pool this weekend, and she always blows up the yellow boat, puts on her Yankees hat so her hair won't turn orange, and paddles around the edge of the pool, leaving a trail of suds.

Last year, as she scrubbed, the diamond from her old engagement ring fell out and sank to the bottom of the pool. She was still married to my father, although they were planning to separate after a last "family vacation" in July. My mother shook the suds off her hand and raised it in front of her face, as if she were admiring a new ring. "Oh, Stephen!" she said. "I think I've lost my diamond."

"What?" I said. I still talked then.

"The diamond fell out of my ring. Look."

I got up from the chair I was sitting on and kneeled beside the pool. She held out her hand, the way women do in old movies when they expect it to be kissed. I looked down at her ring and she was right: the diamond was gone. The setting looked like an empty hand tightly grabbing nothing.

"Do you see it?" she asked, looking down into the pool. Because we had just taken the cover off, the water was murky. "It must be down there," she said. "Maybe if you dove in?" She looked at me with a nice, pleading look on her face. I took my shirt off. I felt her looking at my chest. There is no hair on my chest, and every time my mother sees it I know she checks to see if any has grown.

I dove into the pool. The water was so cold my head ached. I opened my eyes and swam quickly around the bottom. I felt like one of those Japanese pearl fishers. But I didn't see the diamond.

I surfaced and swam to the side. "I don't see it," I said. "I can't see anything. Where's the mask?"

"Oh, dear," my mother said. "Didn't we throw it away last year?"

"I forget," I said. I got out of the pool and stood shivering in the sun. Suddenly I got the idea that if I found the diamond maybe my parents wouldn't separate. I know it sounds ridiculous, but at that moment, standing with my arms crossed over my chest, watching my mother begin to cry in her inflatable boat—at that moment, the diamond sitting on the bottom of the pool took on a larger meaning, and I thought that if it was replaced in the tiny clutching hand of my mother's ring we might live happily ever after.

So I had my father drive me downtown, and I bought a diving mask at the five-and-ten, and when we got home I put it on—first spitting on the glass so it wouldn't fog—and dove into the water, and dove again and again, until I actually found the diamond, glittering in a mess of leaves and bloated inchworms at the bottom of the pool.

I throw my grapefruit rind away, and go outside and sit on the edge of the diving board with my feet in the water. My mother watches me for a second, probably deciding if it's worthwhile to say anything. Then she goes back to her scrubbing.

Later, I am sitting by the mailbox. Since I've stopped talking, I've written a lot of letters. I write to men in prisons, and I answer personal ads, claiming to be whatever it is the placer desires: "an elegant educated lady for afternoon pleasure," or a "GBM." The mail from prisons is the best: long letters about nothing, since it seems nothing is done in prison. A lot of remembering. A lot of bizarre requests: Send me a shoehorn. Send me an empty egg carton (arts and crafts?). Send me an electric toothbrush. I like writing letters to people I've never met.

Lonnie is planting geraniums he bought this morning in front of the A & P when he did the grocery shopping. Lonnie is very good about "doing his share." I am not about mine. Every night I wait with delicious anticipation for my mother to tell me to take out the garbage: "How many times do I have to tell you? Can't you just do it?"

Lonnie gets up and walks over to me, trowel in hand. He has on plaid Bermuda shorts and a Disney World T-shirt. If I talked, I'd ask him when he went to Disney World. But I can live without the information.

Lonnie flips the trowel at me and it slips like a knife into the ground a few inches from my leg. "Bingo!" Lonnie says. "Scare you?"

I think when a person stops talking people forget that he can still hear. Lonnie is always saying dumb things to me— things you'd only say to a deaf person or a baby.

"What a day," Lonnie says, as if to illustrate this point. He stretches out beside me, and I look at his long white legs. He has sneakers and white socks on. He never goes barefoot. He is too uptight to go barefoot. He would step on a piece of glass immediately. That is the kind of person Lonnie is.

The Captain Ice Cream truck rolls lazily down our street.

Lonnie stands up and reaches in his pocket. "Would you like an ice pop?" he asks me, looking at his change.

I shake my head no. An ice pop? Where did he grow up—Kentucky?

Lonnie walks into the street and flags down the ice cream truck as if it's not obvious what he's standing there for.

The truck slows down and the ice-cream man jumps out. It is a woman. "What can I get you?" she says, opening the freezer on the side of the truck. It's the old-fashioned kind of truck, with the ice cream hidden in its frozen depths. I always thought you needed to have incredibly long arms to be a good Captain Ice Cream person.

"Well, I'd like a nice ice pop," Lonnie says.

"A Twin Bullet?" suggests the woman. "What flavor?"

"Do you have cherry?" Lonnie asks.

"Sure," the woman says. "Cherry, grape, orange, lemon, cola, and tutti-frutti."

For a second I have a horrible feeling that Lonnie will want a tutti-frutti. "I'll have cherry," he says.

Lonnie comes back, peeling the sticky paper from his cherry Bullet. It's a bright pink color. The truck drives away. "Guess how much this cost," Lonnie says, sitting beside me on the grass. "Sixty cents. It's a good thing you didn't want one." He licks his fingers and then the ice stick. "Do you want a bite?" He holds it out toward me.

Lonnie is so patient and so sweet. It's just too bad he's such a nerd. I take a bite of his cherry Bullet.

"Good, huh?" Lonnie says. He watches me eat for a second, then takes a bite himself. He breaks the Bullet in half and eats it in a couple of huge bites. A little pink juice runs down his chin.

"What are you waiting for?" he asks. I nod toward the mailbox.

"It's Memorial Day," Lonnie says. "The mail doesn't come." He stands up and pulls the trowel out of the ground.

I think of King Arthur. "There is no mail for anyone today," Lonnie says. "No matter how long you wait." He hands me his two Bullet sticks and returns to his geraniums.

I have this feeling, holding the stained wooden sticks, that I will keep them for a long time, and come across them one day, and remember this moment, incorrectly.

After the coals in the barbecue have melted into powder, the fireflies come out. They hesitate in the air, as if stunned by dusk.

Lonnie and my mother are sitting beside the now clean pool, and I am sitting on the other side of the "natural forsythia fence" that is planted around it, watching the bats swoop from tree to tree, feeling the darkness clot all around me. I can hear Lonnie and my mother talking, but I can't make out what they are saying.

I love this time of day—early evening, early summer. It makes me want to cry. We always had a barbecue on Memorial Day with my father, and my mother cooked this year's hamburgers on her new barbecue, which Lonnie bought her for Mother's Day (she's old enough to be his mother, but she isn't, I would have said, if I talked), in the same dumb, cheerful way she cooked last year's. She has no sense of sanctity, or ritual. She would give Lonnie my father's clothes if my father had left any behind to give.

My mother walks toward me with the hose, then past me toward her garden, to spray her pea plants. "O.K.," she yells to Lonnie, who stands by the spigot. He turns the knob and then goes inside. The light in the kitchen snaps on.

My mother stands with one hand on her hip, the other raising and lowering the hose, throwing large fans of water over the garden. She used to bathe me every night, and I think of the peas hanging in their green skins, dripping. I lie with one ear on the cool grass, and I can hear the water drumming into the garden. It makes me sleepy.

Then I hear it stop, and I look up to see my mother walking toward me, the skin on her bare legs and arms glowing. She sits down beside me, and for a while she says nothing. I pretend I am asleep on the ground, although I know she knows I am awake.

Then she starts to talk, as I knew she would. My mother says, "You are breaking my heart." She says it as if it were literally true, as if her heart were actually breaking. "I just want you to know that," she says. "You're old enough to know that you are breaking my heart."

I sit up. I look at my mother's chest, as if I could see her heart breaking. She has on a polo shirt with a little blue whale on her left breast. I am afraid to look at her face.

We sit like that for a while, and darkness grows around us. When I open my mouth to speak, my mother uncoils her arm from her side and covers my mouth with her hand.

I look at her.

"Wait," she says. "Don't say anything yet."

I can feel her flesh against my lips. Her wrist smells of chlorine. The fireflies, lighting all around us, make me dizzy.